MO xxxx

## Praise for *Plain Killing*

"Delightful."
—*Publishers Weekly*

"The clues will keep readers guessing until the end."
—*RT Book Reviews*

"Very emotional and engaging . . . a real page turner."
—*Fresh Fiction*

"A great mix of Amish fiction and cozy mystery."
—*The Friendly Book Nook*

## Praise for *Plain Murder*

"An excellent addition to the Amish mystery subgenre.
Perfect for anyone seeking a gentle read."
—*Library Journal*

"A good mystery that will keep readers guessing."
—*Parkersburg News and Sentinel*

"Delightful characters."
—*RT Book Reviews*

Books by Emma Miller

PLAIN MURDER

PLAIN KILLING

PLAIN DEAD

Published by Kensington Publishing Corporation

# PLAIN DEAD

# EMMA MILLER

KENSINGTON BOOKS
www.kensingtonbooks.com

This book is a work of fiction. Names, characters, places, and incidents either are products of the author's imagination or are used fictitiously. Any resemblance to actual persons, living or dead, events, or locales is entirely coincidental.

KENSINGTON BOOKS are published by

Kensington Publishing Corp.
119 West 40th Street
New York, NY 10018

Copyright © 2016 by Emma Miller

All rights reserved. No part of this book may be reproduced in any form or by any means without the prior written consent of the Publisher, excepting brief quotes used in reviews.

All Kensington titles, imprints, and distributed lines are available at special quantity discounts for bulk purchases for sales promotion, premiums, fund-raising, educational, or institutional use.

Special book excerpts or customized printings can also be created to fit specific needs. For details, write or phone the office of the Kensington Sales Manager: Kensington Publishing Corp., 119 West 40th Street, New York, NY 10018. Attn. Sales Department. Phone: 1-800-221-2647.

Kensington and the K logo Reg. U.S. Pat. & TM Off.

eISBN-13: 978-0-7582-9177-6
eISBN-10: 0-7582-9177-9
First Kensington Electronic Edition: January 2016

ISBN-13: 978-0-7582-9176-9
ISBN-10: 0-7582-9176-0
First Kensington Trade Paperback Printing: January 2016

10 9 8 7 6 5 4 3 2 1

Printed in the United States of America

# PLAIN DEAD

# Chapter 1

*Stone Mill, Pennsylvania*
*January*

Rachel Mast slid out of the front seat of her Jeep as her fiancé opened the door, and surveyed the crowded high school parking lot with a sigh of relief. This was the opening day of Stone Mill's long anticipated Winter Frolic, and dozens of eager, smiling people, many in Plain dress, were making their way inside. A line of horses and black buggies stood along the side of the building while motor vehicles, some with out-of-state plates, filled more than two-thirds of the parking spaces while others waited bumper to bumper in the street, turn signals flashing.

"Careful. Watch your step," Evan cautioned. "The snow-plows did a pretty good job of cleaning up after the last snow, but it's still slippery in spots."

"I can't believe it! People came out for the frolic." Rachel could hardly contain her excitement. "I hoped they would, but with the storm coming in, I was afraid they might not."

"I'll admit I never expected to see this many visitors." Evan grinned down at her. "I should have had more faith in you, Rache."

"It was a long shot," she admitted. "Most towns only hold festivals in the summer for a reason."

Hosting a big festival had been a risky proposition for the

town, and much of her reputation rested on the outcome. Like so many rural communities, Stone Mill desperately needed any kind of financial boost it could get after years of national economic downturn. Rachel had been born here, which should have made her trustworthy. But she'd left her Amish up-bringing and stayed away for fifteen years, going to college, then joining the corporate business world, which thinned the ties and made her suspect. Stone Mill was an isolated mountain community that held to old ways, familiar faces, and tried-and-true solutions.

Even after some of her previous successes, like the fair they held in the town square on Saturdays in the summer months, it had taken a lot of persuasion to convince the valley residents and business owners that hosting a weeklong craft show and celebration midwinter could be a success. Had the project flopped, she'd have had a difficult time getting people to listen to her next harebrained idea. Luckily, it didn't look to be a flop.

January was usually a slow season for her B&B, but Stone Mill House was booked all week with every room filled. The previous night, she'd seen that Wagler's Grocery, The George, Junior's Diner, and Russell's Hardware and Emporium were all crowded with out-of-towners. So, despite minor glitches in the festivities, the below-normal temperatures, and the threat of a snowstorm, the festival seemed headed in the right direction.

"Rachel! Evan!" A young woman dressed all in black, with both one eyebrow and one nostril pierced, shifted a box of books to one hip and waved. "Wait until you see our table! It looks awesome!"

Rachel waved back. "Is George here?" Ell owned the town's bookstore, but it had once belonged to her Uncle George.

"Are you kidding? I couldn't keep him away," Ell called back.

"Need help with that box?" Evan asked.

"Got it!" Ell shifted the weight to both arms again. "Rachel, don't forget that you promised to help with story time for the kids. I need you at noon for an hour-long shift."

"I'll be there." Rachel returned her attention to Evan. "Be sure to keep an eye on Mary Aaron's strawberry jam, right? Because her mother insisted they were short one jar after the Christmas bazaar."

Evan was wearing his state police winter uniform, which made him appear taller, broader of shoulder, and even more imposing than normal. He'd recently been promoted to detective but had volunteered to serve as security for the Winter Frolic's biggest day, free of charge. Rachel didn't really think that security was needed to guard the tables of whoopie pies and hand-crocheted hot mitts, but she'd learned by trial and error that city folks, visiting for the day, felt more at ease with a tall trooper keeping an eye on things.

"Just doing my civic duty," he replied with a wink. "Serve and protect."

She laughed and gave his arm a squeeze. For two years Evan had pursued her, and she'd finally agreed to marry him when he'd proposed again on New Year's Day. Somehow, making that decision had changed things between them. In a good way. "Would you mind giving a hand with traffic control, first?" she asked sweetly. "Before you start guarding the jam?"

As if on cue, brakes squealed and a car horn sounded from the street. "I'm on it," he said. "See you later?"

"Absolutely," she agreed. "I hope you brought a change of clothes. You promised me a sleigh ride, and I'm not letting you out of it. I'll get tickets."

It hadn't taken much arm-twisting to get her father to agree to let her brother Moses polish up the two-horse sleigh and deck the team with bells so that he could offer old-fashioned Amish sleigh rides during the festival. As she'd suspected, there'd been so much interest that Moses and his wife, Ruth, were taking reservations, and they were attempting to locate a second sleigh and driver.

"Late lunch first and then the sleigh ride," Evan bargained.

"You know how I feel about horses." He squeezed her gloved hand. "You're wearing it, aren't you?"

She laughed. "Of course I'm wearing it." When she'd finally accepted Evan's marriage proposal, he'd slipped an antique diamond ring on her finger. "I haven't had it off since you gave it to me."

"Good. This will be a chance to show it to everybody and let the whole town know you're taken."

Inwardly, Rachel grimaced. Had she had her way, there wouldn't have been an engagement ring. The Amish didn't believe in jewelry, not even wedding rings. And while she was no longer Amish, she knew her family, especially her parents, wouldn't approve. Rings were considered *worldly*, and the Amish were a people set apart from the English world. Although she'd left the faith when she was seventeen, some steps were still hard for her. If she'd had her druthers, she would have settled for a simple wedding band and skipped the diamond altogether, but Evan didn't understand. He'd been so pleased with himself that she didn't have the heart to refuse to wear the engagement ring. And it *was* beautiful, and she loved him for being him. She sighed. Maybe the English world had changed her more than she wanted to admit. But not enough that she felt comfortable flaunting an expensive diamond in front of her Plain friends and neighbors.

As Rachel trudged across the parking lot to the sidewalk, she heard her name being called. She looked up to see an Amish couple standing halfway between the entrance to the school gym and the buggy parking. Since almost all of the Amish women dressed similarly in black dress bonnets, capes, and coats, it was often difficult to tell them apart from a distance, but there was no mistaking Naamah, with her husband, Bishop Abner. He was small and thin; she outweighed him by at least fifty pounds and stood a head taller. The smiling bishop made his way along the sidewalks, weighed down with split-oak baskets of canned goods, presumably to sell at the Plain Pickle and Jam stand her parents' Amish church community was sponsoring.

"Rachel!" Naamah called excitedly. "So many Englishers coming to our frolic. *Wunderbaar*."

Naamah gave a quick hug to a small Amish woman going in the opposite direction, then hurried toward Rachel, her husband trailing three steps behind.

Swooping down on Rachel, Naamah enveloped her in an enthusiastic bear hug, and Rachel was instantly engulfed in the familiar scents of her childhood—damp wool, starch, and dried lavender. "So happy we are that the snow doesn't drive away our visitors," Naamah bubbled. She had a merry voice and eyes that shone with the joy of life. "Lots of people here, it looks."

"Yes," Rachel agreed. "I was afraid the weather would keep tourists away. The road over the mountain into the valley can get slippery, but they must be braver than I thought." She glanced back toward the woman Naamah had embraced. The smaller figure had turned back toward the buggies. "Was that Annie Herschberger?"

"*Ya*, poor Annie," the bishop confirmed. "A difficult time for her and her family."

Annie was a sister-in-law to Alvin and Verna Herschberger, the young couple who made the delicious goat cheeses that Rachel sold in her gift shop. She was also a friend of Rachel's Aunt Hannah, but Rachel didn't know her well.

She watched as Annie walked to one of the buggies and climbed inside.

"Is she leaving already?" Rachel asked.

"Just going back to fetch a pumpkin cake for the bake sale," Naamah said. "She thought either my husband, Joab, or our Sammy had carried it into the school with her raisin bread and *krum kuchen*, but they can't find the cake."

"I wondered where Sammy was," Rachel remarked. A few months ago, Naamah's eighteen-year-old nephew Sammy Zook had come to stay with them. He was a big boy, strong and good-natured, but slow in mind and body. Naamah said that Sammy was full of fanciful tales and couldn't be trusted to give a straight answer if his life depended on it, but as far as Rachel could see, his presence was a great help around the farm to Naamah and Abner. Childless, the two had to perform alone the many tasks living simply demanded, such as chopping wood, building fences, milking and caring for the animals. It seemed a good solution for all three of them as the bishop was growing no younger and Sammy was obviously thriving under his aunt and uncle's loving care.

"*Ach,* Rachel." Naamah shook her head sadly. "Poor Annie said she didn't want to come today, to maybe have people staring at them and whispering behind their back, but Abner insisted they shouldn't hide. If there was fault, it was Joab's, not hers. She has no reason to feel shame, and gossip soon grows cold when idle minds turn to new mischief."

"I agree wholeheartedly," Rachel said.

The bishop turned to Rachel and asked, in a low voice, "Did you have a chance to talk to Bill Billingsly yet?"

She shook her head. "He's been out of the office all week, *supposedly*. I've called three times and I've left messages. I think he's hiding because he's afraid of me."

"I'm opposed to violence, of course, but it might be that he should be afraid of me as well." Bishop Abner stroked his long beard. "I've been praying hard on the matter. Trying to temper my anger. I just can't imagine why that newspaperman would want to hurt good people like Annie and Joab."

"*Ya,* they are both good people," Rachel agreed. "And we need their contributions to the community. Mary Aaron said they were talking about selling the dairy farm and moving out to Wisconsin."

"What a terrible loss that would be." The bishop frowned for a moment but then turned back to her, forcing a smile. "Enough talk of the newspaperman. He's not worth our time to fret over. Congratulations on such a fine turnout. Clever, this idea of yours, Rachel. To bring tourists to our town in the cold of winter." He looked at his wife with obvious affection. "But then, not even Englishers can resist my Naamah's rhubarb jam."

"If any jars are left over next weekend, just drop them by the inn," Rachel said. "You know what a big seller they are in the gift shop. I sold seventeen jars of Naamah's chowchow in December."

"Maybe I should give up raising sheep and learn to make chowchow," he replied. "I would, if I could talk my good wife into giving up her secret recipes."

"No, because if I tell you, you'll hand them out to anyone who asks," Naamah retorted. "I know you. You're a pushover." She laughed again, her round cheeks and the tip of her snub of a nose glowing as red in the icy air as a pickled egg.

"How can I help it?" he teased. "Doesn't the good book tell us to be kind to our neighbors?"

"*Ya,* but it says nothing about giving away my grandmother's recipe for tomato mincemeat or chowchow." Naamah's brown eyes sparkled with good humor beneath the rim of her black dress bonnet. "At the last school fair, I took six jars and Mathiah's Gertie and her sister Agnes brought a dozen exactly the same. They offered theirs cheaper and sold out before me."

Bishop Abner's scraggly reddish-gray beard bobbed up and down as he chuckled again. "And all for the same good cause." He shifted the heavy baskets and rested one in the snow. "Money for the schoolhouse addition, so what was the harm?"

"None, I suppose," Naamah allowed. "But my *grossmama* would not approve."

"Let's get inside before we all freeze," Rachel suggested. "Those baskets must weigh a ton."

"I told him I could carry some," Naamah fussed, "but he wouldn't hear of it. If the bishop had his way, I'd be spoiled rotten."

"And who should I do it for if not my own wife?" He scooped up the basket of pickles and jam and followed Naamah toward the entrance to the school gymnasium.

Rachel trailed after them, thinking what a positive force Abner Chupp was for the community. He was bishop for her family's church and as dear to Rachel as his wife was. He might be diminutive in stature, but he loomed large in the valley both as an example of how an Amish man should live and as a kind and wise religious elder.

Some, even members of her own family, might openly show their disapproval of her choice to leave the faith and become part of the English world, but Bishop Abner never had. All he'd ever offered was friendship, understanding, and an open invitation to return to the Amish way of life. As for Naamah, Rachel adored her. Despite the good-humored bickering that went on between her and her husband, Rachel knew that the two were devoted to each other and never really disagreed.

Rachel paused to greet a few other acquaintances and then stepped through the double doors into the gym. Although she'd been there early that morning, she was amazed by how fantastic the place looked with the addition of big glittery white snowflakes hanging from the ceiling, and twinkle lights looped in all the doorways and overhead. Booths offering everything from hand-woven willow baskets to baked goods, wooden toys, antiques, hand-stitched quilts, and forged iron trivets and fire irons lined the walls. Ell's bookstore, The George, filled two spaces with books for sale, with a third serving hot tea and scones in a reading area and a fourth, carpeted with rugs, designated as a children's story area. There was a double booth offering reproduction colonial- and mission-style furniture and a Mennonite couple's display of one-of-a-kind lighting fixtures.

Rachel spied her friend Coyote's pottery stall and walked over to see how things were going for her. Coyote was the local potter, a talented artist who had transplanted her family from California. Coyote and her husband, Blade, were just the kind of entrepreneurs Rachel hoped to draw to Stone Mill. Rachel didn't see Coyote, but Blade, a rough-featured man with a long ponytail, a scraggly beard, and full sleeves of tattoos, was behind the counter, the newest addition to their family tied to his chest with a colorful baby sling. A small boy in a wheelchair sat beside him, scrolling through an iPad.

Blade glanced up, saw her coming toward him, and grinned. "Rachel. Coyote was looking for you earlier, but she just ran out to the car. This one"—he glanced meaningfully down at the sleeping infant—"just had a major explosion, and I left the diaper bag in the van."

"I'll be around for a while, so I'll catch up with her. Hi, Remi," Rachel said to the small boy. He had a round face; silky black hair cut straight across his forehead; large, dark, intelligent eyes; and skin the exact shade of English toffee. "Are you reading anything good today?"

"*The Giving Tree,* but I read it before. I know how it ends." Remi had an endearing lisp.

"I imagine Ell has some wonderful books over there. Maybe we can find you something you haven't read yet."

"Just what his mama said," Blade agreed. "Although it's hard to keep him in books. He's reading everything he can get his hands on."

Rachel suspected that Remi's IQ, as yet to be formally tested, would surprise even his parents. Not old enough to attend kindergarten yet, Remi had already been reading chapter books for more than a year. "At least you'll never be bored."

Intense pewter-gray eyes lit with pleasure. "Coyote says that, too. Whatever may happen, our kids are our treasure."

Rachel nodded. For all his scary tattoos, her friend's husband was a gentle soul and a model family man always willing to help his wife or his neighbors. She knew Blade had spent four nights that week erecting booths for the festival as well as shoveling fresh snow and ice off the high school sidewalks. "I saw your booth was drawing a lot of interest from visitors this morning. How are sales?"

"Great, so far," Blade answered. "I think Coyote wants me to bring over some more of those blue mugs and the cream pitchers this afternoon. She sold one of the sinks already, the one with the brown swirl."

"It was beautiful. She's going to make one for me for that little half bath I'm making out of a downstairs closet." She smiled at Remi. "Tell your mama I'll stop back by." He nodded and Rachel moved on.

Coyote's pottery booth stood beside a larger display of oils and watercolors featuring work by local artists past and present. Beyond that were candle vendors and stands displaying braid rugs and traditional painted floor coverings. Rachel's own booth was given over to photos and text relating the history of the Stone Mill valley from the seventeenth century up to the present, including a case featuring a local collector's stone spear points, Native American pottery, and models of the type of homes and farming methods used by First Peoples. A friend and neighbor, Hulda Schenfeld, had volunteered to host the booth for a few hours today. It was Hulda who'd insisted that the display include before-and-after restoration photos of Stone Mill House and magnets with the phone number of the B&B listed. Hulda, in her nineties, remained a savvy businesswoman, and Rachel knew she had a lot to learn from her.

More than half of the vendors were Amish. One entire wall of the gymnasium was given over to foodstuffs, with residents offering local goat cheese, honey, apple cider, pickles and relishes, and all kinds of jams and jellies. There were folks selling homemade leather goods, handmade brooms, and wooden rockers and baby cradles. There were also craft projects and face painting for children, a petting zoo in one of the outer garages, and winter activities for all ages, including the horse-drawn sleigh rides, an ice sculpture contest, snowman-building competitions, and Rachel's favorite, a huge ice rink. Visitors could rent skates, glide on the flooded and frozen man-made pond, and warm up with hot chocolate brewed over an open fire.

Rachel was approaching a display of local cheeses when she felt sharp claws on her ankle and heard a familiar yipping. She glanced down to see a small white bichon frise hopping up and down. "Sophie, no," she said. Sophie ignored her as usual and kept jumping and yipping. Rachel knelt and scooped her up, trying to avoid wet kisses as she glanced around for the dog's owner.

"Sophie, you bad girl. Sorry, Rachel. She slipped off her leash." Leaning heavily on a polished walnut cane with a foxhead handle, George O'Day made his way toward her. "Didn't I tell you that you can't do that?" he reasoned with the little dog. "It isn't safe. You could be trampled in this crowd." He gathered Sophie into his arms and held her against his chest while Rachel slipped the collar around the bichon's neck and then lowered her to the floor. Immediately, Sophie began hopping and barking again, but the leash held her fast.

"I doubt anyone would trample her," Rachel said. "I'd say the visitors are more in danger of having Sophie trample them."

"She wouldn't hurt a fly," George defended. "She's just happy to see you, aren't you, Sophie? I think she misses you."

"It was you she missed, George. She was homesick the whole time you were gone." Rachel looked into his puffy, pale face. His white dress shirt, brown bow tie, and brown cardigan sweater were a little at odds with the colorful Scandinavian knit hat that covered his bald head, but his eyes were clear and alert. "Are you sure this isn't too much for you?"

"I'm fine," he said, smiling. "Wouldn't miss it for the world."

"Still, you should take care of yourself," Rachel warned. "Give yourself time to heal." George, a convicted felon recently released from prison, was five weeks out of brain surgery, surgery that few of his physicians had expected him to survive. But he'd beaten the odds and, with the removal of a tumor, seemed to be well on the road to recovery.

"Have you seen Billingsly?" she asked George. She knew he'd been avoiding her since the early-week edition of his paper had come out, but he couldn't hide forever.

"Bill? Not in the last hour." George shook his head. "Sophie doesn't like him, so he stays clear of her. Last time he came into the bookstore, she tried to take a nip out of his ankle. He threatened to sue, but I told him to go ahead and try. Me, an old man with a brain tumor who taught most of the residents of this county. Him, an outsider slandering wholesome Amish families and good townsfolk. Give me a jury of our peers and we'll see how it goes."

Rachel reached out to scratch under the little bichon's chin. "They say dogs are excellent judges of character."

"There you go." George gestured. "If you had been earlier, you would have tried to take a bite out of him."

"Why? What was he doing?"

George shrugged. "The usual. Trying to take pictures of some of the Amish kids in the children's play area. Your cousin Mary Aaron spied him and alerted their mothers. Lickety-split, before you know it, there were a dozen riled Amish mothers surrounding the children, their backs to Billingsly. If he took a picture, it was of a wall of black bonnets and capes. Then, when he backed off, the Amish women started shaking their fingers at him and fussing at him in Deitsch until he made a beeline for the door. Bill's ears were burning, I can tell you that. I doubt if he understands much Amish, but your sister-in-law Miriam called him a thickheaded English mule. Even if Bill didn't get the exact translation, he got the message."

"You know, I've had it with him," Rachel said, her temper rising. "He's lived here how many years? And how many times has he been told that the Amish don't permit photographs? It's rude to invite them to our town festival and then try to take advantage just to sell a few more papers." She glanced around, trying to pick out the local newspaper's owner and editor in the milling crowd. "If you see him before I do, tell him that I'm looking for him."

"Wish I could watch," George said. He glanced at his iPhone. "But I promised to take a turn in the toddlers' reading corner."

"Just don't let Sophie bite any of the little kids."

"You know she'd never do that," George said. "She loves children. It's Billingsly she hates." George turned away toward the children's reading section. "Call me later. I want to hear all about the showdown."

Rachel didn't find Billingsly, but she did run into her best friend, Mary Aaron. She was down on her knees, pulling a crate of canned peaches out from under a table. Leaving the family egg, peaches, and treenware stand in the capable hands of her sister Elsie, Mary Aaron adjourned with Rachel to the cafeteria for coffee. Mary Aaron was wearing a new apple-green dress with a white *kapp* and apron and black stockings and shoes. Rachel thought she looked exceptionally attractive, but then Mary Aaron had always been the cutest one in her family. She was younger than Rachel, but the two had become fast friends since Rachel had returned to Stone Mill.

"So, is Timothy here?" Rachel asked. She had removed her coat and thrown it over a chair and was now devouring a raisin-cinnamon sticky bun and sipping strong Kona coffee. Timothy was the personable young Amish man who often squired Mary Aaron to singings and other young people's frolics. Mary Aaron insisted he was just a friend, but Rachel suspected that Timothy wanted to court her cousin.

"*Ne,* he had to take his uncle's place at the farm auction in Delaware today. His uncle had several teeth pulled and he didn't feel like going. His cousins are teenagers and their father didn't trust them to bid on the team of Percherons. Timothy's staying over until Monday with another uncle, but he'll be here later in the week."

"How's Timothy going to get the team back to Stone Mill if he buys them?"

"His uncle will arrange to have them trailered after the weather clears. Provided, of course, that Timothy—" Mary Aaron broke off in midsentence. "Look who just walked in."

Rachel had seen Billingsly come in to the coffee area at almost the same instant her cousin had. "He won't get away from me this time," she said, getting to her feet.

Mary Aaron used her napkin to brush away the last crumbs of her cinnamon bun and grabbed the empty coffee cups. "I better get back to the stand. I'll hope he'll listen to reason."

"He will." Rachel stood as well. "Or I'll give him and his paper more trouble than he knows what to do with."

# Chapter 2

Billingsly was looking at his cell phone and didn't see Rachel until he nearly collided with her. He stopped short inches from contact, and his face reddened. He knew he was in trouble. "Rachel."

She glared at him. "I called the office several times for you this week. I left voice messages and I emailed you. You haven't gotten back to me, Bill."

"I've been busy. I get a lot of emails." He made a dismissive gesture. "And I was out of town on business. It's been hectic. You know. All the news that's fit to print and so forth," he joked.

She didn't smile. "And some that isn't." She indicated the cafeteria table she and Mary Aaron had just vacated. "We need to talk. Now."

His phone alerted him to the arrival of a text message, and he looked down at it. "This really isn't a good time." He glanced up and around the room as if looking for someone, then back at her. The smirk was gone from his face. "Why don't you drop by the office? Later in the week, maybe?"

"I've already been to your office, Bill. I went Wednesday. Then again yesterday. The receptionist keeps saying you were out."

"As I said, out-of-town business."

"Right." She nodded as if in total understanding. "The odd thing is, your Lexus was parked in your usual spot."

"Honestly, Rachel, I really don't have time to chat right now. Unless . . ." His tone became playful, though his pale eyes remained flat and expressionless. "Unless you've stumbled upon another dead body. In that case—"

She made fists and clamped them tightly against her sides. "That's not even a little bit funny."

He smiled thinly. "Murder's always good for selling newspapers. And Amish murders are better yet. Newswise, I mean. Bad for the victim, of course."

As a child, she'd been taught forbearance and forgiveness, but she doubted that she could ever extend grace to Billingsly. Right now, Rachel wanted desperately to smack his smirking face. "Has anyone ever told you what an egotistical jerk you are?"

His mouth pursed. "I think you've said quite enough."

"I haven't said nearly enough." She raised her voice, and several strangers sitting at the next table over drinking hot chocolate looked their way. "You've been avoiding me because you don't want to talk about that nasty gossip column you've been printing."

"You're making a scene, Rachel. People are staring."

"Let them. Let them hear what I think of your disregard for this town and the Amish community." She took a step closer to him, feeling her cheeks grow hot. "Do you have any idea how much damage you've caused, printing your hearsay? Why someone hasn't sued you for libel, I don't know."

"It has to be untrue to be libel," Billingsly responded coolly.

His arrogance made her even angrier. "How can you sleep at night, putting things like that in print? Maybe it's because you're a bully at heart. Is that why you enjoy this sort of thing? You enjoy taking advantage of vulnerable people who won't fight back? Is that it, Bill? Because it's not like this is the first time we've seen this from you. Last summer you used Beth Glick's murder to sell papers. And you didn't care how deeply you hurt the Amish doing it."

"The citizens of Stone Mill deserve to know the truth of what's happening in their neighborhood. If it's news, I publish it. I'm not responsible for people's dirty secrets. I just print it. Not my fault if it sells papers."

"Whose business is it that Joab and Annie's son broke with the Amish? So what if he's living in a trailer park with his girlfriend? Why would you shame Joab and Annie in front of their church?"

"You're not putting that on me. Joab shamed himself when he lied to his wife and his friends," Billingsly argued. "We're supposed to think the Amish are such good people. The Amish are no different from the rest of us. Joab lied to his bishop, his neighbors, and his wife. And that's news." He lifted a shoulder. "Besides, Aunt Nellie never uses names. Readers come to their own conclusions."

"Doesn't use names! What does that matter? Your gossip column identified Joab as a bearded miller who drives a piebald horse." She raised her chin defiantly. "How many millers in this valley still make stone-ground flour? How could it be any other man but Joab Herschberger? He and his wife are good people. Joab's brothers and his elderly parents live in Stone Mill. Their grown kids are here. Now Joab and Annie may sell and move west because of what you did."

"Not because of what I did," Billingsly flung back. "Because of what *Joab* did."

Rachel was so angry now that she felt like steam was going to blow out her ears. "It's going to stop." She pointed forcibly at the floor, ignoring the fact that she'd now drawn quite an audience. "And it's going to stop now. Your column has caused enough heartache in this community. Promise me that you'll never print it again, or—"

"Or what?" he scoffed. "What are you going to do? Have your cop boyfriend arrest me for telling the truth?" His eyes narrowed, and he lowered his voice so that no one around them could hear him. "Let me give you some advice, Rachel. Can I do that?"

He went on before she could respond. "You need to stop worrying so much about your Amish friends' reputations and start worrying about your own. You know why? Huh? Because Nellie has plenty of material and there's one column she's eager to see in print. A juicy tidbit about a nosy innkeeper with an insider trading conviction . . ."

Rachel blanched, suddenly feeling nauseated. "What did you say?" she breathed.

"You heard me. How would you like seeing your B&B on the front page of next Saturday's edition? You think that might dent your halo in this town? I bet the Associated Press would pick up *that* story." He thrust his head forward so that his nose was almost touching hers. "How good would that be for your business?"

She caught her breath, feeling as though she was going to implode or explode—she didn't know which. "Are you threatening me, Bill Billingsly?" she demanded loudly, not caring who heard her.

"Not threatening," he said quietly. "Promising." He turned as if to walk out of the cafeteria in the direction of the gym, then halted. A strange expression flickered across his features.

She glanced past him to see what had distracted him. Striding into the cafeteria was a burly, bearded man in green camo pants and an army jacket, a beret pulled over his head. She instantly recognized him as Jake Skinner, one of her guests at the B&B, a Vietnam War veteran who hadn't spoken more than twenty words to anyone since he'd checked into Stone Mill House.

Abruptly, Billingsly turned and strode away in the opposite direction. He walked between several tables to the service area, where kids picked up school lunches and placed them on trays. Without looking back, he pushed through a half door, and disappeared in the direction of the school's industrial kitchen.

Rachel looked back in Jake Skinner's direction, but lost sight of him in a party of tourists being herded toward the refreshment area by a tour guide waving a flag stamped with the outline of an Amish buggy.

"This way," the guide called to his charges. "We meet back here in half an hour for the buggy tour."

Rachel circumnavigated the group, her curiosity at the editor's flight quickly vanishing under a wave of anger. Billingsly had just threatened to publicly expose an incident that she'd thought was behind her. Would he do it? Would he plaster her face and Stone Mill House on the front page of his vicious rag? And if he did, what would it mean for her future?

"The snow's really coming down outside," Rachel observed, staring out the kitchen window for a moment, then turning back to Mary Aaron. "Glad my guests are all settled in for the night. I don't think anyone ought to be driving in this."

"*Ya,*" Mary Aaron agreed as she filled a thermos with milk that would be placed in the dining room for guests who rose early in the morning. "And a good thing I don't have to walk home in this weather. Listen to that wind. *Dat* said the almanac was calling for a blizzard this weekend."

"According to Evan, the weather service isn't expecting a blizzard, but there may be whiteout conditions in some parts of the county."

It was after nine p.m. Evan had taken Rachel and her cousin out for dinner at the local Mennonite diner, which had been packed, then dropped them off at the B&B and headed home. Rachel had invited him in for a cup of tea, but he'd declined, saying he wanted to get to bed early. He was starting a week on the seven-to-three shift the following day.

Mary Aaron had offered to spend the night at the B&B

and help Rachel do whatever needed to be done the following day. Ada, Rachel's cook and housekeeper, wouldn't be in the next morning because it was a Sunday, and Rachel would have her hands full. Usually on Sundays, Rachel could count on her part-time, non-Amish, high school girls, but one girl had taken the weekend off to go to a cousin's wedding in Philadelphia and the other had called in sick. Rachel and Mary Aaron would be on their own seeing to the needs of the inn.

Stone Mill House offered a buffet brunch daily, and afternoon tea some days of the week, but not regular sit-down meals. Still, if snow kept everyone indoors, Rachel's guests would need to eat. Her fridge and cabinets were well stocked, but she was no cook. Mary Aaron was technically bound by the same rules Ada and the other Amish women of the community followed. She was expected to refrain from unnecessary work on the Sabbath, but not being baptized yet, she was allowed a little leeway.

"Would you like a cup of tea before bed?" Rachel asked, filling a glass jar with homemade biscotti. She was standing beside Mary Aaron at the kitchen counter. "A cookie maybe?"

Rachel was half hoping that Mary Aaron would decline and head to bed once they had the dining room ready for morning. Rachel was feeling as if she could use a few moments to herself, just to get her head straight. It had been a great day, all in all. The Winter Frolic was off to a better start than anyone, including her, had expected. And she'd really enjoyed the horse-drawn sleigh ride with Evan. But she couldn't get Billingsly's threat out of her mind.

It wasn't something she wanted to discuss with Evan or even Mary Aaron. The incident Billingsly had referred to had happened a long time ago. In a different lifetime, really. When she'd lived in a high-rise apartment complex, worked for Lehman Brothers, and dated Christopher. In corporate business, actions weren't always black and white, especially in those days. Rachel didn't want to have to get into a conversation with Mary Aaron or Evan or any of her friends or relatives about what had happened because they could so easily misunderstand . . . and think the worst of her.

"*Ne,* I'm stuffed like a Christmas goose after all I had to eat at the frolic, and then the chicken stew and biscuits at the diner." Mary Aaron patted her abdomen, then picked up the thermos and carried it out of the kitchen and into the dining room.

Rachel followed her with the jar of biscotti. A coffeemaker and a stack of Ada's muffins covered in plastic wrap were already on the elegant oak serving buffet that Rachel had refinished herself after buying it at a yard sale. As Rachel arranged a set of mugs near the coffeepot, the light from the wall sconce reflected off her diamond, and Mary Aaron exclaimed with delight.

"Pretty, it is, your betrothal ring," she said, switching to the familiar Deitsch they often reverted to when they were alone. "Has your mother seen it yet?"

"No," she admitted. "But I'm not going to hide it from her and my father. I'm not Amish anymore. There's nothing wrong with wearing a ring given to me by the man I'm going to marry."

Her cousin patted her arm. "Poor Rachel. Caught somewhere between your world and mine."

Rachel closed her eyes for a second, suddenly feeling tired. "Something like that."

"Hard it must be." Mary Aaron paused. "You're really going to do it then? Marry your Englisher policeman? We wondered. The two of you have been walking out for what? Two years?"

"Something like that," Rachel admitted. She removed her apron. "It's been a while."

"And you're sure he's right for you?"

She opened her eyes to look at her cousin. "And you don't think he is? I thought you liked Evan."

"I do." Mary Aaron straightened a wicker basket of paper napkins. "I'm just asking if you're absolutely sure. Because for a long time—"

"Yes?"

"You weren't," Mary Aaron said gently.

"Evan's the right man for me. He's the man I want to marry," she said. Mary Aaron was right. For a long time, Rachel hadn't been sure about her relationship with Evan. But, looking back, she knew that was more a reflection of her own indecision than him.

"And he makes you happy?"

Rachel nodded. "He does. He's a wonderful man, and I hope that my mother and father will understand and come to love him as I do."

"It will be hard for them, Aunt Esther and Uncle Samuel. So long as you are single, they can still hope that you will come back to the church . . . to the community."

"I won't. I can't. It's not me anymore. I respect the faith"—Rachel sighed—"but I can't live like that. Not ever again."

Mary Aaron's lips curved into a gentle smile, one that lit her eyes with affection. "Then you should marry your Evan. Our life is not an easy one. It's not for everyone. But it will take time for your mother and father to accept him as a son-in-law. When he becomes your husband, they must face that there is no more chance."

Rachel shook her head again. "I know *Mam* wants me to come back. And I know she loves me. But she has to realize that I made my choice when I walked away from the farm all those years ago. I'm not the daughter—" She broke off as a man materialized in the hall doorway. "Mr. Skinner."

She walked toward him. "Is there something I can get you?"

He was wearing his coat. A pair of thick leather gloves dangled from a beefy hand. "I don't suppose you can offer me anything stronger than coffee?" he said brusquely.

Mary Aaron smiled and made herself busy checking to be sure the sugar bowls were full.

"No, Stone Mill House doesn't have a liquor license." *And I wouldn't sell it if I could*, Rachel thought. She did have an occasional glass of wine, but some habits die hard. The Amish didn't partake. Ever. And they would never serve alcohol to friends. Or strangers.

"Figured as much. But there must be a place in this town where a man can get a decent draft."

"The Black Horse. That's the tavern in town. It's right on the main street, just past the old theater that's a bookstore now." She hesitated. She didn't usually monitor her guests' comings and goings, but that didn't mean she never worried about them. "Have you looked outside, Mr. Skinner? It's really not a night to—"

"A little snow doesn't scare me, ma'am. I'm from Colorado." He tugged a black watch cap over his head and walked out of the dining room.

"Only an Englisher would be so foolish," Mary Aaron said when the front door closed behind Jake Skinner, "to go out in such a storm for beer."

"I agree," Rachel said. "But I could hardly tell him so."

"I suppose." Mary Aaron yawned and covered her mouth with her hand. "I was up before dawn this morning, so I'm ready for bed. Anything else you need me to do?"

"Not a thing. You go on up," Rachel said. "Pull the trundle bed out from under my bed. It's already made up with sheets and blankets."

"You're not coming?"

"In a bit. I want to check my email," she hedged. She did want to check her email, but she felt too restless to turn in yet. She knew she couldn't sleep, and she could hardly keep the light on and read with her cousin trying to nod off.

Rachel couldn't stop going over her encounter with Billingsly in her head. Had he really been threatening to publish information about her past? Or was he just running his mouth? She didn't know what she was going to do about it, but she couldn't let him get away with trying to intimidate her—no matter the personal cost.

A gust of wind rattled the windows, and they both looked in the direction of the front of the house. "Hope we don't lose electricity tonight," Rachel said. "I'd hate to have to depend on the fireplaces and woodstoves to keep my guests from freezing."

"At least you have them," Mary Aaron said. "Is good you don't forget all the lessons you learned growing up in a Plain household." She opened a closet door and removed a kerosene lantern. "I'll take this lamp up with me, just in case."

More than an hour later, Rachel was still puttering around in the small office. She'd checked her email and found a cancellation for the next night, which was just as well because the elderly couple in the first room on the second floor had already told her that they weren't attempting to drive home the following day and would be staying on.

It was getting late. Rachel knew that she should get to sleep herself because the following day would be hectic. Even though the Amish members of the community wouldn't be participating in the celebration, there was still an array of events scheduled. The one she was most excited about was the ice sculpture contest. Entrants, locals and out-of-towners, had signed up to create ice statues of animals. The creations could be sculpted anywhere in the town limits, and part of the fun was that visitors were asked to locate as many of the statues as possible. The winning sculptor would receive a hundred dollars and bragging rights, and the visitor who found all of the sculptures would win a free night at Rachel's B&B for the following year.

Sunday's forecast was for below-normal temperatures and sunshine by midafternoon. Rachel was expected to be a judge for the ice sculpture contest. And without enough sleep and with the extra work of so many guests, she would be lucky to make it through the day on her feet. She really did need to go to bed.

But she kept thinking about Bill and what he'd said. Would he really tell the town she'd been convicted of insider trading?

She stood in the middle of her office for a moment, thinking. She needed to talk to Billingsly. And the fact of the matter was, she wouldn't be able to sleep until she did. She stood there listening to the howl of the wind for a moment. Last time she had checked, it was still snowing. Weather reports were for heavy snow and high winds all night, tapering off sometime after four a.m.

It really wasn't a good idea to be driving during a storm like this. But Billingsly lived only three blocks away. And he made a point of telling anyone who would listen that he never dined until ten or went to bed before midnight. Billingsly would still be awake. He'd be home because of the storm, and she could make a rational attempt to talk some sense into him. Or at least know if he really was going to tell everyone what she'd done. Because if he was, she needed to tell those closest to her before the news got out. Resolutely, she donned boots, her warmest parka, and mittens, and let herself out by the back door.

The cold took Rachel's breath away. Not only was it snowing hard, but the wind was piercing, too. It howled around the house, whipping the tree branches and heaping up drifts around the house. Rachel shoved her hands in her coat pockets, put her head down, and started walking.

Hulda's house, behind her, was lit up like a Christmas tree. Her elderly neighbor would no doubt be curled up in her bed, reading a book, and the sons and grandsons would be watching sports on the multiple TVs in the house or playing billiards in the basement.

No vehicles were moving on the road to town. Rachel was so glad that Evan wasn't on duty tonight because the highway would be littered with accidents: fender benders and worse. It happened every time they had a major snowstorm. Did average people ever consider how much the police sacrificed to protect them in this kind of weather? Did they ever consider how often public servants like the police and paramedics put their lives on the line?

The snow was piling up fast, making it hard to see where the sidewalk ended and the street began. Rachel kept walking, but began to wonder if she'd come out on a fool's errand. Not only did she have another block and a half to walk, but she'd have to make her way back, too.

Of course she had no intention of staying long. And maybe Billingsly, despite being the cold fish that he was, would hear her out when she walked into his house looking like Frosty the Snowman.

Her feet were getting numb, and she wished she'd thought to wear a scarf. Luckily, lights were on in a few of the houses, and here and there a yard light shone. She concentrated on how the lights sparkled in the falling snow. Unlike her B&B, which was a hundred years older than most of the structures in Stone Mill, the houses were mostly early Victorian, with large yards and elaborate front porches. Pretty houses.

She turned onto Billingsly's street and spotted his house; the front porch light was on. Third on the right. She thought she could make out . . . Yes, there were definitely lights on downstairs in his house. He had to be at home because he never wasted electricity by leaving lights on when he wasn't there.

It was impossible to find the brick walk that led to the front porch, so Rachel cut across the lawn. Shivering with cold, she reached the house and made her way carefully up to the front door. The house had been magnificent in its day. Six pillars marched across the front, and the porch roofline was edged in gingerbread trim. The stained glass windows were large, almost floor to ceiling, and the elaborate front door boasted another pane of stained glass and an antique doorbell. Rachel reached out to ring the bell, but then hesitated.

Was this really a good idea? She was still so angry.

And a little scared.

She lowered her hand. Through the stained-glass sidelights on the door, she thought she could make out Bill's silhouette in the doorway that she knew led into his kitchen. His back was to her. He appeared to be wearing a bathrobe. A fire flickered on the hearth in his living room fireplace.

She raised her hand to ring the bell again. Then dropped it. *Face it, Rae-Rae,* her inner voice mocked. *This isn't one of your better ideas. Better to think on this a day or two. Go home, get warm, and climb in your bed* . . . which was exactly what she did.

# Chapter 3

As predicted, the snowfall ended by sunrise the following day, and while Stone Mill did get about nine inches, it was not hit by the blizzard that everyone had been talking about. At seven thirty, after Rachel had fed her goats, she and Mary Aaron set out a breakfast of fresh fruit, pastries, and cereal and went outside to begin shoveling the sidewalks. There was a heavy pewter sky, and the air was cold, but the wind had driven much of the new-fallen snow into drifts at the edge of the house, so the task wasn't as bad as it might have been. They'd worked about fifteen minutes when Rachel's brothers Danny and Levi came walking up, each carrying a snow shovel.

"I didn't expect you two here this morning," Rachel said, leaning on her shovel to catch her breath. "But I'm glad to see you."

Levi was a sturdy boy of twelve with dark hair and a sweet smile, her favorite among her brothers, even though a sister wasn't supposed to have favorites. Danny, soon to be fourteen, was just entering the difficult teenage years when an older sister, especially one who had shamed the family by leaving the church, could be a source of embarrassment. Lately, she'd been making an effort to get to know him better, but so far, he'd resisted.

"How did you convince *Dat* to let you come shovel snow for me?" Rachel asked Danny, but Levi answered.

"Didn't tell him that's why we were coming. It's visiting Sunday. We've come to visit our sister."

Danny averted his gaze and dug his shovel into the snow.

"Of course, it being the Sabbath," Levi continued, "we're not supposed to do work except what has to be done."

"Like clearing snow for safety reasons," Mary Aaron put in with amusement. She was wearing a blue scarf over her head and a man's black beanie over that.

"Right," Levi agreed. "So we can't take money, but we *can* take breakfast." He grinned, his nose and cheeks a bright red. "I'll bet you've got something good in that kitchen."

"Fair enough," Rachel agreed. "And next time you come to help out, I'll be sure to—" A distressed cry caught her attention, and she turned toward the street. Eddie, the boy who delivered the Sunday Harrisburg newspaper, was stumbling along the street, slipping, falling, and weeping.

"What's wrong?" Rachel called. Eddie was a sensible youth, about the same age as Levi. "Are you hurt?" She stuck her shovel in a drift and ran through the snow, wading through drifts to reach the street. Mary Aaron, Danny, and Levi abandoned their shovels and followed her. "What happened to you?" she asked as she reached Eddie. His face was bright red with cold, his face wet with tears. The child looked terrified.

"Something wrong?" Jake Skinner had appeared on the front steps of the B&B in his coat and hat.

"We're trying to find out," Mary Aaron called back to him.

Rachel grabbed both of Eddie's arms, forcing him to look at her. He was almost as tall as she was. "Do you want me to call your mom?" she asked calmly.

The paperboy nodded, wiped at his running nose with his coat sleeve. "Yeah. Could you call my mom? Please? I left my cell phone at home."

Rachel let go of him and inspected him closely. She didn't see any blood; he seemed more frightened than injured. "We'll go right inside and call her, but you have to tell me what's wrong. Are you hurt?"

Tears began to run down his red cheeks again. "It's Mr. . . . Mr. Billingsly," Eddie sobbed. "He's—" The boy pointed with a shaking hand in the direction he'd just come.

"Take a deep breath and calm down." Rachel took him by his shoulders. "What about Mr. Billingsly?"

Eddie's wide eyes stared into her face. His normally fair skin had turned a pasty gray, his freckles standing out like raindrops on a dusty windowpane. He looked as if he'd seen a ghost.

Jake Skinner approached. "Is the boy hurt?"

Rachel shook her head. "I don't think so." And then to Eddie she said, "What were you saying about Mr. Billingsly?"

"I think he's . . . he's dead." Rachel heard one of her brothers gasp behind her. "Outside . . . on his front porch," Eddie managed. "I was delivering his paper. He . . . he wants it on the porch by the front door. Not in the yard. No tip for the month if you forget."

"You think he's dead?" Rachel repeated, trying to cut through the boy's rambling. She could hear the faint wail of sirens.

"He's got to be dead. I . . . I didn't know it was him. I saw this . . . this *thing*—" Eddie choked. "On the porch. I thought it was an ice statue. You know, the ones for . . . for the contest today. But . . . but when I got closer, I saw that it wasn't. It was a real person. All covered in ice. His eyes were open and he was . . . was staring at me." The boy lowered his head and began to weep uncontrollably. "It was aw-awful."

Rachel looked at Mary Aaron. "Could you take Eddie in the house and phone his mother to come and get him?"

"*Vat is?*" Danny asked. Both he and Levi were standing a few feet away, staring at Eddie. "Somebody's dead?"

"Of course I'll take him." Mary Aaron smiled kindly at the paperboy and reached for one of his gloved hands. "Come on, Eddie. You can have something hot to drink while you wait for your mom."

"Go on," Rachel urged, glancing in the direction of Billingsly's house. "She'll call your mother for you. Don't worry. It'll be all right."

"No, it won't," Eddie said, shaking his head slowly. "It won't. Because he's dead."

Rachel watched as Mary Aaron led Eddie toward the house. "Danny, you and Levi wait here. I'm going to go and see for myself."

She glanced at Jake Skinner. He had picked up one of the snow shovels and started clearing the sidewalk, which struck her as odd since she was sure he had heard Eddie's claim that Bill Billingsly was dead. And she was also certain her guest somehow knew Bill.

"You don't have to do that," Rachel called.

The man shrugged. "Needs doing."

Rachel headed for Billingsly's, deciding to walk on the street. A snowplow had been through already, so it was easier going than the sidewalk would have been. She quickened her pace as the wail of emergency vehicle sirens cut louder through the peaceful, tree-lined neighborhood. Could Billingsly really be dead? From what? Had the man suffered a heart attack shoveling snow?

As Rachel hurried, she became aware that Levi and Danny were following her; she heard their boots crunching on the new snow. "Go back to the house," she called over her shoulder. They ignored her, catching up, then surging ahead. Other neighbors were coming out of their homes, some still in bathrobes and slippers. Staring. Talking excitedly. Rachel broke into a trot. Billingsly couldn't possibly be dead.

Billingsly was definitely dead.

A few minutes later, Rachel stood in the midst of a gathering crowd of horrified onlookers. Although there were a few strangers, people in town for the Winter Frolic, she knew most of them, both Amish and English—among them several Amish couples; Jerry the mailman; Dr. Patterson the dentist; two of Eli Rust's sons; Blade, who lived with his family a block away; and a Canadian couple who were staying at Stone Mill. She had no idea how the Canadians had beat her there.

Two uniformed state troopers were already at the scene, trying to keep civilians out of the yard and away from the house, but it was a lost cause. A minute ago a paramedic vehicle had come to a halt in the middle of the street in front of the house, but they made no move to approach the victim. One of the troopers had met the paramedics on the sidewalk and was talking to them.

Rachel, like everyone else, couldn't stop staring. The entire scene was so bizarre that it was hard to believe it was real. Billingsly's stately home and the yard surrounding it looked like a painting on a calendar. Snow frosted the roof, the porch, and the surroundings, and ice coated the trees and shrubbery, making a beautiful winter montage. The yard was a pristine white, the perfect tableau, broken only by the curve of a small, dark object lying half buried in the snow at the side of the house.

Rachel's gaze kept returning to the front of the house. There were only two sets of footprints in the snow leading to the porch, one made by Eddie, Rachel assumed, and the other made by one of the troopers, who must have gone up the steps to check for a pulse. Eddie's tracks hadn't gone all the way up the stairs. It was obvious from his footprints where he had stopped, stared, then turned and run. His canvas bag of newspapers lay half buried in the snow at the bottom of the steps.

Everyone was talking excitedly, but in hushed tones. As Eddie had related, at first glance, Rachel would almost have taken the grotesque figure on the porch for one of the ice sculptures that had been springing up all over town all week.

The thing had the distorted shape of a man. Upon closer inspection, a naked man. She glanced away, attempting to convince herself that this wasn't some publicity stunt that Billingsly had conjured up to cause a commotion and sell papers. But she couldn't help herself; she had to look again.

This was not an ice sculpture or a stunt.

Bill Billingsly was dead and not of natural causes. He was seated, his back to one of the large supporting pillars of his porch, his hands behind his back tied to the gray column. His legs were outstretched, as if he were lounging on the edge of the porch, his body parallel to the street. There was a length of rope wrapped around his ankles and calves.

Encased in ice.

And through ice, she could make out blue-and-white fabric tied around his mouth. A gag.

Rachel hated herself for standing there gawking at him, but she couldn't look away as the macabre image burned into her consciousness. She took in more details: Billingsly's dark, hairy legs and chest were as bare as his feet. He wore no hat or coat, though she could see now that he was wearing blue-and-green boxer shorts. And his eyes were open, as Eddie had reported. In fact, it was worse. Billingsly's eyes and mouth gaped as if in a final scream, crying out for help that never came.

Rachel couldn't help but begin to put together the facts she could assemble from the scene. Someone had obviously tied him to the porch; no one could do this to himself. She wanted to think that maybe he'd been killed and then left on the porch, but she suspected that wasn't the case. This looked too . . . staged. Staring at Billingsly's frozen body, she got the immediate and distinct impression that someone was making a statement.

"Could you step back, please?" One of the two troopers on the scene was trying to control the growing crowd. She was tall and attractive, even with her long blond hair tied back severely and no makeup on her face. Rachel had met her at a Christmas party she'd attended with Evan. She'd recently transferred from a troop farther west. Evan liked her; he said she was smart and had good instincts, that she was a good cop. Her name was Lucy . . . Lucy . . . Mars.

"Please," Trooper Mars repeated, speaking with authority but not unkindly. "I need you to take a few steps back. If you could move to the sidewalk, that would be best." She looked up and called out to several people cutting between the house next door and Billingsly's house. "We're asking that everyone stay off the property," she insisted, waving them out of the side yard.

Rachel took a couple of steps back to stand on the sidewalk that had yet to be shoveled, her gaze still fixed on Billingsly's hideous form. When she'd first reached the house, she'd been aware of no sounds but the creaking of snow-clustered boughs and the steady pulse of her own heart. Now, she was almost overwhelmed by the noises around her: the familiar click of photos being snapped with smartphones, more sirens, the clang of a fire truck, a dog whining, and Jerry's disjointed voice, hoarse and rasping: ". . . I called it in. It was me . . . Walking my dog and the paperboy . . ." He walked toward the police cruiser with Trooper Mars, and his words were lost in the gathering hubbub of arriving firemen and more tourists and locals.

Rachel glanced to her left, and her gaze settled on her brother Levi, then on Danny. "You two need to go home. *Mam* and *Dat* will be very upset that I let you see this." She herded them out of the crowd.

"Are you coming?" Danny asked.

"In a few minutes." There were people everywhere now. Cars were pulling up, not just out front but on the side streets, too. In the alley behind Billingsly's house. People were walking all over the yard. "You two go on now," she told her brothers. "Have Mary Aaron get you some breakfast. I'll see you for supper."

"You're still coming?" Levi asked.

"Of course." She stood there after the boys walked away, watching as several state troopers and the paramedics approached Billingsly's porch. They all stopped and studied the body. This had to be difficult for the paramedics, she thought. Being called to a scene where there was obviously nothing that could be done. She was no pathologist, but from his appearance, he'd been dead for hours.

A trooper and one of Billingsly's neighbors began to hastily put up crime scene tape, and she was pushed back farther by the crowd. There were people everywhere. Where had they all come from? she wondered. She didn't want to be there. She wanted to be anywhere else . . . but she'd been here last night. The thought came to her suddenly. She'd been here last night and would have to tell the police.

Billingsly hadn't been on the porch when she'd come the previous night, obviously. But he'd been home—she was sure of that. She stared at the house, taking notice that there were no lights on as there had been the night before, neither the porch light nor any interior lights; it was a dark enough day that had there been lights on inside, she would have been able to see them. So this had happened after he went to bed?

Rachel made eye contact with an Amish woman standing near her. Mary Yoder, a distant cousin of her mother's. She wore a heavy black wool cloak and black bonnet, her Sunday church clothes. She and her husband must have been passing through town on their way to services. There were several Amish church groups in Stone Mill and they had different Sunday schedules; while this week was a visiting Sunday for her parents and Bishop Abner's flock, folks from another church district a mile away might soon be gathering for day-long services.

Rachel nodded and Mary nodded back, but Rachel made no attempt join the group of Amish, even though she knew most of them. They were family friends, cousins, cousins of friends. Some people might have been surprised to see their Amish neighbors there, but Rachel wasn't. They cared as much about what happened in Stone Mill as the Englishers did.

An unmarked car pulled up behind the paramedics' van. Two men got out. One was Evan. He wasn't in uniform this morning. He was wearing dress pants under his parka. As a detective, he didn't wear a uniform.

"Are they taking Billingsly to the hospital?" a bearded Amish man asked her in Deitsch. It was John Glick, Beth Glick's uncle.

"Why would they do that if he's dead?" Mary Yoder asked.

"Who knows what Englishers would do?" commented another man. "But who would do such a thing, even to him? It is a terrible thing to happen here in our valley."

"I don't understand it either," Rachel agreed. "It's unbelievable. I wouldn't believe it if I didn't see it with my own eyes."

"After last summer, you can say that?" Rachel's cousin Ruth asked. "After that poor girl you found drowned in the quarry?" She shook her head sadly. "You live as long as I have, you learn that there is much wickedness in this world."

" 'Whoever diggeth a pit shall fall therein,' " someone quoted.

Sounds of agreement rippled through the small group dressed in black.

Rachel's throat constricted. It was a quote from Proverbs her mother had always used when Rachel was a child. You get what you deserve was what it meant. But no one deserved this. Her gaze went to Bill's body and then to Evan. Who would do something like this? she thought. Who had a problem with Billingsly? A lot of people, and she was at the top of the list. But who hated him enough to kill him?

She immediately thought of Jake Skinner. He was a stranger in town, a stranger whom Billingsly obviously had a history with, enough history to duck out of the school the previous day through the kitchen to keep from running into him. And then his behavior a few minutes ago, when he'd heard Bill was dead, was even odder. And suspicious. Who, upon hearing of the death of someone he knew, responded by shoveling a stranger's snow?

Rachel walked out onto the street, wove her way around the police cars parked haphazardly and then back onto the sidewalk. When Evan saw her approaching, he said something to the other plainclothes detective and came toward her. She held up her hand. She knew what he was thinking. She shouldn't be here. "I'm going," she said when he stopped in front of her. "I just wanted you to know that I saw something odd yesterday. You need to contact a man named Jake Skinner staying at my B&B and tell him not to leave town." She looked up into his eyes. Eyes she had fallen in love with at some point, though when she didn't exactly know. "He shouldn't leave until you talk to him, Evan."

# Chapter 4

"Such a terrible thing," Bishop Abner said as he took a seat at Rachel's parents' kitchen table that evening, "to have another murder here in our Stone Mill. Like them big cities with all the shooting of guns and stabbing with knives."

"No better than Sodom and Gomorrah we'll be soon," Rachel's Uncle Aaron intoned. "Not that Bill Billingsly was ever a friend to us, but no man should die in such a way."

"Frozen solid, they say." Rachel's father, Samuel, stood at the head of the long kitchen table that easily sat twelve. "You think he just went onto his porch and got locked out?"

"Locked himself out and then tied himself to his front porch?" Aaron gave a snort. "Not even an Englisher would be so *mupsich*."

"Tied himself to his front porch," Naamah's nephew Sammy repeated and nodded. "*Ya,* stupid to do such a thing."

Rachel's Aunt Hannah made a clicking sound between her teeth as she set down a butter plate. "No man should die in such a way. Not even the newspaperman who has said such terrible things."

Rachel couldn't agree more, but she remained quiet, helping her mother and her little sisters bring food to the table. Uncle Aaron, Aunt Hannah, Annie and Joab Herschberger, Bishop Abner, Naamah, and her nephew Sammy had come to share a light supper with the family, as had Rachel's brother Moses and his wife, Ruth.

Since Rachel's mother and father still had three sons and two daughters living at home, the additional company made quite a crowd for the evening meal. The younger children were all scattered through the house, playing with an assortment of cousins. Rachel's mother's kitchen was large, like most Amish kitchens, but rather than set up additional tables and still not be able to seat everyone comfortably, they had decided that only the adult guests and Rachael's parents would eat in the first sitting. Once their meal was finished, Rachel's parents would retire to the sitting room with the others and Rachel, Mary Aaron, and the younger children could have their turn at supper.

In remembrance of the early days of persecution, Amish worship services were held in private homes rather than a church, but this Sunday was a visiting Sunday for Bishop Abner and his flock. These pleasant days of rest and relaxation were reserved for time with close friends and family. There were no chores other than those absolutely necessary, such as caring for the farm animals. Hard work was a natural and welcome part of Old Order Amish life, but visiting Sundays were a cherished and much anticipated break from everyday life, one that Rachel missed as part of the English world. Too often, at the B&B, her Sunday afternoons were consumed by housecleaning, laundry, and catching up on her bookkeeping on her computer.

Though Rachel no longer attended Amish religious services, she was always invited to come on visiting Sundays. She liked spending time with her family and Amish friends, especially her siblings, and she enjoyed being part of the family's challenges and successes. She missed so much in her day-to-day life at the B&B. Being here, in the home she'd been raised in, grounded her and filled her with a quiet peace. Lately, Evan had even been joining her on visiting Sundays. He liked both of her parents, and he enjoyed interacting with her large and noisy family, so different from his own. Evan had been invited for supper today, which always made for an interesting evening, but he hadn't been able to get off due to the urgency of the murder investigation.

Rachel sliced a loaf of whole wheat bread and carried the platter to the table. The bread had been baked the previous night, but still smelled rich, yeasty, and heavenly. Not even having the bishop and his wife to supper would warrant making bread on a Sunday. The meal would be mostly cold: sliced ham, potato salad, pickled beets, coleslaw, an assortment of cheeses, and canned fruit. The only thing served hot today was a hearty pepper pot soup that had been prepared Saturday and kept warm on the back burner of the woodstove.

Rachel's father scraped the floor noisily as he pulled out a chair at the head of the table. "We should pray for Billingsly. He may not have been a friend to our people, but he deserves our compassion."

"*Ya,*" Bishop Abner agreed. "At a time like this, it isn't our place to judge." He turned an empathetic gaze on Joab and Annie. "You must extinguish the anger in your hearts, despite the harm he's done to your family."

Joab's expression remained wary, but he nodded. Annie pursed her lips and looked down at her plate. The unnatural stiffness in her neck and shoulders told Rachel that she was not ready to forgive Billingsly.

"Shall we bow our heads for grace?" Rachel's father asked.

Quietly, Rachel's mother slid into a chair between Annie and her daughter-in-law Ruth. Rachel, Mary Aaron, and Rachel's sisters paused and closed their eyes during the silent prayer of thanksgiving. When grace was over, her father began to pass the food, and everyone settled in to enjoy the simple meal. There would be no more discussion of the murder during supper and probably not for the rest of the evening. Of course, even if there were discussion, Rachel wouldn't be included because she wasn't welcome to sit at the table with them.

Her relationship with her mother and father was complicated. She had never been baptized in the church, so she'd broken no laws by leaving the faith as a young woman. But in her parents' eyes, or at least her mother's, there had to be consequences to her abandoning the church and Amish life. At her mother's insistence, one of those consequences was that she could not eat with her parents. While Evan and other Englishers found this hard to believe, Rachel understood it wasn't a lack of love that made her parents treat her this way. It was a desperate attempt to force her to return to her faith and roots.

Rachel was just getting ready to slip out of the kitchen when her mother held up an empty serving plate and announced, "I think the pickled beet dish is running low."

"I'll get more from the pantry." Rachel took the plate, knowing very well that the statement had been intended for her. Since Rachel had returned to Stone Mill, her mother had refused to speak to her directly, which made for some awkward moments. But some funny ones, too. Sometimes Rachel would stand next to her mother and have a whole conversation with her via one of her siblings or her father. Her mother would speak to the go-between, who would then repeat what had been said.

Rachel headed for the pantry.

"Need something?" Mary Aaron followed Rachel out of the kitchen.

"Beets. I can get them."

Mary Aaron was her closest friend, closer to her than even her brothers and sisters, but Rachel had a lot on her mind, things she wasn't comfortable talking about, even with Mary Aaron. Like her unwise decision to go to Billingsly's house to confront him the previous night. She hadn't told Mary Aaron; she hadn't even told Evan. She wasn't sure why she hadn't told, but the longer she waited, the more difficult it would be. She'd look as though she was deliberately concealing what she'd done rather than simply being unwilling to admit she'd been so rash.

Inside the small room, lined floor to ceiling with shelves, Rachel stood on tiptoes to grab a Mason jar off a shelf.

Mary Aaron let the heavy wooden door swing shut behind her. "Where's your engagement ring?" She kept her voice low. "It's not on your hand."

Rachel curbed her impatience and tapped her skirt to be sure it was still there. "In my pocket." She didn't want to talk about this now, but she knew her cousin. When Mary Aaron got a notion in her head, she usually wouldn't let up on it.

"You still haven't told them?" Mary Aaron stared at her, clearly displeased. "Rae-Rae, you promised. It's been two weeks. You *have* to tell them." She grabbed her cousin's hand. "You haven't changed your mind, have you? About Evan?"

"No. No, of course not." Rachel pulled away and tried to unscrew the ring on the jar. She didn't want to be cross with Mary Aaron, but this was really none of her business. The thought that her cousin was probably right made her position hard to defend, though. "It took me such a long time to agree to marry him because I wanted to be sure." Frustratingly, the jar lid wouldn't loosen.

"You have to tell them," Mary Aaron insisted. "Your parents are going to find out from someone else and then their feelings are really going to be hurt."

Rachel sighed. She'd been putting off the announcement of her engagement because she knew how disappointed her family was going to be. Even though they all liked Evan, they were all still hoping that she would *come to her senses* and return to the Amish faith. If she married an Englisher, that would pretty much mean they had lost their daughter. At least in the sense of their faith. "I'm going to tell them." She tried the lid again.

"Tonight? Are you telling them tonight? Here, give it to me."

Rachel slid the jar across the painted wooden countertop to her cousin. "Probably not tonight," she admitted.

Mary Aaron cut her eyes at her as she tried to twist the lid.

Rachel gestured in the direction of the kitchen, where everyone at the table was in quiet conversation as they ate. "Not with everyone else here. Not with what's happened today. Me getting engaged to someone I've been dating a year isn't all that monumental considering the fact that Bill Billingsly is lying in the morgue right now."

"I'm sorry he's dead, but you had nothing to do with that. I'll pray for him. But whatever happened, I don't think it was a random killing. He probably brought the evil on himself because he hurt so many people."

*She's right,* Rachel thought, not voicing a reply. *I had nothing to do with Billingsly's death, and I didn't see anything at his house. I have nothing to add to the investigation.* Saying something to Evan would only muddy the water. Unconsciously, she rubbed her palms together.

"And it's not a year. It's more like two years," Mary Aaron corrected. "You and Evan have been dating *two* years." She slid the jar back. "I can't get it, either."

"We've got one of those rubber thingies somewhere." Rachel avoided eye contact with Mary Aaron and began to dig around in a wooden box on top of the counter that held spare jar lids, rubber bands, and other assorted objects.

"So why haven't you told them yet?" Mary Aaron persisted. "Is it the whole idea of becoming engaged to an Englisher, or is it the fancy ring?"

Rachel found the rubber gripper at the bottom of the box. "You know I'm never coming back to the church. *Mam* and *Dat* know, too, I think." She met her cousin's penetrating gaze and then returned her attention to the stubborn jar lid. "And it's not the ring, either. I've just been busy, and—"

"You're stalling," Mary Aaron put in.

"It's just that I want to tell them in the right way." Rachel gave the lid a good tug. "There it is!" She set aside the little rubber mat and unscrewed the lid.

Mary Aaron handed her a can opener. "You *have* to tell them this week."

Rachel popped the lid off the beets. "I will."

"You will," Mary Aaron insisted, using a fork to move beets from the jar to the plate. "Or I'll tell. I feel bad enough as it is, me knowing when they don't; a girl's parents should know these things first."

"You wouldn't dare." Rachel met Mary Aaron's gaze again. "*I'll tell them,*" she insisted. "This week. I'll come over one day this week, I'll sit them down, I'll tell them. I'll even wear the ring."

"Good." Mary Aaron picked up the plate. "Now you better get back to the kitchen or your mother will be coming to see what happened to you."

"No, she'll probably send Amanda or Lettie." She offered Mary Aaron a conspiratorial smile. "Because coming herself might force her to speak to me."

At the table, Naamah, Aunt Hannah, and Rachel's mother were discussing plans for the next quilting bee, and the men were quietly eating. Rachel's sister-in-law Ruth threw her a look that said, without words, that she would rather have been in the pantry as part of whatever Rachel and Mary Aaron had been up to than on her best behavior seated among the older women.

Ruth was shy around the bishop's wife and her mother-in-law, but full of fun in her own house or when she was with women her own age. She was a perfect match for Moses, and managed to get her way most of the time while making him think that he was in charge. Rachel wished she could learn a few tricks from Ruth because, as well as she and Evan liked each other, they often butted heads.

The atmosphere in the kitchen was warm and friendly, despite the pall cast by Billingsly's death. Only Joab and Annie seemed on edge. Rachel noticed that Annie had taken food on her plate but had hardly touched a morsel, while her husband ate but had little to say. Poor Joab. He seemed to have aged ten years in the week since Billingsly's column had exposed their son's true circumstances and the deception Joab had perpetrated.

Folks in Stone Mill had known that Joab and Annie's son had left suddenly the previous fall, but Joab had told everyone, including his wife, that their Wayne had simply needed to *sow some oats* and had moved to an Amish community in Delaware. He told everyone that his eldest son was working for a construction company and living with an Amish family while he searched for a wife. The truth, Billingsly had reported in the paper, though no one knew how he'd found out, was that Wayne had left the faith and was living in sin with an English girl in Delaware.

When the newspaper column had been published, Joab had told Annie what he'd done and then gone to the bishop and confessed his sin of lying. What had gone on in that conversation only Joab and Bishop Abner would ever know, but Joab had been forgiven. Forgiveness was one of the cornerstones of the Amish faith. And while the community as a whole was surprised by Joab's deception, there wasn't anyone who didn't understand why he had done it. As he had explained to Annie and his family and friends, he'd lied because he hoped their son would see the error of his ways and return to his faith without having to worry his mother unduly.

Wayne's transgression was more serious than Rachel's. She had left the faith before baptism, whereas Wayne had fled several years after he'd joined the church, leaving his family and community no way to accept his new life. Upon hearing the news from Joab's own mouth, Bishop Abner had been forced to immediately deliver a sentence of shunning.

With Wayne under the *bann*, should he return to Stone Mill, no one in the community, including his parents and brothers and sisters, could allow Wayne into his or her home, eat with him, or speak with him. It was a bitter pill for those who loved him, a last resort, not intended as punishment but as a final attempt to save him. If he repented of his sin, confessed in front of the congregation, and returned to his Amish life, he would be forgiven and could join the family again with no repercussions. If he didn't, he would be cut off from everyone for the rest of his life.

Touched but helpless to do anything about the Herschbergers' grief, Rachel was suddenly overcome with a need to be with Evan. Joab's dishonesty with his wife, family, and friends was almost more devastating to the community than Wayne's abandonment. And now Rachel suddenly felt guilty about her own dishonesty. Even if she wasn't being outright deceitful about her engagement to Evan, she was certainly withholding information. Had he been here tonight, he would have been sorely disappointed in her. Maybe he'd even think she was ashamed that she'd agreed to marry him. It wasn't that at all. She loved him and intended to spend the rest of her life with him.

On impulse, Rachel slipped into the pantry, pulled her phone from her pocket, and texted Evan.

**Hey.**

It only took him a few seconds to respond. **Hey yourself.**

**I miss you.**

**Me too.**

**Dinner?**

**Still at the troop,** he responded a couple of seconds later.

**You need to eat and rest,** she texted. **Want me to bring you a plate?**

**Leaving soon. Your place?**

**See you in an hour,** she responded. Then she slipped her phone into her pocket and waved to Mary Aaron to join her in the pantry.

"I think I'm going to go home," she told her cousin, keeping her voice low. "Evan's just getting off and I'm sure he hasn't eaten all day."

"You're not going to stay and eat?"

"No, I think I'll go now. It's had to have been an awful day for Evan. I don't want him going home to cold dinner out of a can."

"Rachel?" Her father's voice made them both turn toward the kitchen. "Rachel, are you woolgathering in there? Bishop Abner has a question for you."

"Coming!" Rachel hurried out of the pantry and approached the table. She smiled, smoothing her skirt. "*Ya?* Sorry, I didn't realize you were calling me."

Gazing at her with affection, the bishop stroked his bearded chin with gnarled fingers. "We were just talking about how successful the Winter Frolic is going to be," he said in perfect English. "I wonder if you might have a count of how many visitors we had yesterday."

"That's a good question. I'm not sure," she admitted. "But I'll find out. George will know. That's the kind of thing that he would keep track of."

"*Ya*, I suppose he would, poor man," her father said. "There's another who carries a terrible weight on his shoulders."

"It's not our place to judge," Uncle Aaron intoned. "A cancerous tumor of the head might cause a good man to do anything."

"I agree," Naamah said gently. "George has a good heart."

Sammy paused in his chewing. "I like George. He gave me a book about kites. I made forty-seven kites and I climbed up on the windmill and I tied forty-seven hundred kites to the blades."

Abner smiled kindly at his nephew. "Enough talk, Sammy. You didn't tie kites to the windmill." He glanced at the others gathered around the table. "Sammy's afraid of heights. I can't even get him to stand on a ladder. If I've got a problem with my windmill, I'm the one going up. I can't even get him to go up to the hayloft to throw down bales."

"I can throw forty-seven bales," Sammy said cheerfully.

"Our Rachel has a good heart, too," Aunt Hannah said,

returning to the conversation they were having before Sammy spoke. "No wonder she's not herself tonight. We should save some of our pity for her. No wonder you are in a daze, child."

Naamah nodded. "True words. My heart goes out to you, Rachel. To discover poor Beth Glick last summer and then to witness Billingsly's remains this morning. With your own eyes to see such a thing."

"*Ya,*" Annie said with a sigh. She laid her fork down beside her plate. "To see such a thing, and still she comes here to be with us and help her mother. Such a good girl you are, Rachel, even if you have strayed from the fold."

"Your daughter does look exhausted." Her mother glanced at her husband. "I hope this has not made her ill. A sickness of the mind seeps into the body."

"I'm not sick, *Mam,*" Rachel assured her. "But I am tired." She untied the apron and hung it up. "Please excuse me if I don't stay any longer. I think I need to go back to Stone Mill House. I have a house brimming with guests, and I think I'll turn in early."

"Without your supper you must leave us?" Her father rose to his feet and looked at her with a furrowed brow. "Are you sure you are not getting sick?"

"I'm not sick." She offered him a half-smile. "It's only that—"

"Samuel," her mother interrupted, "tell your daughter that, sick or not, she can't go away hungry. Amanda, Lettie." She stood and clapped her hands twice. "Don't just stand there like geese. Pack now some supper for your sister. And for her friend. On a Sabbath he must work to find the killer in our valley, but he should not do so with an empty stomach."

"You don't have to—" Rachel began.

But her mother waved her hand impatiently and talked right over her. "What are you waiting for? Lettie, dip a quart of that soup. Amanda, fetch that half of a blueberry pie."

Her mother might not speak directly to her, but that didn't

prevent her from looking after her. By the time Rachel drove out of her parents' farmyard, the back of her Jeep contained several plates and Mason jars full of food. Sinner she might be, but she wouldn't go hungry to bed so long as Esther Mast was in charge.

It was almost ten when Evan's SUV eased into the driveway of Stone Mill House, and she couldn't help feeling a sense of relief that he was safe. Usually, she managed to push her concerns for him being on the street to the shadowy corners of her mind, but Billingsly's murderer reminded her that there was evil everywhere, even in Stone Mill. She'd have to be a fool not to worry some when Evan was forty-five minutes late. It was something she'd have to get used to, though, if she was going to be a policeman's wife. That was a hard truth with which she was still coming to terms.

Oblivious to the blast of cold air that whooshed into her kitchen when she opened the door to the porch, Rachel greeted him eagerly. "You must be starving," she said as he stomped the snow off his boots and ducked his head to enter the house.

"Yeah, I guess I am." Evan pulled off his leather gloves. "Didn't have time for lunch." He straightened up to his full height, pushed back a lined hood, and shrugged out of his heavy parka. His medium-brown hair, cut in a no-nonsense style, was still damp from the shower, and he was wearing a pair of jeans and the thick tweed fisherman's sweater that she'd given him for Christmas.

She waited as he hung his parka next to her white one on a pegboard on the wall. Then he took off his boots to leave them near the door.

Dark smudges shadowed his intelligent gray eyes, and her pulse quickened as he pulled her against him and brushed her lips with a tender kiss. "Sorry to have kept you waiting. I ran home to jump in the shower and then I got a call from the troop and . . . here I am now."

She pressed her face against his chest and inhaled deeply.

He smelled faintly of Pasha de Cartier and a clean whole-some scent that was his alone. Wrapped in the security of his strong arms, Rachel felt some of the day's tenseness ease out of her body. "You don't need to explain," she murmured, patting his chest before stepping away. "You're here now, and my mother sent tons of food."

"It's late, I know."

"Not that late, and the last of my guests went up only twenty minutes ago." She waved him toward the table. "I've kept the soup warm on the stove. Wait until you taste it. Delicious, as always. Perfect for such a cold night." Something brushed against her ankle, and she glanced down to see her cat, Bishop, giving Evan the *Siamese stare.* So far Bishop had resisted all of Evan's attempts at friendship, the cat contenting himself with the occasional *hiss* and impatient swishes of his long tail whenever Evan was present.

"All your guests accounted for?"

She nodded.

"Including Mr. Skinner?" He stood there, dominating the old kitchen, the crown of the massive hand-hewn beams clearing his head by only a handsbreadth.

She turned to the stove to dip out a bowl of the soup. "I think so. I saw a light on under his door when I was taking extra towels to another room. I could hear his TV."

Evan paused at the sink to wash his hands and dry them on the hand towel. "Smells great, but I'm so hungry I could eat Bishop there."

"Shhh," she teased. "Don't let him hear you say that." A half dozen questions surfaced in her mind as she placed the bowl in front of him and removed a prepared plate of food from the refrigerator.

She wanted to ask Evan if he'd taken her advice and questioned Jake Skinner yet, or if they had a suspect in Billingsly's death. She was curious as to exactly what had killed him and when his death had occurred. She couldn't help wondering if the murderer might have been watching the house or even been inside when she was there. She knew from past experience that an autopsy would have been ordered, but the report certainly hadn't come back yet. It was possible, however, that the coroner had already provided a preliminary report that revealed some details. But as eager as she was to learn what was happening with the case, she knew better than to question Evan when he hadn't eaten since early morning. He had a hearty appetite and, like her Uncle Aaron, he could be a bear when he was hungry. His mood would be much improved when his stomach was full.

Realizing she was hungry, too, she helped herself to some of the soup and took a seat across from him at the small table under the windows. She eyed the man she was going to marry sitting across the table from her, not sure how long she could keep quiet about the case. The trick was to get Evan to share information on an investigation without directly asking questions. Fortunately, she didn't usually have to pry too much because he did some of his best thinking by using her as a sounding board.

"How was supper at your parents' house?" Evan asked, shaking pepper on his potato salad. "Your father buy that draft horse he was looking at?"

For the next half hour they talked about nothing in particular: her father's hesitation to buy the horse he wanted, her brother Danny's desire to continue with his schoolwork after he completed the eighth grade, her frustration with the water heater that kept throwing a breaker in the electrical box. None of the topics were all that important, but it made for a gentler dinner conversation than the discussion of the autopsy report, which was what she really wanted to talk about.

"It's nice, being here like this," Evan said later as she cleared away the empty pie plate and forks. Scandalously, they hadn't even sliced it and put it on dessert dishes, but had shared the blueberry pie like two kids who'd filched it off a windowsill, washing the pie down with tall glasses of ice-cold buttermilk. "With you, I mean," Evan clarified. "I keep thinking how happy we'll be when we can spend time alone every day, after we're married."

"Mmm." She leaned across the table and wiped a dab of blueberry off his lower lip with a napkin. "It will be nice." They hadn't set a date yet. She'd gotten as far as knowing that she wanted to marry Evan, but she wasn't ready to commit to when. It was important to be absolutely certain when they took their vows. They both wanted to be parents, someday. And they both wanted a forever marriage. She might not be Amish anymore, but for her, taking a husband meant pledging herself wholly to him so long as they both should live.

"So, how was your day?" she finally asked because she couldn't stand it another moment.

He glanced meaningfully toward the door that led to the dining room.

# Chapter 5

Without another word, Rachel got up to close the door. As she rested her hand on the doorknob, she paused to listen. The house was silent, not a creepy quiet like in movies but the peaceful stillness of walls that had protected and nurtured its inhabitants for two centuries. "Not a creature or a houseguest stirring," she assured Evan as she pulled the door shut and returned to her place across from him at the little table.

"Still, we're not alone," he reminded her. "We can't be too careful. Anything I say to you has to remain between us. I'm not supposed to ever say anything to anyone about what I'm working on." He took a drink of water from his glass. "But most cops . . . if they're totally honest, will admit they have *someone* to talk to." He looked up at her. "Someone they know they can trust."

"You know you can trust me."

She could tell by the look on his face that he wanted to talk about the investigation. He might have been trying to carry off the pretense that this was just another routine day in the life of a policeman, but Rachel knew better. Evan had wanted to be a Pennsylvania state trooper for years, and he'd worked hard to get where he was. His promotion to detective so early in his career had been a combination of being good at the job and being in the right place at the right time, when his respected mentor, sidelined by ongoing cancer treatments, recommended Evan to fill the position.

"I've pretty much been given the case," he said. "I'll report to higher-ups, but for all intents and purposes, I'm the lead officer on this one." His obvious pride in the assignment was shadowed by a hint of doubt. "It's a lot to take on, but they think I'm ready."

"I know you are." She placed her hand over his. "This is your town. Who knows the people here better than you do? You have the full support of the community, something an outsider might not."

"Yeah, that's what I keep telling myself." He looked down at the table, then back up at her. "Right now, I'm trying to come up with a solid plan for my investigation. This isn't going to be an open-and-shut case. There's almost no evidence; whoever did this was careful not to leave any behind. There are no obvious suspects. And the snowstorm last night makes things more difficult. No one was out and about to see anything suspicious in the area of Billingsly's house. And who knows what kind of evidence could have been covered by the new snow?"

"Was there sign of a break-in?"

"No. In fact, all the doors were closed and locked."

She frowned. "Locked? You mean someone lured him out onto the front porch and locked him out?"

Evan shrugged. "The front door was dead-bolted."

"So it was locked from the inside. Or . . . the person had a key," she mused. "Did Billingsly have a girlfriend? I know he was divorced."

"My understanding is that he was between girlfriends. I talked to the last woman he dated, a woman from Pittsburgh. Saw a photo on his refrigerator with her name on the back. I got her number from his cell phone. She's at a business conference in Florida."

"Well, she's got a solid alibi."

"Yup. Although she told me she would have *liked* to have killed him. Apparently he was a pretty big jerk to her. But she didn't do it. She gave a speech last night in front of two hundred people." He leaned back in his chair. "The whole thing is strange. We're checking fingerprints in the house, but that's a long shot. The place was neat, everything tidy. No overturned furniture and nothing disturbed anywhere. Shoot, Billingsly was about to cook a steak for himself. It was right on the stove in a frying pan." Evan began to crack his knuckles. "Got names and numbers of his ex-wives. I'll talk to them tomorrow. My next step will be to start looking at those closest to him. Work my way out. FBI statistics from a couple of years ago say a victim knows his murderer seventy-three percent of the time."

"Wow. So . . . you'll look at people who worked for him? People he saw regularly?"

He nodded. "He has a daughter in California who doesn't speak to him. I had to notify her today, as next of kin."

"That must have been a difficult call to make."

"Not as hard as I thought it would be. She didn't seem to be too upset. She didn't have much information for me. He didn't have any other living relatives, and she didn't know anything about his life in the last five or six years."

She picked up a crumb of piecrust from the table and popped it in her mouth. "You question Jake Skinner?"

"I did, just briefly. An odd duck. Not hostile, but not particularly helpful either. He said he didn't know Billingsly." He looked at her from across the table. "Why did you think I should to speak to him?"

She studied Evan's face. "He said he didn't know Billingsly? That's interesting because I saw him at the frolic yesterday, in the cafeteria. When Billingsly spotted him, Billingsly had a strange reaction, almost as if he was frightened. And then Billingsly abruptly left through the kitchen." She got up, went to the cupboard, and returned to the table with a bowl of walnuts and a nutcracker. "Why would he do that unless he was trying to avoid Skinner? And why would he be avoiding him if he didn't know him?"

"Good question." Evan took a nut, cracked it, and removed the meat. "Mr. Skinner said he would be around all week. I got his information. Running a background check. We questioned all the neighbors on Billingsly's street. No one noticed anything out of the ordinary, other than the nasty weather. Except for Mrs. Abbott."

Rachel knew a Louise Abbott from church; she lived with her daughter and son-in-law on Billingsly's street. She was a feisty woman in her late eighties and suffering from dementia. She was always getting lost in the church and social hall and being returned to the sanctuary by kindly parishioners.

Evan removed a small notebook from his jeans pocket. "Yes. Mrs. Louise Abbott reported a snowman coming down the street sometime between ten and eleven last night. She knows that it wasn't before ten because she never misses a favorite TV program that ends at that time."

"A snowman?" Rachel chuckled. "Walking?"

Evan nodded. "Mrs. Abbott says that she goes to bed after her show but has trouble getting to sleep. Sometimes she wanders around the house. Last night, she said, she sat by a window, watching the pretty snowfall. She claims the snowman walked up onto Billingsly's porch, knocked, and went inside." His serious demeanor cracked as his lips twitched. "Not sure how reliable she is. Apparently, she sent several letters to the troop last summer complaining about Frank Sinatra mowing her front lawn." He chuckled. "Now mind you, Frank drives a horse and buggy. And he's grown a long beard."

"Well, Mrs. Abbott is right, sort of."

Evan lifted his eyebrows. "About Frank Sinatra growing a beard?"

"No, about the buggy. One of Eli Rust's brothers-in-law mows lawns on that street on Saturday afternoons. He might even have done Billingsly's."

"I thought the Amish didn't use power mowers."

"They don't *own* them," she said. "But they don't have a problem operating them. He uses his clients' mowers."

Evan made a notation on his pad. "His name isn't Frank by any chance, is it?"

She chuckled. "No. But Frank Sinatra may still be a suspect if he's prowling around Mrs. Abbott's house."

"Especially if he's building snowmen that can walk."

The mention of someone wandering around in Billingsly's yard gave her a twinge of guilt. Should she just tell Evan she'd been there last night? But to what end? So he'd know for sure that his fiancée was an idiot?

"As you know, Billingsly wasn't all that loved in the town," Evan went on. "Even before he started running that ridiculous gossip column. The photos he published last year from Beth Glick's funeral still have some people seething, Amish and English. I have a feeling I'm going to be chatting with a lot of people who were holding a grudge against him. Seems like he was in a public argument with someone at least once a week."

She exhaled. "Well, you can add me to that list. I had a disagreement with him yesterday in the cafeteria just before Skinner showed up."

"I know. Your argument's old news." He reached for another walnut. "Several people told me all about it yesterday. What were you arguing about?"

"About the column and the harm it was doing to the Herschberger family. We got pretty loud."

"I suppose I need to speak with the Herschbergers just to cross them off my list." He took pains in selecting another walnut. "I was thinking maybe you could go with me, just to make them feel more comfortable."

"Sure." Bishop jumped up on her lap. She stroked the cat until he curled up and rested his chin against her hand. She and Bishop sat in silence while a thoughtful Evan cracked and ate two more walnuts.

"It's probably smart to talk to his two ex-wives," she suggested. "I gathered from things Billingsly said in passing that there was a lot of hostility between them."

"Three ex-wives," Evan corrected. "I'm going to talk to them, but I think it's just a formality. It's doubtful his assailant could have been a woman. Billingsly wasn't a small man. He was in his sixties, but in good shape. It's more likely that his murderer or murderers were male."

"You think maybe it was some random psycho passing through town?"

"Who wanders around small towns tying editors to front porches in a snowstorm?" Evan shook his head. "Just as unlikely. It's too soon to make any assumptions, but off the top of my head, I believe that whoever killed Billingsly went to his house with a specific intent, maybe not to commit murder but not to bring a gift basket either. Someone had a grudge against him. Big time."

She thought about Billingsly's body on the porch. She'd gotten the same impression when she saw him. She got the feeling that his murder was very personal.

"The assailant probably possessed a great deal of physical strength," Evan went on. "Blunt force trauma to the back of the head. He was in the living room when he was hit. We found a smear of blood on the floor."

"So his killer dragged him dead out onto the porch?" she asked. "That doesn't make sense. At least, tying him up doesn't. Are you sure the injury killed him?"

"Don't know what killed him yet. Still waiting on the coroner's report. I agree with you. If he was killed inside, why drag him outside? I hate to say it, but my guess is that the cause of death was exposure. And whoever tied him to the porch post dumped water over him."

"I can't believe whoever did it left him half naked," she said.

"We found a flannel robe in the living room. Not sure if Billingsly had removed it or his killer did."

"Creepy." She shivered at the thought. Who could do such a thing? Even to a man like Billingsly?

"I should have a cause of death by morning." Evan glanced down at his cell phone. "It's getting late. I should go. We both have to be up early in the morning. Thanks for dinner." He got to his feet. "I mean it, Rache. I really appreciate—"

"Evan," she interrupted, the images of Billingsly on his porch coming back to her. Images from the snowy yard. "This may not be anything, but I can't get it out of my head."

"Okay."

"Something I saw at Billingsly's house this morning." She got out of her chair. "There was something black lying in the snow, almost covered up. I just saw it in passing, and there was a lot of confusion: The rescue squad was arriving, there were people everywhere. And when I thought to look again, it wasn't there."

"Something black? What do you mean? How big?"

"I don't know. I couldn't really tell. Not big." She measured with her hands in the air, showing him the length of a loaf of bread.

"I didn't see anything in the snow. I walked around the perimeter of the house when I got there, looking for weapons, footprints, whatever. I didn't see anything."

"Do you think the killer could have been there this morning? Been there, saw something he dropped last night, and grabbed it?"

"I guess anything is possible, but it's not likely. You probably just saw a dead branch sticking up through the snow. There were a couple of branches lying around from the elm tree in the side yard."

She followed him to the door. "No, it wasn't a branch."

He stepped into his boots. "Then a mitten. We found a child's mitten in the snow right on the sidewalk in front of his house after we got everyone cleared off." He took his coat from the pegboard. "I'll touch base with you sometime tomorrow if I can." He leaned toward her and brushed her lips with his. "Lock your door behind me. And try and get some sleep."

"Be careful," she warned.

He pulled on his coat. "You do the same, and if you have any ideas what you saw . . ."

She sighed. "I'll tell you. I promise."

"And no playing detective on this case." He waggled his finger under her nose. "Your job is to take care of your guests. Mine is to catch the bad guys."

"I hear you."

"Good." He kissed the crown of her head and then opened the kitchen door to the porch. "And keep your eyes out for walking snowmen," he teased. "Sighting one would be great for the Winter Frolic. A guaranteed tourist attraction."

Rachel hadn't finished her first cup of coffee the following morning when Evan reappeared at her back door. He'd come to speak with Jake Skinner, though why so early she didn't know and he wasn't saying. Evan asked if he and Jake could talk privately in her office, but she showed him to the small parlor in the oldest wing of the house instead. He rang Skinner's cell phone to tell him he was waiting downstairs to speak with him. Rachel put them in the parlor because it wasn't a room open to her guests or likely to be invaded by one of the Amish friends and family who worked in the kitchen or cleaned for her.

Rachel wished she knew why Evan needed to speak to Skinner first thing this morning, but she knew better than to ask. Whatever transpired between Evan and Jake was part of the official police investigation and none of her business. She told herself that as she got to work.

For a Monday morning, Stone Mill House was quiet, but quiet didn't mean she could remain idle. A couple had checked out two days early due to the imminent arrival of a first and long-awaited grandbaby, and the D'Silva sisters had wanted their coffee and blueberry muffins to go before hurrying out to catch the Amish Countryside horse-drawn sleigh tour. And besides offering her usual Monday morning cold-breakfast buffet, she made a hot menu available, so she was kept busy taking guests' orders.

Once Rachel was satisfied that the morning at the B&B was running smoothly, she needed to get over to the high school to meet with the festival committee to reschedule the judging for the ice sculpture contest, which had been canceled the previous day after Billingsly's body had been discovered.

Later in the morning, she had an interview with a local cable TV personality who was doing a feature on Stone Mill's Winter Frolic and had showed interest in featuring the ongoing restoration of the town. She hoped she could keep the content focused on the festival and not on the gruesome murder of the town's editor. She knew she should be thinking of something sensible to say to the host if questioning veered to the crime rather than the event, but she couldn't keep her mind from wondering what Evan and Jake were saying and if Evan was as suspicious of him as she was. She was certain that Skinner's presence in Stone Mill at the time of Billingsly's death wasn't a coincidence, not after the way Billingsly had behaved when he'd caught sight of Skinner on Saturday. Had Billingsly been afraid of Skinner? Was that why Billingsly had hightailed it out of the cafeteria through a back door?

Rachel threaded her way through the kitchen, carrying an empty sugar bowl, stepping around Minnie, who was turning sausages on the griddle, and taking care not to collide with Dinah as she brought a tray of sliced oranges, grapes, and grapefruit from the oversized refrigerator. Ada had a batch of cheese biscuits in the oven and was whipping up pumpkin pancakes. The kitchen was toasty warm, and the sizzle of the pork sausages and their wonderful odor made Rachel's mouth water.

The sleigh bell on the door jingled, and her brother Levi came in, his cheeks and nose rosy from the cold. "Morning. Something smells good in here," he said cheerfully, in Deitsch. "Already, I fed up the ducks and the goats for you." He removed his wide-brimmed black hat, pushed his unruly hair out of his eyes, and hung the hat on a peg by the door. "And I dug the ice out of the water troughs."

"Thanks," Rachel said, refilling the sugar bowl from a crock canister on the counter. "That was sweet of you, but shouldn't you be in school?"

Levi was a good student, but he was also creative about finding ways to play hooky from class. His teacher was a young woman not much older than her students, and Levi complained that she gave too much busywork instead of seriously challenging his reading and math skills. As much as she liked having Levi at the house, she couldn't condone skipping school.

"No school today," he said. "Teacher's going with her grandmother to the hospital in Huntingdon. Her grandfather fell on the ice and broke his hip. Everybody has to write a paper about the Winter Frolic, due tomorrow. Two hundred words."

"Did you wipe your feet?" Ada interrupted brusquely. "I won't have boys running in and out muddying clean floors."

Levi winked at Rachel. "Left my boots on the porch, Ada." He lifted one thickly stockinged foot as proof.

Ada scowled, seized a tea towel, and pulled a pan of biscuits out of the oven. A fantastic cook, Ada wasn't known for her patience with people who interfered with her schedule, especially boys. "Hands off these biscuits," she warned Levi. "They're not for the likes of you. They're for the paying guests."

"Go on upstairs," Rachel urged her brother, giving him a meaningful look that told him he'd have a cheese biscuit and some sausage as soon as the coast was clear. Strictly speaking, it was her kitchen and Ada worked for her, but crossing Ada wasn't always the best policy if she wanted things to run smoothly at the B&B. "I imagine there'll be plenty of food left. There always is."

"That may be," Ada grumbled, "but if we run short and your guests go hungry, who will you blame?"

"I'd never blame you," Rachel soothed. "If those biscuits were any lighter, they'd float off the baking pans." She and Levi exchanged glances, and he grinned at her.

Her little brother came to Stone Mill House whenever he got the chance because she had an extensive library and he loved to read. He was working his way through *Tom Sawyer* this week. She wasn't certain that her parents would approve. Her father would rather that Levi spend more of his free time studying his German, but Rachel didn't have the heart to refuse Levi. The two of them shared a passion for the written word. She told herself that so long as she didn't provide any books explicitly forbidden by the church or that were too mature in content, she was doing her brother no real harm. And there were a lot of things worse a boy could get into than Mark Twain.

Levi hurried off, and Rachel returned the sugar bowl to its place and then, on impulse, gathered a tray with coffee for Evan and Jake Skinner. Neither had asked for coffee, but she thought they might appreciate it. She almost added muffins to the tray, but serving coffee and pastries in a murder investigation interview didn't seem appropriate.

Rachel was at the closed door, lifting her hand to knock, when she heard Jake's gruff voice.

"Who says I knew Billingsly?"

Evan's deep reply was calm and professional. "Did you come to Stone Mill to see him?"

"Maybe I came for the sleigh rides and ice sculptures."

"So, Mr. Skinner, you're stating that you didn't come to town *specifically* to meet with Mr. Billingsly?"

There was a pause in the conversation, and Rachel raised her hand to knock again.

"You have a conviction for battery," Evan said.

Rachel froze.

"Long time ago," Skinner answered.

"Can I ask you about the conviction?"

"You can ask," Skinner barked. "Nothing says I have to answer. You got access to my arrest record. Look it up yourself, you want to know so bad."

Rachel let out her breath, rapped twice, and opened the door. "Sorry to interrupt, but I thought you might like some coffee." She stepped inside and placed the tray on an antique wedding chest that functioned as a table.

Jake stood by the fireplace, face hard, shoulders rigid, arms crossed over his chest. He ignored her. "You arresting me, Detective?" he asked Evan, not seeming to care that she was there to overhear.

"No, I'm not." Evan frowned at Rachel. "We're not quite done here."

"I didn't mean to intrude. I just assumed you'd be finishing up."

"Yeah, we're finished," Jake said gruffly. He looked at Evan. "Unless you're prepared to charge me. In which case I'll be calling a lawyer."

"No need to get upset, Mr. Skinner." Evan held up both hands.

Evan looked nice this morning in khakis and a gray sweater over a shirt and tie. Professional, but not too dressy. Nothing fancy, she'd warned him weeks ago when he'd been shopping for clothes for his new job as a detective. The people in Stone Mill would automatically be suspicious of him in a suit and tie.

"I'm just talking with everyone who knew Mr. Billingsly," Evan explained. "Friends. Family. Ex-wives. Anyone who can help us figure out who might have done this."

"I'll leave you two alone." Rachel backed toward the door.

"No need." Jake was wearing the same clothes she'd seen him in since his arrival. The only thing that ever changed was the hat: Sometimes it was a beret, sometimes a knit watch cap. "Nothing I've got to say that you can't hear. I didn't kill Billingsly, Detective."

"Call me if you need anything," Rachel murmured.

"Mr. Skinner said you sent him to the Black Horse," Evan directed to her.

"I did." Rachel glanced at Skinner. "He wanted to know where he could get a beer. About . . . what? Close to nine o'clock, Mr. Skinner?"

"Something like that," he muttered. "It's not like I had an appointment."

"And you walked?" Evan turned back to Skinner. "It was snowing pretty hard by that time."

Jake shrugged. "I walk a lot. In all kinds of weather."

Evan wrote something in his notepad. "And if I ask at the pub, they'll remember you?"

"They should. It wasn't exactly crowded, but it wasn't empty either. The bartender and I were talking about 'Nam. He should remember me."

"And what time will he say you left?" Evan asked.

"I don't know. Ten thirty, maybe eleven."

Evan raised his head. "And you went where?"

"Walked around some."

"In a snowstorm?" Evan lifted his brows.

"Like I said, I walk a lot. Then came back here. Went up to my room and stayed there the rest of the night."

"Anybody see you come in?"

"Don't think so. It was pretty quiet." Jake looked at Rachel. "You see me come in?"

Rachel shook her head.

"Guess nobody saw me. Are we done?" Jake asked.

"Almost." Evan gave her a look that told her to beat it, and she quickly made her exit.

As Rachel went down the hall, she wondered if Evan had come this morning because he'd learned of Skinner's criminal record. Or was there something else? What could he have done that would have made Evan suspicious of him? And to think, he was staying under her roof. But that came with running a public inn. It wasn't like she could run background checks on all of her guests before they arrived. And to be fair, a person's criminal record didn't tell the full story. She, of all people, knew that.

Rachel entered the kitchen to find it empty. With Ada out of the kitchen, she realized it was the perfect time to snitch a biscuit and some sausages for Levi. Glancing in the direction of the dining room, she took two biscuits and a good-sized serving of sausage and put it on a plate. As she turned to make off with her booty, her gaze fell on Levi's hat hanging on the peg.

Something just clicked in her head, and it came to her. She knew what she'd seen in the snow beside Billingsly's house. The object that had been there, then disappeared. It was an Amish man's hat! If it hadn't been nearly buried by the snowfall, she would have recognized it immediately, but the snow had altered its apparent shape.

So why was it there? And then not there? Who could have dropped it there? And equally as important . . . who had taken it?

A few moments later, Jake Skinner entered the dining room and gave his breakfast order to Minnie. Since Evan hadn't appeared, Rachel went back to the parlor. "Evan?" she asked.

"Hey, Rache, I'm just about done here." He was sitting on the leather sofa, scribbling notes in his notebook. "I hope I haven't driven off Skinner. I don't want to be responsible for running off your guests. I told him I might have a few questions later, but . . ." He shrugged. "Not overly friendly, is he?"

"No, he's not." She joined him on the leather sofa. "But he isn't rude either. He doesn't use inappropriate language, and he's respectful to Minnie and the other help."

"And most people aren't?"

She shook her head. "That isn't what I meant. It's just that Jake seems like a rough sort. He's certainly not my typical guest, but he's not a bad guy. He even helped to shovel the sidewalk yesterday." She dropped her voice. "Which I have to admit I thought was strange, because I know he heard the paperboy say that Billingsly was dead on his front porch. You would think that he'd go down to take a look like half the town. But he didn't. He just started shoveling. Almost as if he already knew what had happened."

"Or . . . maybe he'd seen enough dead men in the war. People react differently to emergencies," Evan said. "And it would have been a lot better for the investigation if more people had followed his example and stayed away. The crime scene was a circus." He rose to his feet. "I gotta go. I'm going to talk to Billingsly's receptionist and a couple of guys who work at the paper, and I have that phone appointment, and then this afternoon I'm going back to Billingsly's house to have a look around again. There were so many people there yesterday. I'd like to have a look on my own." He glanced at his notebook.

"I remembered," she said. "What it was I saw. In the snow?"

He looked up at her blankly.

"I told you last night. I saw something black in the snow. It was there when I first arrived at Billingsly's house, and then it was gone."

He waited.

"It was a man's hat, Evan. An Amish hat."

"I saw several Amish families there. Someone dropped it and then picked it up."

"Amish men don't take their dress hats off outside," she insisted. "And this one had definitely been in the snow. It was there, then someone picked it up."

"Not much in the way of hard evidence." He smiled at her as he rose. "But I'll make a note of it, if it will make you happy."

"It won't make me *happy*." She tried not to be annoyed that he wasn't taking her seriously. "It's just odd, out of place."

"Maybe." He gave her a quick kiss on the cheek. "I'm still waiting for the medical examiner's report. We'll know more once that comes in."

"I've got to go, too. I need to go to the school. We're rescheduling the ice sculpture contest."

"Just one thing more," he said, turning back to her. "Did you know Blade Finch had a recent falling-out with Billingsly?"

She thought for a minute. "I did. Coyote told me. Something about work Blade did for him that Billingsly refused to pay for. I'm not sure of the details."

"You know Blade Finch well? You're friends with him?"

"I wouldn't say I know him well. I'm friends with his wife. He's really good to Coyote and a great father to the kids." She frowned. "You don't think he could have had anything to do with Billingsly's death, do you?"

"I'm just gathering information at this point. I'll call you later. After work, if it's not too late." He paused again in the doorway. "Be careful, Rache. Don't go wandering off alone."

"I thought you said you were looking for someone who knew Billingsly and had a grudge against him," she reminded.

"I've got a hunch that's what we'll discover, but meanwhile, I don't want you to take any chances. It took me long enough to convince you to marry me. I don't want to lose you now."

"You won't," she promised. "And the same goes for you. Use common sense."

He grinned. "I always do."

# Chapter 6

The school gymnasium was busier than Rachel had expected. Some of the booths wouldn't open until noon, but most of the Amish stalls were already doing a brisk business. She paused to greet her sister-in-law Miriam, who told her that she'd sold two willow egg baskets and taken an order for one of her husband's wooden baby cradles. Rachel considered her brother Paul's woodworking skills to be superior, but he'd been dubious that anyone would pay what he was asking for his one-of-a-kind pieces. She was pleased with their success. As it was for most young Amish families, winter was a tough time financially for them, and the sales would be a well-earned reward for the long hours and effort they put into their crafts.

Naamah and Annie were already restocking their Amish food booth by the time Rachel reached them. "We had our first customer at eight thirty," the bishop's wife proclaimed cheerfully. "One Englisher woman bought a dozen jars of my chowchow for her church bazaar."

"They like Naamah's jams and jellies, too," Annie said. "We'll make a lot of money for the school, I think." She had dark circles under her eyes, and her face was pale. She looked to Rachel as though she hadn't had much sleep the night before.

"We sent Sammy to Annie's house with Joab to bring more

pickled eggs and canned peaches," Naamah explained. "Give
those two something to do. Your mother has promised us
two shoofly pies. The tourists love them, and we sold every
one we had on Saturday."

"Too sweet for me." Annie pursed her lips. "But your
mother's are very good."

"Too sweet for me, too," Rachel agreed. She exchanged a few
more words with the women and then moved on to speak to
Verna Hershberger, who was putting out a display of goat cheese
on a bed of ice. "Did Alvin bring any of your goats for the petting zoo?" Rachel asked her. Verna nodded shyly. "I'm so
glad," Rachel said. "I know the goats will be a big draw for
the tourists. If you need anything, please ask me or someone
on the committee," she added before she moved on to chat
with one of Hulda Schenfeld's granddaughters.

As Rachel strolled from booth to booth, saying hello and
checking to see if anyone needed anything, her mind kept
drifting back to her conversation with Evan that morning.
Regardless of his cavalier disregard for her suspicions, she
just couldn't shake the feeling that the hat in the snow was
important.

The fact of the matter was, it was definitely a wide-
brimmed Amish wool hat she had seen in Billingsly's yard,
and it shouldn't have been lying there. Amish men didn't *lose*
their hats; at least, it wasn't likely. The hats were expensive,
so most men only owned one, and a person would certainly
know if his blew off his head.

So what was it doing there on Billingsly's lawn, and why
did the owner or someone else whisk it away? Evan might
have thought she'd misremembered what she'd seen, but she
hadn't. There was no way it was a mitten or a tree branch or
anything other than what it was. It had just taken a while for
her to realize what it was because of the angle from which
she'd glimpsed it.

"Rachel!" Ell waved to her from the book booth. "I've
been waiting for you to get here. George said to tell you that

they decided to reschedule the ice sculpture contest results for six. He hopes that works for you. He wanted to wait until you arrived, but he had a doctor's appointment that he couldn't miss. He's still having migraines, and the meds aren't doing anything to help."

"Six is fine." Finally warm, Rachel slipped out of her white parka and threw it over her arm. "I think he's pushing himself too hard. He's not that long out of surgery. He's got to give himself time to heal."

"Exactly what I said, but you know George. There's no telling him anything." As usual, Ell was dressed all in black. This morning's attire was a knee-length black lace dress over black leather boots and leggings, worn with a fringed shawl, also in black. Her shoulder-length hair and severe bangs were blacker than black, accented by sterling silver eyebrow and lip rings.

"What have you got here?" Rachel asked. She picked up a hardcover children's book from a stack on the counter and flipped through the pages. It was a collection of traditional Scandinavian fairy tales with beautiful watercolor illustrations. Another book appeared to be about whales and dolphins, and a third was a preschool retelling of "The Fox Went Out on a Chilly Night."

"Aren't they scrumptious?" Ell fanned the other books out so that Rachel could see them. "George donated them as prizes for the kids' games after school today. Every one is autographed by the author."

"Wonderful," Rachel said. "Do you have anything suitable for Amish children?"

"We sure do. I have an illustrated nonfiction on beginning beekeeping and another about raising sheep. I made sure George remembered. No make-believe and no talking animals."

"Super," Rachel agreed. "Nonfiction or stories about children's lives in other countries are always welcome. So long as there's no violence." Rachel glanced around the gymnasium.

"There are more people here than I thought there would be on a Monday morning."

"Tell me about it. Lots of locals, but a lot of unfamiliar faces, too. I thought after what happened to poor Mr. Billingsly that visitors might stay away from the town, but it seems to be just the opposite. I've talked to several people who weren't here for the weekend festivities, but came today after reading about the murder in their morning paper."

"I'm not sure if I should say I'm glad to hear it or not." Rachel grimaced. "I mean I'm glad people are coming—"

"But not exactly how we wanted to get word out," Ell finished for her.

A browser picked up a book off one of the tables and held it up. "I'm looking for something by this author on Amish quilts," the woman said to Ell.

"I think I have exactly what you're looking for, but it's back at the main store. I can call the desk and ask one of the girls to bring it over, if you'd like." Ell smiled at the customer. "Talk to you later," she said quickly to Rachel.

"No problem. I'm just going to leave my coat here with you, if you don't mind. I'll be back for it."

"Of course."

Ell took her coat and Rachel moved on. At Coyote's pottery booth, she found Blade with Remi and two small, very blond daughters. Remi had a real stethoscope hanging around his neck, and the girls were taking turns pushing a doll carriage with a stuffed monkey in it.

"I'm the pediatrician," Remi declared. He rolled his eyes. "Mama said I have to be nice to them until she comes back. The *baby* needs his shots."

"Remi is the doctor," one girl proclaimed.

The stuffed monkey was wearing a pink baby hat and infant sleeper. One of the girls nodded and patted the monkey's head in sympathy.

"You're holding down the fort again?" Rachel asked Blade.

"It's what I do." He opened his arms wide and grinned.

"But Coyote should be back any minute. Some lady from Harrisburg wanted to take some of Coyote's pieces on consignment. The two them went to the studio to see what the woman might be interested in selling, but they've been gone a while." He motioned toward an empty space on a table. "We sold that green pitcher you liked this morning."

"Great," Rachel said.

He smoothed the hair of his long ponytail. "I heard congratulations are in order. You and Evan Parks?"

"Yes." She gave him a quick smile. "Thank you."

From behind the counter came the wail of an infant. Rachel hadn't even noticed him there.

"And another country heard from," Blade quipped.

The baby was swaddled in blankets in a large woven basket behind the display table. Blade fumbled in the front pocket of his flannel shirt and fished out a pacifier. He squatted down and popped it in the baby's mouth. He grinned at Rachel. "Works every time. Whoever invented those things, she should have gotten a Nobel Peace Prize."

Rachel smiled and turned to watch as one of the girls pushed the carriage forward, nearly colliding with a lady in a black peacoat and a fur hat.

"Easy there, Shoshone," Blade warned. But he hadn't spoken soon enough. The carriage tipped over, and the stuffed monkey slid out.

Shoshone's sister snatched up the baby and ran with it, and Shoshone scrambled after her. "No fair! My turn to be the mama!"

"Excuse me," Blade said to Rachel. He went after his daughters, picked them up, and returned with the carriage in tow. "Behind the table, both of you," he said. "Or there will be no ice cream after lunch for any of you. You, too, Remi."

"But, Papa," Remi cried, "I didn't do anything."

"Sorry, son. Them's the breaks," Blade said.

"Listen," Rachel glanced around and said quietly, "Evan is the lead detective in the investigation into Bill Billingsly's death. I was talking to him this morning, and he may want to ask you some questions about that problem you two had."

"He does, does he?"

Rachel felt the temperature drop significantly as Blade's friendly banter became serious.

Blade set his square jaw. "He wants to question *me* after Billingsly shortchanged me more than a thousand dollars?"

She shrugged, beginning to wonder if it had been a mistake to say anything. She had a feeling that this kind of thing was exactly what Evan had been talking about when he had asked her to stay out of the investigation. "I think he's talking to anyone who had a problem with Billingsly recently." She gave a little chuckle, trying to lighten the conversation. "Shoot, I had a public argument with Billingsly Saturday. I'm probably at the top of the list for questioning."

"Right." Blade's mouth tightened. "But it's not really police business. I didn't file a complaint." He crossed his arms over his chest. "It's an invasion of privacy, if you ask me."

"But it isn't personal," Rachel reasoned.

"What's he want to know?"

Now Rachel definitely wished she hadn't said anything. It had never occurred to her that Blade would react this way. "Just, oh, I don't know. Like, where you were on Saturday night."

"So, now I'm a suspect?"

Rachel felt her cheeks grow hot. "No, of course not. He just needs to account for people's whereabouts. It's how you investigate a murder."

Blade's face was hard. Clearly she'd struck a nerve. "I'm not crazy about cops," he said. "Nothing personal."

"But . . . you were at home on Saturday night. Right? Home with Coyote and the kids, like always? Especially with all the snow."

"Who wants to know where you were Saturday night?"

Rachel turned to find Coyote walking up behind her.

"I was just telling—" Rachel began.

"Evan Parks wants to know." Blade kept his voice low so the kids wouldn't hear.

Coyote looked at Rachel. Coyote was a pretty woman, tall and thin with long blond hair. She looked every bit a Californian, and she was gorgeous, even when she frowned. "He was at his book club. Every second Saturday of the month. He never misses book club. Why does your Evan want to know where Blade was Saturday night?"

"Apparently he's talking to everyone who had a problem with Bill."

"Well, that list's going to be long." Coyote walked around the table to put down her coat and the canvas sack she was carrying.

"That's what I said." Blade tucked one hand under his arm and gestured with the other. "Could be anyone in Stone Mill. And there were plenty of people out Saturday night. Parks is going to have a hard time questioning everyone in town who had a problem with him." He was clearly angry now.

"Blade." Coyote rested her hand on her husband's arm, her tone suggesting he needed to calm down.

This was a side of Blade Rachel had never seen before. But she got the impression Coyote had.

Blade didn't calm down. "What's Parks going to do, go door-to-door?" he asked, loud enough for people at the booth next to them to look in his direction. "He'll have to go to every house in the valley. And not just Englishers. Amish, too. Hell, Saturday night on my way home I saw a buggy in Wagler's parking lot. Everything was closed up and there was this horse and buggy tied there."

Rachel frowned. "What time was that?"

He shrugged, still clearly aggravated, but he had lowered his voice again. "I don't know. Late. Ten thirty, maybe?"

"Are you sure there was a horse?" Rachel was certain he had to be mistaken. By that time of night, most Amish families were snuggled in their beds in the winter. And certainly during a snowstorm. "It wasn't just a buggy?"

He lifted his dark brows. "Just a buggy?"

"Broken down? Maybe someone left it there with a broken wheel or something?"

"I know what I saw, Rachel. I saw a horse and a buggy at Wagler's, which is, what, a block and a half from Billingsly's house?" Blade turned to walk away. "So if your boyfriend is going to check alibis of anybody in town Saturday night, you'd better start looking for whoever was driving that buggy."

Rachel arrived at the ice rink at five thirty that evening, soon after Olympic hopefuls brother and sister Neal and Chelsea Katz of Allentown finished their figure skating demonstration. She hadn't heard from Evan all day. She called his cell, but it went to voicemail and she left a message reminding him that she'd be at the Winter Frolic, first at the ice sculpture judging and then at the Amish supper.

Again, there were far more people at the event, both English and Amish, than Rachel had ever expected, and everyone seemed to be having a good time despite the cold. The fire company had cleared the snow from the makeshift ice rink and carried portable bleachers from the softball fields so that visitors would have places to sit. There were skates available to rent, and one of the local scout troops was running a hot chocolate stand. Whole families were enjoying the novelty of a safe place to skate, and both expert skaters and novices shared the ice.

To Rachel's delight, Bishop Abner, as well as three other Amish men, had joined the open skate after the demonstration. The bishop's old-fashioned skates were laced high over his ankles, a broad wool hat clamped firmly on his head. His hands were behind his back as he skimmed effortlessly over the surface of the pond.

"Look at him," Mary Aaron said, coming up to stand beside Rachel. "Did you know he could skate like that?" The bishop's long beard and trailing scarf whisked out around him as he executed a graceful turn into the cold wind.

"He shows off, that one," came the jovial comment of Naamah. Breath exhaling in great puffs, the bishop's wife joined them. "I tell him, 'Bishop Abner, some may think it shows *hochmut,* what them Englishers call pride, to skate so in front of all these people.' And what do you think my *goot* husband says to me? He says, 'Naamah, exercise is *goot* for the health. I cannot be responsible for what other people think, only what I think. And not always can I control that.' Have you ever heard the like from a bishop?" She laughed, a deep and unrestrained outpouring of joy. "I did not know my Abner when he was in *rumspringa,* but I think that one, he was a handful to his parents. *Ya?*" She tilted her head. "Of course, you know he was born in Wisconsin. Lots of ice and snow they have there, so he learned to skate almost before he could walk."

Mary Aaron crouched to unlace her boot and slip her foot into a white leather ice skate. "No one will say I'm showing off, and that's the truth." She looked up at Rachel. "Aren't you joining us?"

"Not tonight. Maybe tomorrow if I get time." Rachel chuckled. "I'm as *doplich* as a sheep on the ice. Evan can skate rings around me."

"A clumsy one, are you?" Naamah laughed again, so hard that her bonnet slid back and nearly tumbled off the back of her head before she caught her dangling bonnet strings and pulled it firmly into place again. "No one is as *doplich* as me," she continued, "but . . ." She patted her ample stomach, made even more substantial by a padded black coat and a thick, hand-knit sweater beneath it. "When I was a girl, I was light on my feet."

"Rachel!" George waved to her as he made his way out of a throng gathered around the hot chocolate stand. In one hand, he carried an insulated mug, in the other arm his bichon frise, attired in a red-and-black faux-fur coat and matching doggy boots and earmuffs. "Isn't this marvelous?" he said. "Look at this crowd. You know this is going to have to be an annual event." He lowered his voice and leaned close. "Of course, next year we won't have the notoriety we have now. From what I've overheard in the bookstore today, a lot of out-of-towners came because Stone Mill made the evening news again."

Mary Aaron finished lacing up her second skate, glanced at Rachel, and grimaced. "A little creepy."

"I'd say," Rachel agreed. She wondered if George's brain tumor had done more damage to his rational thinking than was first thought.

"Creepy, but human nature," George said. "People are fascinated by violence. Look at how they stare at traffic accidents." He nodded to give weight to his statement. "Seriously, don't you think we should hold the Winter Frolic again next year?"

"As long as you're going to be the chairman, George, not me." Rachel petted the dog's head. "Nice earmuffs, Sophie."

Taking no offense at her teasing, George smiled broadly. He was fashionably dressed for the slopes of Aspen in a hooded red-and-black Obermeyer ski jacket and matching pants. Rachel wouldn't have recognized the brand, but George had agonized over the purchase, and she'd had to spend most of an evening examining choices on the website while he tried to make up his mind. "I had her bathed and clipped for the occasion," he said. "Had to look her best for the tourists." He motioned toward a raised platform constructed of snow and ice and fitted with appropriate electronic gear. "We should be ready shortly. We're running a little late on the judging results."

"We'll have to do it before seven," she reminded him. "That's when the talent contest begins." The school board had been good enough to allow them to hold the competition in the high school auditorium. Thankfully, she wasn't in charge of the talent show.

"Look at him now," Naamah said, pointing at her husband. He was skating beside the paperboy, Eddie Millman, his head bent to hear what the boy was saying.

Rachel was glad to see that Eddie was out and about; she'd been concerned about him, after what had happened the previous day. Worried enough that she had considered calling his mother to check on him, even though she didn't know her that well. It was good to see him smiling; stumbling upon a corpse could traumatize anyone.

"I think Bishop Abner is enjoying himself as much as Eddie," Mary Aaron observed.

"*Ya*, he should have had sons and daughters of his own. He would have been such a *goot* father." Naamah thrust her hands into her coat pockets against the cold. "But it was not God's will for us. And we must bear our lot." She forced a tremulous smile. "It does my heart *goot* to see my Abner taking pleasure in his neighbors' children."

Mary Aaron took Naamah's arm. "You may not have children born to you, but they are all children of your hearts. And you have your nephew with you now," she murmured. "They all love you."

"I hope they do." Naamah slipped a mittened hand out of her pocket and patted Mary Aaron's cheek. "Now go and have some fun yourself."

"It looks as though they may be ready for us." Rachel indicated the ice podium. "There's Hulda and Polly." She started walking in their direction and George followed. She had reached the bottom step when she caught sight of Evan standing near the hot chocolate stand; she waved to him. "I'll just be a few minutes," she called, waiting to let George and Sophie ascend the steps ahead of her. The music from the speakers stopped, started again for a few seconds, and then cut off abruptly as George reached the podium.

"Welcome, all of you," George said, his cultured voice carrying over the audio system. "Friends, neighbors, and all of our guests from out of town. We're so happy to have you here to share the fun at our first annual Winter Frolic. And now, without further ado, we'd like to announce the winners of our ice sculpture, but first . . ."

Rachel smiled and tucked her hands into her pockets. George was just warming up. For all his rhetoric about *without further ado,* he enjoyed the limelight far too much to simply announce the winners and move on. He began to thank the fire company members and the festival organizers and then to name everyone who'd volunteered to make the event special. Rachel glanced around, trying to locate Evan, but didn't see him in the milling assembly. Minutes passed and George was still talking, waxing on about the history of the valley. Rachel's mind wandered, and again she thought about the hat in the snow. Did it have anything to do with Billingsly's death, or was she letting her imagination run wild?

"Rachel," Hulda whispered, giving her a little nudge, "you're on."

". . . Our terrific town innkeeper and an inspiration to all, Rachel Mast!" George proclaimed. "Let's give her a well-deserved hand." He motioned to the onlookers, and everyone began to clap.

Rachel closed her eyes and wished she were back in her small parlor, cuddled up with her cat on her lap, fire crackling on the hearth. She wasn't afraid to stand up in front of an audience, but neither did she enjoy it. She forced a smile and took her place at the microphone. "I'm pleased to announce that third place goes to . . ."

A few minutes later, Rachel stood with the winners and the runners-up while a nervous young man with a bad complexion lined them up to snap photos for the town newspaper. "Is there even going to be a paper?" She tried to recall his name. Vaguely, she remembered him as either the son or nephew of Billingsly's surly receptionist. It was Greg. That was his name. "I just assumed, Greg, that with Bill Billingsly's death . . ."

"We're putting out the Saturday edition, as planned," he said. "With extensive coverage of the Winter Frolic. Most of the content was already set to go to press. Advertisers already paid for their ads. Aunt Lulu said the show must go on." He motioned to the group. "Move in a little closer, please."

Once Greg had all the pictures he wanted, Rachel congratulated the contestants again and reminded the visitors to check out the nearly two dozen ice sculptures all over town. Smiling for real and pleased that her duties were complete and she could hunt down Evan, she excused herself.

As Rachel gratefully made her way down the steps and into the crowd, she heard Hulda reminding everyone over the PA system of the family style Amish feast about to begin in the school cafeteria and the talent show in the auditorium.

Rachel hadn't gone more than twenty paces from the judging stand when Evan found her. "We have to talk."

She looked up at him in surprise. From the tone of his voice and the expression on his face, he was clearly upset. "What's wrong?"

He grabbed her arm and moved her through the crowd. "Not here."

# Chapter 7

"You want to go have something to eat?" Rachel looked at him, wondering what was up. "I should make an appearance at the Amish feast."

"Not the cafeteria. I need to speak to you alone." There was no hint of a smile.

She took in her surroundings; there were still plenty of people milling around, but many were heading for the warmth and good food of the cafeteria, where Amish women would be serving typical Amish fare family style at long tables. "It's a little cold to stand here."

"My car." He nodded in the direction of the parking lot.

She didn't know that she'd ever heard him use this tone with her before. "What's wrong?"

"I don't think you want an audience."

She followed him across the parking lot to his SUV. He opened the passenger's door for her, and she climbed in. She wondered if he'd found out she went to Billingsly's Saturday night. Had Mrs. Abbott realized it hadn't been a snowman she'd seen at Billingsly's door but rather an innkeeper in a white parka? Rachel *knew* she should have told Evan. She shivered, the cold seeping up from the soles of her boots.

He went around to the other side, slid into the driver's seat, and slammed his door. "Why didn't you tell me about your criminal conviction?" The interior light shone on his face, illuminating rigid lines and the hard set of his mouth.

This was the last thing she'd been expecting to hear. The first words out of her mouth should have been an apology, but her reaction was one of irritation. "How did you find out?"

"Does it matter?"

She had started to shiver. She wrapped her arms around herself. "It matters to me."

"I'm not in a position to give you information on an ongoing investigation."

"Billingsly. You found something at his office." She gave a heavyhearted sigh. When Evan didn't reply, she leaned back against the seat, letting the implications sink in. "He was going to do it, wasn't he? He was going to tell everyone. He threatened me, but I didn't really believe that he'd—"

"Is it true?" Evan's words fell like stones between them.

It had been a long time ago. Another life . . .

Numbness spread through her. If it came out in the paper, no one in this town would ever look at her the same way again. Her parents would have to live with the shame of having a criminal for a daughter. "So it's coming out in the next edition?"

The interior light went out, but she could still see the outlines of his features. "No. We found the information, along with dirt on other people in town, on his laptop. He had the column featuring everyone's favorite Stone Mill innkeeper half written. There was a different, completed 'Over the Back Fence' scheduled for Saturday." One gloved hand clenched into a knot, and he slammed it against the steering wheel. "Why didn't you tell me, Rache? Didn't you think I had a right to know?"

She turned to him. "It was a long time ago. I wasn't the same person I am today."

"You didn't answer me. Is it true or not?"

Her mouth tasted of copper. "What did it say?"

"That you were convicted of insider trading."

She glanced out the window; it was beginning to fog up. Townsfolk and strangers, Amish and English, were laughing and talking as they stomped the snow off their boots and entered the school. She could imagine the delicious aromas coming from inside. "It's true."

"Rachel." His voice was laced with a mixture of anger and hurt feelings. "You should have told me. I would have told *you* about something like this."

"No, you wouldn't have." She was angry now, and she wasn't even sure why. He hadn't done anything wrong. She had. She was the one who would carry that stain on her name for the rest of her life. "You would never have had to tell me because you never would have been in the situation I got myself into." Straight-arrow Evan. A man who saw everything in black and white. No gray. But the world held a lot of gray, didn't it?

"I want to hear your explanation, not what Billingsly wrote."

She put her hand on the door. She didn't want to be here. She didn't want to talk about this. Not tonight. Not ever. "It's complicated."

"I'm sure it is." His voice was tight . . . a stranger's voice. "Which is why I want to hear it from you and not from some sleazy would-be tabloid writer."

"It's freezing in here." She took her hand off the door and gestured to the dashboard. "Can you at least turn the heat on?"

He started the engine and pushed buttons. The air coming out of the vents was only lukewarm. "I'm waiting."

"As I said. It was a long time ago. Basically, I pled no contest to insider trading. But . . . unless you understand the nuances of finance . . ." She stopped and started again. "Lay people don't understand what insider trading really means, that it can mean a lot of things. And I was going to tell you. It just never seemed the right time."

He raised his voice again. "In two years?" He shook his head and didn't look at her. "I'm a cop and my girlfriend—

the woman I asked to marry me—has a criminal record and I don't know about it? And now I find out that you lied to me about the argument you had with Billingsly hours before he was murdered?"

"I didn't lie to you about my conversation with Billingsly. He *did* threaten me. But that wasn't really what we were fighting about. It was about what he'd done to Annie and Joab—what he was doing to this town. I told him he had to stop it."

"Or what?" He groaned. "Him threatening you, you getting angry, that changes things, Rache." He turned to her. "Do you understand what I'm saying?"

She met his gaze. "What? I'm a suspect now? You think I'd kill him over his stupid gossip column?"

"No, I don't think you'd kill him. But I'm a detective. I don't get to decide, based on personal relationships, who's a person of interest and who isn't. I have to follow an established protocol." He looked away and then back at her. "Anyone else hear the argument? Was Mary Aaron there? Anyone who can vouch for you?"

"No. Lots of people heard us arguing. But nobody heard what we said. Mary Aaron had walked away."

"Do you understand that to an outsider, it might look as though you had a reason to silence him?" He brought his fist down on the dashboard, hard. "Damn it, Rachel. Your name is going to have to go on my list of possible suspects."

Her hand found the door handle again. She couldn't believe what he was saying. She couldn't believe he would think for even a second that she could kill someone, much less that she could kill a man the way someone had killed Billingsly, leaving him to freeze to death like that. She didn't know what flew into her when she spoke again. "Well, if I'm a suspect, Detective Parks, then you may as well know it all. I went to Billingsly's house that night. I—"

"Don't say any more," he interrupted sharply.

"Why?"

He raised a hand, fingers spread. "I need to think about

how I have to proceed, whether it's ethical for me to even continue with this case or—"

"Evan? You don't seriously think I could have done that to Billingsly? That I could take a man's life in such a cruel way?" Her voice dropped to a whisper. "For *any* reason?"

"Of course I don't think you killed Billingsly," he snapped angrily. "I said that, didn't I? Of course I know you better than that. But I have to do my job. You argued with Billingsly and he threatened you. You go on the list. Blade had a beef with him. He goes on the list until his alibi checks out. Same goes for Skinner. I can't pick and choose."

"No. You can't." She yanked off her glove. "And the lead detective on a case can't be compromised by a relationship with a convicted criminal—especially one who's just become a suspect." She grasped her ring and struggled to remove it.

"Rache, no," he protested. "Don't—"

"This was a mistake, Evan. My mistake. Apparently, I make a lot of mistakes." She opened the car door, thrusting out her hand. "Take your ring."

"Rachel."

She slapped the diamond ring on the dashboard and got out of the car. She didn't bother to slam the door but walked away as fast as she could. Behind her, she heard Evan calling her name, but she didn't stop. Sobbing, tears cold on her cheeks, she plunged into the shadowy parking lot, headed for her Jeep.

Later—she wasn't sure if it was fifteen minutes or fifty— Rachel pulled off the street on the edge of Stone Mill, dug in her purse for a tissue, and blew her nose. She'd left the ice rink parking lot with the intention of going out to her aunt and uncle's farm to find Mary Aaron, but then had decided against it. If Rachel went there, she would have had to deal with her aunt and uncle and the family. They'd want to know why Rachel was at their house and not at the frolic, and she'd have to give some excuse and act cheerful, at least in front of them. And she couldn't do it. Not tonight. She was just too emotionally wrung out from her explosive exchange with Evan to put on a good face.

She felt empty. She had no more tears left, just a hollowness inside.

She rested her hands on her steering wheel. She couldn't just drive around all night; she ought to head home. But if she went home, she might have to play hostess to some of her guests, something she normally loved doing. But not while she was so upset.

She glanced up the street; it was mostly empty. Businesses were closed; everyone was either at the Amish feast or tucked safely in warm houses or hotel rooms. But not everyone had gone home. Rachel spotted the lights from The George still on. Maybe Ell was there. Even if she was busy with customers, the bookstore would be a warm and welcoming place to sit down for a few minutes and catch her breath. No one would expect anything of her, and she could gather her thoughts and decide what she was going to do about Evan. She didn't want to even consider that the engagement might really be over, that their relationship might be over. But how could she marry a man who could think she could kill someone?

Rachel shifted her Jeep into gear and pulled back onto the street. A light dusting of new snow covered the sidewalks and streets. She found a parking space in front of the bookstore and hopped out into the cold. Fat snowflakes drifted down, dreamlike in the light from the old-fashioned street lamps, and the ice crunched under her feet as she made her way to the first pair of double doors.

The George had been a theater in a former life, closed and falling into disrepair like so many small-town America cinemas. George O'Day had possessed the imagination and the financial means to buy and restore it as an independent bookstore. Books were George's first love, after Sophie. And to everyone's surprise and against all odds, the store had been a huge success, drawing customers from far-flung communities in this part of the state and aiding in the rejuvenation of Stone Mill's downtown.

Just walking into the marble lobby of the stately structure always gave Rachel a thrill. The concession stand now served as the register counter, and rows of bookshelves had replaced the theater seating, but the velvet drapes, the painted plaster ornamentation, and the ambiance remained. The spacious stage once trod by actors had been transformed, minus the screen, into a coffee shop/tea room, complete with tasty Amish-baked delicacies and scattered seating. Alone with a book, doing homework, or sharing a chat with friends, townspeople and visitors were charmed by The George's hospitality.

Rachel had expected to find Ell or one of the employees at the register, but instead, it was George O'Day ringing up a purchase for the high school principal. They both smiled and called out a greeting when they saw Rachel. LeRoy Sawyer, a portly gentleman with curling dark hair and a bristling mustache, complimented her on the success of the Winter Frolic. She thanked him, reminded him that it was a joint effort by dozens of residents, and George repeated his hope that the festival would become an annual event.

"I'd love to stay and discuss it," Sawyer said. "Our student council came up with some ideas you might want to consider for next year. I have to run, though. I'm meeting my wife and her parents at the Amish feast."

Sophie whined, and he stooped to scratch her head. The little dog wriggled with pleasure and then jumped up and down, wanting more attention.

"Enough," George said. "Be a good girl."

Sawyer chuckled. "And as usual"—he grimaced—"I think I'm running late. Better go before I get into even more trouble."

George and Sophie followed the principal to the double doors. "Watch the sidewalk," he cautioned. "We sprinkled salt on it, but it's still slippery." He closed the door behind Sawyer, turned the lock, and pulled down the shade. He repeated the routine with the other two sets of doors, and then dropped the blind in the old ticket booth that read *Closed*.

Rachel glanced up at the ornate clock over the register and then at George.

"Closing early tonight," George declared. "LeRoy was the only customer who came in after six."

"I can go if you like. I just stopped by to say hi. You could tuck in early for the night."

"It's one of the perks of being an independent. You can close when you want to." George threw her a compassionate look. "And you look as though you need a cup of tea and a friendly ear . . . unless I miss my guess."

"I could use both," she admitted.

"Switch out the lobby lights, will you?" George removed his cane from behind the register counter and led the way into the book room, Sophie bouncing along behind. "I hid two cinnamon twists," he said. "Ada's mother makes the best I've ever eaten. With black walnuts."

"Thanks," Rachel said. "I don't think I'm hungry. The tea does sound good, though."

"Nothing like peppermint tea on a cold night."

When they reached the refreshment area, Rachel ran fresh water and flipped on the electric kettle. "Tea bags or leaf?"

George snorted. "Need you ask?"

She smiled. "You're right. I shouldn't have." She took a porcelain English teapot, rinsed it with hot water, then added tea leaves from a glass container on an antique sideboard. She filled the pot with water and carried it to the table, where George had already assembled teacups, cream, and a small dish of raw sugar cubes. A crystal saucer held the famed cinnamon twists.

"I had an argument with Evan." She slid into her chair. "I'm not sure if I broke up with him or not." She stared at her hands in her lap and the finger missing her engagement ring. "I may have."

George nodded knowingly. " 'The course of true love . . .' " he quoted. "Tea first. It will make you feel better."

She smiled again. George believed that a cup of peppermint tea could remedy just about anything, and usually he was right. She didn't think that the solution to this problem would be found so easily, though. "It hasn't been the best of weeks."

"No." He poured tea into her cup and then his. He'd chosen dainty English cups and saucers with porcelain so thin that you could see shapes through them. Using a silver sugar spoon, he dropped a single lump into his tea and stirred. "I don't suppose we needed the cream. Foolish of me." He stirred again, put down his spoon, and cradled the cup in his hands. "Tea warms twice, outside and in." He smiled at her. "If you need to talk, I'm here, Rachel. If you'd rather just sit in the quiet, we can do that, too. I'm learning patience in my old age." He reached for a cinnamon twist.

"I hardly think you've reached your dotage yet."

"Not yet. At least I hope not. But some days, I wonder."

"I thought Ell would be working tonight." She added sugar to her tea.

"I sent her off to have dinner with that nice Aldritch boy. She works too hard, and she could stand with a little more meat on her bones. An Amish meal with gravy and biscuits is just the thing for her." He set his cup down. "Ell needs to learn to relax and enjoy herself more. What's life if we don't enjoy ourselves?"

Rachel hadn't thought she was hungry, but the cinnamon twists George had put on the table between them were calling her name. She reached out and slid one onto the plate he'd given her, *just in case*. She took a nibble. It was good. Amazingly good. Her guests would love them. Ada had never baked them at the house. She wondered if Ada had the recipe or if she'd consider winging it. Maybe her mother hadn't shared it. Amish cooks were as territorial with their prized recipes as any other women.

Idly, Rachel gazed around the sitting area. One table had been set aside for a display that included blown-up book covers of Harper Lee's *To Kill a Mockingbird* and *Go Set a Watchman*, as well as a photo of the author. Copies of both titles were stacked in front of it. "I haven't read *To Kill a Mockingbird* since . . . well, not in years, but it was always a favorite."

"You read the sequel yet?" George smiled. "We decided to combine the two for our book club selection this month."

"I haven't read the second book yet, but I've been meaning to. I bet the discussion was great." She would have liked to be in George's book club, but they met on Saturday nights, which were usually busy for her. "I'd have loved to have joined the discussion Saturday night."

"Still a chance. We had to cancel for the bad weather, so we're meeting this Saturday night. You're welcome to come then. Always room for one more reader."

*Postponed,* she thought. But Blade had told her he'd been at book club Saturday night. Or, rather, his *wife* had said he'd been at the meeting. She knew her eyes must have widened.

Had Blade lied to Coyote? Why would he do that? Surely it couldn't have had anything to do with Bill Billingsly's murder . . . could it?

She sipped her tea. "Um . . . how many regulars do you have?"

He paused, considering. "Eleven if you count Hulda, but she misses a lot in winter. Says she's ready for bed by the time we're just getting warmed up."

Rachel chuckled. "Is Teresa still a member?"

"Absolutely. She kept it going while I was away." He named off the people who rarely skipped a meeting. "I know because Teresa kept excellent attendance records."

"And Blade Finch. He comes regularly, too, doesn't he?"

"Blade? No." George shook his head. "He's hit-or-miss." His gaze met hers. "Why do you ask?"

Rachel shrugged slowly. She didn't want to jump to conclusions. "No reason, just someone told me that he was a serious reader. You wouldn't expect it, looking at him. But—"

"You mean the long hair and the tattoos?" George chuckled and wiped his mouth with a napkin. "What do I always tell you, Rachel? You can't judge a book by its cover." And they both laughed together over that old saying.

George finished up his cinnamon twist and asked, "Want to talk about Evan?"

She licked sugar from her fingertips, almost wishing George had saved a few more of the pastries. "I don't think so."

"Well, just remember, I'm here if you need me. You, Sophie, and Ell, I consider you my family. You know that." He reached for his teacup. "I understand that you saw Bill's body. Before the police shooed everyone off." He met her gaze across the table. "I imagine it was bad."

"Awful," she agreed. "It was ghoulish of me to go down there, I suppose, but when Eddie Millman told me Billingsly was dead, I don't think I believed it. It seemed impossible that anyone would do such a thing."

"He died of exposure, you know." George took a last sip and set down his empty cup. "He was alive and probably awake when they tied him to that post and doused him with water."

The full horror of Billingsly frozen on his porch came back to her. "How do you know that? I thought . . . I assumed there was a possibility he'd been killed inside and then . . . dragged out."

George patted his lap, and Sophie jumped up into it. "I have my sources. I won't say who, but let's say someone in the medical examiner's office is a bit of a gossip. The knock on the head wasn't fatal. Bill died tied to his front porch. No doubt about it."

"But you said *they*. The police think more than one person was involved?"

"That's just conjecture on my part. Bill wasn't a small person, and he should have been fighting for his life. I'd imagine that it would have taken two assailants or at least one formidable one to overcome him. There was a concussion. He was struck in the head by a hard object—some sort of bar, but they don't know what. No weapon was found on the scene. He was either disabled or knocked unconscious and carried or dragged onto the porch." He thought for a minute. "Although I guess he could have been held at gunpoint and made to walk out there."

"But then why hit him with something?" she asked.

He nodded. "Good point. He was gagged, and there were ligature marks on his wrists and ankles. He struggled against his bonds, and he probably was very aware that he was in danger of freezing to death. Which proved true."

She sighed. "It's just so bizarre. Killing someone that way, so . . . indirectly."

"Right," George said thoughtfully. "Why leave him outside to die like that? If you were going to hit him over the head, why not just hit him a little harder and be done with it?"

"I think Evan is right to look at people Billingsly knew. This wasn't a random killing. It was too . . . too personal."

"Exactly what I thought," George agreed. "A crime of passion." He stroked Sophie's head. "Do you think Evan is up to this investigation? He's new at this. No offense intended. You know that I'm very fond of Evan, but this is going to be a high-profile case. It could make his career or . . ."

"Break it." She finished her tea. "Evan's good at procedure. He's studied the guidelines and worked under other detectives, so I think his foundation is good." She hesitated. "It's his intuition that I worry about. At some point, I think you have to go with intuition, and I don't know that he believes that. I don't know if he has intuition." She looked up at George. "And if he did, would he recognize it?"

George didn't say anything and Rachel went on. "Evan says that the argument I had with Billingsly in the high school cafeteria the afternoon before he was killed puts me on the *persons-of-interest* list."

"You?" George frowned. "He can't seriously believe that you could *kill* anyone?"

"That was my first response. I got so angry that I just lost my temper. I gave him back his ring. He said it didn't matter what he thought personally, that he had to follow all leads, but—" She put her head in her hands. "He didn't want me to take it personally? How could I not?" She lowered her hands and looked up at George again. "I'm so confused. I don't want to marry a man who thinks I could kill someone, do I? Only . . . in all fairness to him, that's not what he said." She exhaled. "What do I do, George?"

"You're an intelligent woman, Rachel." He reached across the table and patted her hand. "You'll figure it out. Evan will solve the murder, and the two of you will patch up your differences."

"You think so?"

"I'm sure of it."

They chatted for a few more minutes, and Rachel got up to go. She thanked George for the tea and for listening, and left him with a hug and a kiss on the cheek. She was just getting into her Jeep when her cell phone vibrated. She glanced at the screen, saw Evan's name, and almost didn't answer. But she did.

"Rache. I just . . . I was calling to see if you were okay."

She started the engine but just sat there. "I'm okay," she said softly. "But I'm not ready to talk about this. I think that both of us are too—" She cut herself off. Too what? Too headstrong? Too emotional?

"Right," he said. "It's better if we wait. We're both wound pretty tight. But I was worried about you. I went by the house. Your Jeep wasn't there."

"I stopped at the bookstore and had tea with George. I'm going home now."

"Well, drive safe."

There were a few seconds of silence and she wondered if he'd hung up, and then he said, "I have to go and talk to Joab and Annie Herschberger in the morning. I'd appreciate it if you'd still come along, break the ice for me."

"You're sure that won't compromise the investigation. Me being one of the suspects?"

He exhaled. "I wouldn't ask you if I did. So, will you?"

She felt ashamed of her childish sarcasm. "If you think it will help . . ." It was her turn to be silent for a long second. "Of course."

# Chapter 8

❧

Evan had the heater running when he picked her up the following morning in his SUV, but the mood was still as cool between them as when she'd gotten out of his vehicle the evening before. A crisp "Good morning," followed by "I don't think this should take long," was the extent of Evan's greeting. She murmured something in reply and then stared out the window as he pulled out of her driveway.

Hulda was on her step retrieving her out-of-town paper from the boxwood where the deliveryman had thrown it. She waved, cheery in a red-and-white robe and furry slippers.

Rachel waved back. "At least the sun's out today," she remarked to Evan.

He grunted.

He didn't look as if he'd slept any better than she had. The wrinkles at the corners of his eyes and the puffiness beneath them made his features stoic. Rachel doubted that her own appearance had benefited from her distress.

Because they were going to Annie and Joab's home, Rachel had taken pains to dress in a manner that wouldn't offend the Herschbergers. They knew and accepted that she was no longer Amish, but interaction in the Plain world went smoother when she covered her head with a scarf and wore modest clothing. Today she was wearing a long denim skirt, black tights and boots, and a hand-sewn, padded Amish-style coat. She wore no makeup; her red hair was bound up and pinned in a neat bun at the back of her head and covered. Evan hated her getup, as he called it, but in the past he'd agreed that, as odd as she might appear to an outsider, the Old Order Amish responded to her appearance in a positive manner. When she was dressed plainly, they spoke to her not as an Englisher but as one of their own. Almost.

"How's the case going?" she asked after a few blocks of silence.

He didn't respond to her question, but after a minute or two glanced at her and asked, "What do you know about Blade Finch?"

"I know he's a skilled woodworker, a good father. He seems extremely responsible, hardworking, and appears to adore his wife and children."

When Evan made no comment, she continued, "I gather he may have come from a rough background, but he attends church regularly with his family and he must have convinced the State of California that he was a decent man because they allowed him and Coyote to adopt Remi."

"He's the boy's stepfather, did you know that? He was married before. The mother's dead, and the child had no other relatives."

She smoothed the fabric of her skirt. "I never asked anything about Remi's background. I assumed that if Coyote and Blade wanted me to know, they'd have told me." She looked at Evan. "But it says something about Blade's character, doesn't it, that he'd want to adopt Remi?"

"It might." Out of town now, he took a narrow country road. "Were you aware that he'd spent time in jail?"

"No." Her mouth went dry, and the impossibility of Blade's story about going to the book club meeting when it had actually been canceled surfaced in her mind. "I didn't. What did he do?"

Evan hesitated and slowed as the road descended to a single-lane bridge over a rocky stream at the bottom of a hill. "I don't think that's something that I should be sharing with you."

"I'll just look it up on the Internet."

He exhaled. "Not jail. Prison. Dennis Lee Finch, alias *Blade* Finch, served nine years for manslaughter."

Rachel wouldn't have been any more surprised if Mrs. Abbott's walking snowman had crossed the road in front of them. "Manslaughter?" Blade had killed someone? The gentle and good-humored man who carried his newborn around in a baby sling and tenderly cared for a physically challenged little boy had been convicted of causing someone's death? "I had no idea," she admitted. "But manslaughter could mean a lot of things." She hesitated. She of all people knew that, with matters of the law, definitions of crimes could be broad. "Couldn't it?"

Evan didn't respond. He slowed the SUV again and turned onto a lane marked by a large black mailbox with the name J. Herschberger painted on the front. The driveway hadn't been plowed, but a heavy motor vehicle had recently driven over it, packing down the snow. The path led to a tidy farmyard with a large barn, two-story stone house, and well-maintained outbuildings. Bare cornstalks sprouted from a blanket of white in a large enclosure ringed by a painted picket fence and boasting a scarecrow in threadbare trousers and a battered hat.

"You should see this house in May," Rachel said. "Annie has hundreds of yellow tulips and daffodils. And by July, the rosebushes around the house will all be in bloom."

Above the farmyard, a windmill creaked and turned, the white paddles stark against the blue of the winter sky. A dog barked a friendly welcome and trotted out of open double doors on the barn. Just inside, sheltered from the wind and warmed by a patch of sunshine, stood a patient workhorse. One bearded Amish man stood at the animal's head while a young man inspected a massive hind hoof.

Evan parked his vehicle and turned off the key. "Is that Joab Herschberger? The older man?"

Rachel nodded and climbed out of the SUV. She walked over to the dog and patted its head, then waited for Joab to recognize her. His companion, younger and wearing glasses, studied her but said nothing. Rachel thought she had seen him before, but she wasn't certain of his name.

Joab slowly released the horse's halter and gave his full attention to Rachel. "Morning," he said in Deitsch. "That's Evan Parks with you, isn't it? The policeman?"

"*Ya,*" she answered. "But he's not wearing his uniform or driving his police car," she replied, also in Deitsch. "He's come to speak with you, if you are willing."

Joab frowned. "And if I'm not? This is about the newspaperman's death, isn't it? Does the Englisher think that I'm the one who committed this terrible crime?" He ran a hand down the horse's neck and came toward her. "Did he bring his gun?"

Rachel shook her head. "No guns. He was hoping to ask you and Annie a few questions. It's his job to find who did this murder in our community, and he has to talk to everyone who might have been angry with Billingsly."

"Then he has come to the right place," Joab said. His eyes narrowed. He was a spare man of medium height, but he moved easily, evidence of a lifetime of manual labor. Joab's face was weather-beaten and his eyes fierce above his graying beard.

"Mr. Herschberger?" Evan came to stand beside her. "Would you mind answering a few questions?"

Joab frowned, but when he spoke again, it was in heavily accented English. "You want to know if I hated him enough to take his life. Maybe I wanted to, but—"

"But my Joab could never do such a thing." Annie appeared from the shadowy interior of the barn, a bucket of chicken feed in one hand. She was dressed for the cold in men's boots and a heavy coat, and a wool scarf much like the ones Rachel wore. "My husband told an untruth to protect me and our other children. He also wished to protect our foolish son and keep him from being shunned." She used the Amish word *mei-dung*, meaning *bann*. "He was angry, so angry that he did this to this bucket." She turned it so that Rachel could see the dent in one side. "Joab was wrong to shelter us, but he has lamented his error and received forgiveness."

"I don't wish to cause either of you trouble. My questions are routine. I promise not to take much of your time," Evan said. "I just need to know Mr. Herschberger's whereabouts Saturday night after the festival closed."

"Has he come to arrest my husband?" Annie asked Rachel in Deitsch. "Is there a law that says he must answer these questions?"

"It would be better if Joab did," Rachel answered in Deitsch. "You know I argued with Billingsly at the school. I had to say where I was Saturday night, too. But you don't have to say anything. And you have a right to ask for a lawyer if—"

"No Englishman of the law." Joab spoke firmly in English. "I am an innocent man and have nothing to hide. Ask your questions, Evan Parks."

"I can say where my husband was that night," Annie said quickly. "Where else would he be but here with me in our home? We came back early from the frolic because of the threat of bad weather and we did not wish to risk the horse on a slippery blacktop."

Evan glanced at Joab for confirmation. "So you came directly home. And your wife was with you all evening?"

"Not only my wife but my brother Barnabas; his wife, Belinda; three of his sons; and his new daughter-in-law and their baby. They were on their way to his wife's family, but when the snow started to fall they came here for the night."

"So all those people would state that you were here at home all Saturday night?" Evan asked.

"He was," the younger man said. He eyed Evan suspiciously. "Uncle Joab never left the house again that night."

"What did my husband just say?" Annie asked sharply. "His

three nephews slept in the living room. Joab could not have gone out of the house without waking us all. He did not stir from the house until morning."

"We were driving through Stone Mill when we heard that there had been a death and stopped to see." Joab shook his head. "I saw what had happened to Billingsly, and I will never forget it, not if I live to be a hundred."

"It's all true," the younger man, holding the horse's bridle, said.

Evan glanced at him. "And you are?"

"Little Joe Herschberger. This is my uncle. My wife, my brothers, and my father and mother will all tell you the same thing. Uncle Joab was with us in this house. He harmed no one." He spat onto the barn floor. "Maybe you should go look for the killer instead of pestering my uncle, who has such a gentle heart he cannot even cut the head off his own chickens."

"So, you can cross Joab off your list," Rachel said a few minutes later as they drove away from the Herschberger farm. "That's good, right?"

"Good for Joab," Evan said, making no attempt to hide his grumpiness. "Not so good for you."

The ride back to Stone Mill House was as awkward for Rachel as the trip out to the Herschbergers had been. It was so awkward that she was relieved when Evan dropped her off at her house.

"Thanks," he said as he pulled into her driveway. It was the first word he'd spoken for the last several miles.

"I didn't really do anything," she replied.

His face showed nothing of what he was thinking. "I doubt they would have spoken to me at all if you weren't there."

It was true, but she saw no sense in repeating what they both knew. She wanted to say something that would make things right between them, words that might bridge the distance and the hurt, but she was still numb. This wasn't an Evan she knew, this scowling, brooding man. She suspected that he was aching inside as much as she was.

She mumbled something noncommittal and watched, dry-eyed, as he drove away. Inside, she found Ada bustling around the kitchen, rolling piecrust and roasting a chicken. The expression on her face told Rachel that her housekeeper was in no mood for small talk, so Rachel moved on to the dining room, where Mary Aaron was giving instructions to Minnie and seeing to the guests.

"Hulda's in the office," Mary Aaron supplied.

"Oh, good."

No one seemed to have noticed that Rachel had been gone for an hour. She should have been pleased that everything at the inn was running smoothly. Instead, she felt a vague discomfort that she was dispensable in her own inn these days.

*Pull up your stockings and be a big girl,* she told herself. Wasn't that the whole idea of having a dependable staff?

Hulda came every Tuesday morning and sometimes on Thursdays and Saturdays as well. Wanting her son and grandsons to take more responsibility, she was spending less time at Russell's Hardware and Emporium and more time at Stone Mill House. That was a tremendous help to Rachel because having Hulda's help for a few hours several mornings a week freed her from the routine office duties. Age aside, Hulda was computer literate and a savvy businesswoman, and although she'd never been an innkeeper, Hulda had been able to give Rachel a lot of pointers on running the B&B more efficiently. For the first year, Rachel had tried to do almost everything herself, and the task had been overwhelming. But now that she could hire more help and had Hulda volunteering, Rachel had more time to devote to the growing craft shop and her greater plans for improving the town's prospects.

But she couldn't do much toward those goals if she couldn't even remember what day of the week it was. She was definitely not herself. Since Billingsly's death, she'd had trouble keeping track of the hours. It shocked her to think that his body had been discovered only two days earlier on Sunday morning. And since she'd seen the editor's frozen corpse on the front porch of his stately Victorian, she'd broken her engagement with the man she loved and found herself on the list of murder suspects. How could her life change so completely in only forty-eight hours?

"I forgot you were coming in today," Rachel said to Hulda as she walked into the office, with Mary Aaron following behind. "Billingsly's killing has me rattled. I don't know whether I'm coming or going."

"No wonder." The elderly woman peered over her glasses. These were her new ones, Rachel noticed, electric pink with rhinestones. At least she thought they were rhinestones. With Hulda you never knew. They might be genuine diamonds.

"I really appreciate you coming to help out in the office," Rachel said. "But I feel guilty for not paying you for your time. Not that I could compensate you properly for all the hours you put in here."

Hulda scoffed. "Nonsense. At my age, I do what pleases me. And why should I waste my time staring at television in that museum of an empty house when there are so many interesting people over here?" She lowered her voice. "That Mr. Skinner. I think he likes me; he was in here a few minutes ago, trying to butter me up. But I'd never be interested in him. He reminds me of a terrorist, or maybe one of these survivalist types who hides in the mountains and hoards canned food, waiting for the end of civilization."

"Jake Skinner frightens you?" Mary Aaron asked.

Rachel didn't comment on Hulda's remark about Jake Skinner liking her. According to Hulda, lots of younger men found her so attractive that they wanted to marry her.

"No, he doesn't *scare* me." Hulda adjusted her glasses again. "I just call them as I see them, and there's something suspicious about that man." Today Hulda was wearing a gold-and-white pantsuit with a puffy red vest. Her close-cropped white hair, makeup, and manicure were as flawless as always. "Now you girls go along and let me answer these emails from prospective guests. I think we're going to be full through next month, at least on the weekends."

"As long as they don't expect Amish tours of the murder scene," Mary Aaron said.

Rachel wondered if the notoriety was attracting visitors. "We can hope not," she said. Was it ghoulish to imagine that her business might prosper because of Billingsly's death?

Of course, the inn's popularity might come to a screeching halt if Billingsly's spiteful column became general knowledge or if there was reason for people in Stone Mill to start examining her background. The thought that she might be an official suspect in Billingsly's murder was chilling. Evan might not believe that she could be guilty of committing such a crime, but if he didn't make progress in solving the case soon, her personal future would be in serious trouble. Evan would do his job, and if it meant involving her, he would, especially now that she'd admitted that she'd gone to Billingsly's house the night he was killed.

She wasn't sorry that she'd told Evan. She hadn't stopped loving him, and no matter what happened with their relationship, she was determined not to keep any more secrets from him. As crazy as it seemed, she was relieved that he knew the worst about her because secrets didn't lie quiet. They had a tendency to rub at your conscience in the dead of night.

"Do you need me for anything right now?" she asked Mary Aaron.

Her cousin gave her a thoughtful look. Mary Aaron always seemed to be able to read her. She didn't ask questions; she just smiled. "*Ne,* Rae-Rae. We're good. You go do whatever it is you need to do. I should be finished up with the things I want to get done by noon. And if you could give me a ride home after that, I'd appreciate it. I caught a ride here with Aunt Hannah's driver this morning."

"No problem." Rachel tucked a lock of hair that had escaped from her bun behind her ear. "After I change, I wanted to walk down to the post office. Mail off your Evening Star quilt to the woman in South Carolina. I'll just wrap it and—"

"Best to slip it in one of those priority boxes. I wrapped it in plastic and printed out the accompanying letter and a mailing label," her cousin told her. "That makes three quilts we've sold since Christmas. The craft shop business is doing great, and the website is bringing customers from all over."

"What would I do without you?" Rachel said.

She was soon out of the house and walking briskly through the residential streets toward the post office. The holidays had passed, but the snow on the ground and the twinkle lights that many people had left up for the Winter Frolic gave the town a festive air. The heaps of snow, the sharp scent of evergreens, and the ice sculptures and snowmen in front yards raised her spirits and made her smile. And for a few minutes, she could almost push her worries away. Almost.

She loved Stone Mill, with its old homes and small-town American values. It was a place where everyone knew your name and there were always neighbors ready to lend a helping hand. The valley was a good place for families, and despite the recession that had made life in the valley more difficult financially, there was a general sense of optimism and hope for the future. Stone Mill didn't have to wither and die like so many small towns in America's heartland, not if she could help it.

"For every problem, there's always a solution," her father always said. "Prayer and hard work carry us through life," she'd heard him say many times as she was growing up. She wished she could go to him now for advice. She'd prayed on it, but she was too much a coward to explain to him about the insider trading conviction. She couldn't bear it if *Dat* was ashamed of her.

Walking in the fresh air *did* help her put her thoughts in

order and put things in perspective. There was no way around it. It was foolish of her to blame Evan for following procedure. She couldn't take it personally. It was his job to follow up every lead. Her arguing with Billingsly and then going to his house just before he was murdered were leads, even if they led to a dead end.

She shuddered. Why couldn't she get the word *dead* out of her head today?

She really needed to cut Evan a break. He must have been shocked to learn about her past, and he had every right to be angry. Putting her name on his list of possible suspects was the right thing to do, no matter how much he might regret it. Her name couldn't be cleared until Evan found the real killer . . . or until she did.

She couldn't rid herself of the hunch that Evan wasn't looking in the right direction. The wide-brimmed hat *had* to be a clue. The more she thought about it, the more she was certain that it might lead to the killer. As difficult as it was to believe that one of the Amish might be involved in a crime of violence, a man's hat being there was all wrong. It stood out like a blue cow in a herd of black-and-white Holsteins. But Evan showed no signs of listening to her advice, and he definitely didn't want her involved in yet another investigation.

Not that he would get far getting information from the traditional Amish without her. They might like Evan, but he was an Englisher, and few of them would trust him. Fewer still would give information that might reflect badly on another of their people. Hundreds of years of keeping apart from the world had added to the suspiciousness of a naturally private people. Joab's nephew's attitude toward Evan's questions was mild compared to the wall of silence he could expect from the general community.

If she did do a little investigating on her own, she'd have to keep it from Evan. He was upset enough with her as it was. It certainly couldn't do any harm for her to ask a few questions . . . eliminate a few possibilities. Naturally, if she did learn anything substantial, come up with any hard evidence, she'd hand it over to Evan at once . . . But where to start?

Blade had mentioned seeing a buggy in Wagler's parking lot long after the grocery was closed. It wasn't like the Amish to be out late at night, and there wasn't a good reason for any of them to be downtown at that hour. And certainly not in a snowstorm. Maybe she would stop by Blade and Coyote's and see if Blade was there, or if he'd gone to the school gym already that morning. She could ask him about the buggy. The vehicles all might look alike to non-Amish, but they weren't. Buggies were as individual as different horses were. If Blade had a good sense for detail, which she suspected he did, she might be able to discover who owned the buggy and why it was still in town so late on the night of a snowstorm.

Rachel mailed her package and was able to extricate herself from the postmistress in less than fifteen minutes, a record. The post office was often a gathering place for locals. There were even several benches where townspeople would sit and chat. Not surprisingly, the talk this morning was of Billingsly's murder and the crime wave that was overtaking Stone Mill. In addition to Billingsly's death, someone was missing a cat, two trash cans had been overturned at the curb, and the priest at St. Agnes's had found the gas cap removed from his pickup and a quarter tank of gasoline missing. Rachel pleaded urgent business and made her getaway before Mabel Grooper could relate the gruesome details of Billingsly's appearance to a tourist from Harrisburg.

Blade and Coyote lived a short distance away from the post office in one of the many Victorian-age homes in town. The downstairs was given over to a studio and shop, the kiln was out back in the barn, and the Finches and their children lived in an apartment on the second floor. Donna, an aspiring painter who displayed some of her watercolors on one wall of the shop in return for clerking, was dusting the shelves when Rachel came in.

"Coyote's at the school working the booth, but Blade's upstairs with the kids," Donna said when asked.

Rachel nodded and let herself in to the wide hallway. At the foot of the stairs, a door led to the apartment. She buzzed the intercom, and when Blade answered she identified herself. "Hey, Rachel. Coyote's already gone to the school."

"I know, but it's you I'm looking for."

"Is this more questions?" He didn't sound friendly.

"Just a few."

"Then I guess you'd better come on up and get it over with."

# Chapter 9

Blade was waiting for her at the top of the stairs. Rachel never entered the Finch apartment on the second floor without being amazed by the transformation the two of them had made on the rambling Victorian. When they bought it, it had been empty for more than fifteen years and slowly slipping into decay. Bats, wasps, and honeybees reigned in the attic, and broken windows had allowed the once-grand rooms to be littered with rotting leaves and squirrel nests. The cedar-shingled roof leaked. Modern plumbing and electricity were practically nonexistent. But Blade had worked tirelessly to restore the structure: replacing the roof, adding modern plumbing, rewiring the entire house, and installing an open kitchen with open shelving, marble-topped counters, and a freestanding island. He'd knocked down non-load-bearing walls so that light streamed in through stained glass windows and made the hardwood gleam. Now colorful posters and handcrafted furniture coexisted comfortably with antiques that had languished in the attic, and children's toys filled the homeschool area.

Remi smiled and waved before returning his attention to the papier-mâché volcano that he and his sister Shoshone were constructing, while the baby watched, wide-eyed, and cooed from a baby seat on the floor.

Blade glanced at the kids and motioned to Rachel. "We can talk in the library. Latte?"

"That sounds good."

He took two mugs created by Coyote's hands and hit a button on the fancy coffeemaker on the countertop.

Rachel watched with fascination as steamed milk shot into the mug, followed by a stream of dark liquid. The room was immediately filled with the heavenly scent of fresh coffee.

"Raw sugar? Honey?" Blade asked as he made a second mug of coffee.

"No, thanks," Rachel answered.

"Remi, you're in charge," his father instructed, handing Rachel her coffee. "Call me if the baby fusses."

Remi nodded vigorously from his wheelchair, beaming with pride.

"The other one is napping," Blade explained as he led the way into a paneled room with bookshelves running from floor to ceiling along three walls. He closed the door behind them and waved her to a church bench. "Have a seat."

She sat down, cradling her coffee, and met his gaze. Now that she was here, she was having second thoughts. Maybe she really did need to mind her own business and let Evan solve the case.

Blade leaned against the boarded-up fireplace, a project Coyote had explained was next on her husband's restoration schedule, and regarded her coolly. "Your fiancé told you about me serving time, didn't he?" Behind him, over the marble mantel hung an old wooden bow and intricately beaded quiver.

"He did. But I . . . That's not my business, Blade." She glanced around the room, noticing a long-stemmed stone pipe with feathers dangling from it hanging from one of the bookshelves. "Are you Native American?"

Blade's expression remained unchanged. "My mother was half Swede and half Arapaho. I never met my old man. She claimed he was a Marine who had heavy Indian blood. But he didn't hang around long enough for anybody to tell what tribe." He rested his coffee on the mantel and folded his arms over his chest. "Did Parks tell you why I went to prison?"

She really hadn't come here to ask him about his past. It wasn't her business, and honestly, she didn't want to know. She wanted to appreciate Blade for the man he was today, not judge him for what he might have done in the past. But the look on Blade's face told her he wanted to tell her. "He said you killed someone."

"Manslaughter. Twelve years, three off for good behavior. Not something I'm proud of or something Coyote would want people talking about around the teapot at The George." He shrugged. "It was a long time ago. Long story, but I was trying to keep a buddy from ending up being another homicide statistic. But the other guy ended up dead."

"So you were responsible?" Rachel asked.

"No guilty men in prison." Blade's thin lips twisted into a semblance of a smile. "Prison humor." He looked down and then back at her again. "Can't say about the others, but I was guilty."

Rachel waited, letting him speak.

"Coyote was volunteering at the prison in Stockton where I'd been sent. Teaching an art class. We hit it off, started writing to each other, and when I got out, she helped turn my life around." Blade's husky voice rasped with emotion. "We built a life together. It would be tough on her and the kids if Billingsly's murder—which I did not commit—jeopardized it."

"You two had a falling-out," Rachel said. "You and Billingsly."

"We did. I built some bookcases for him, fancy cabinet-work. Did a great job, took me more than a month. Floor to ceiling. Go to his office if you want. See for yourself if it was first-rate. He paid me half of the agreed-upon cost up front. Wanted only the best, old-growth Pennsylvania cherry. He raved about my work. But once I finished and wanted what was due, he changed his tune. Claimed it was shoddy work. Refused to pay the rest. I didn't take it too well. Had a few choice words with him. But I didn't lay a hand on him. Not then. Not later." A muscle twitched along the line of Blade's jaw. "Not that I wouldn't have taken pleasure in decking the jerk. But he wasn't worth the trouble. What I have here . . ." His gesture took in the house, his wife, and his kids. "I've spent enough time behind bars. I'm never going back to that life." His complexion darkened. "And it might sound corny, but I've made my peace with the guy upstairs. One death on my conscience is all I can handle."

She drew in a long breath. "You said that when you were walking home Saturday night, you saw an Amish buggy in Wagler's parking lot. Just sitting there empty? No one around?"

"No. I looked inside. Wondered if somebody had trouble. But it was empty. I thought it was odd. You know, the bad weather. And it was late, like I told you. Nobody on the streets."

"You think maybe some young *rumspringa* kid drove it there so he could go to the tavern?"

"Could be." Blade shrugged. "But why is it important?"

"As I said, just following up on things various people have told me. You said there was nothing unusual. Do you remember what color the horse was?"

"Brown, just a typical brown horse. Reddish-brown maybe."

"Probably a bay. Any markings?" She sipped her coffee. It was as good as she could get in a big-city coffee shop. "A white foot? A blaze on his forehead?"

Blade chuckled. "I'm no cowboy. They all look the same to me. It had a blanket on, but if the horse had white feet I didn't notice. The buggy was one of those funny ones, sort of an Amish pickup truck."

"A long bed with a closed-in cab?" Her interest was immediately piqued. "That's called a top-hack."

"One of those ones with an open bed for hauling stuff."

The type of horse-drawn carriage Blade mentioned was rare in the Stone Mill valley. Much more common around Lancaster. Rachel could think of only half a dozen in the valley, maybe less. It was going to be much easier for her to find out who was out late that night.

"A top-hack," she repeated, trying to think about who had one.

He glanced toward the door. "Look, I've got stuff to do. But I'm telling you, I had nothing to do with offing Billingsly."

"I believe you, for what it's worth." She rose from the bench. "Just one more thing and I'll be out of your hair. You told me that you were at a book club meeting Saturday night. But you weren't, were you?"

Blade's visage darkened.

"Blade, there was no meeting that night. It was canceled due to the snowstorm."

He picked up his coffee mug, but he didn't drink from it.

"Can you tell me where were you? And why Coyote thinks—"

"It's personal, Rachel," he interrupted. "Nothing that hurts her. And nothing she needs to know about."

"So you *did* lie to a police officer?"

He motioned toward the door. "I think maybe you've worn out your welcome today."

"I'm not accusing you of murder. I'm simply asking where you were."

"None of your business. And none of Evan Parks's either." His heavy-lidded eyes narrowed. "You want to share what you know about my past with people in this town, do it. But know you'd be causing unnecessary hurt to my wife and my kids. You've never seemed to me like somebody who could do that. But it's a free country." He opened the door. "You do what you have to."

\* \* \*

As she walked back to Stone Mill House, Rachel kept mulling over her conversation with Blade. Her instincts told her that Coyote's husband really didn't have anything to do with Billingsly's death, but if he didn't, why had he lied about where he'd been Saturday night? And why had he been unwilling to say where he'd really been? She refused to believe that he was seeing another woman. His love for his wife and children was obvious. But what would Evan say if he knew? Did gut feelings have anything to do with solving a crime? And was she withholding evidence by not telling Evan about Blade's phony alibi?

As Rachel walked, she was almost oblivious to the cold. Blade had obviously been shaken by her questions, and she hoped it wouldn't spoil her friendship with the family. Everyone had things in his past he didn't want to share. Certainly she did. Prying into her neighbors' lives made her uncomfortable, but how else was she going to find the killer? Certainly a few bruised feelings were a small price to pay to clear her own name and see justice done.

Mentally, she began to construct a chart on the whiteboard in her bedroom, the same way she'd done the year before when another murder had been committed in their community. The vanishing hat would begin her list of things that didn't sit right. And directly below it, the top-hack that Blade had seen in Wagler's parking lot, the buggy that shouldn't have been there.

There had to be logical explanations, and she hoped that they didn't involve Billingsly's murder. Both the hat and the buggy were nails that stuck up when all the others were nailed snugly in place. Evan had brushed off her concern about the man's hat, and she had the sinking feeling that he'd do the same with the late-night buggy. But she knew someone who would listen, a person she trusted who might help her unravel this ball of tangled wool.

At the B&B, Rachel found Mary Aaron upstairs just finishing

vacuuming one of the guest rooms. "Hi," Rachel said in Deitsch once her cousin had switched off the vacuum. "Wasn't this supposed to be Dinah's job today?" Mary Aaron could turn her hand to anything, but she was normally working in the gift shop or giving instructions to housecleaning.

Mary Aaron's pretty face creased into an amused expression. "It was, but the machine was getting the best of Dinah again today." She chuckled. "I won't repeat all she called it, but *stupid goat* was the mildest. She said that when she kicked it. And the poor vacuum cleaner was as innocent as a new-hatched chick. Poor Englisher machine can't eat dirt if the bag's full." She used the Englisher word for the vacuum because there wasn't one in the Amish dialect.

Rachel shook her head as she gathered up the furniture wax and cleaning cloths. Dinah's rocky relationship with electrical appliances was much like Ada's war with the telephone. More than once, Rachel had caught her stepping over the vacuum cleaner and sweeping the rug on the stairs with a broom. And the multiple choices on the washing machine confused her. It wasn't that Dinah was stupid, far from it. She simply had taken such a strong dislike to the appliances that she refused to learn how to properly operate them. Evan often asked Rachel why she didn't dismiss Dinah and hire someone more useful, but he didn't understand. Dinah was a good girl, and her mother depended on her wages. Firing her would be an insult to the family and ultimately the community. And besides, Dinah was cheerful, industrious, and always good with the guests.

"This is the last room," Mary Aaron said. "Would you mind giving me that ride home?" She removed a spiral notebook and pencil from her apron pocket and drew a line through the final entry. Mary Aaron loved her lists and rarely was without her small notebook.

"Sure, I'll be glad to drive you," Rachel answered. "But I was hoping you didn't need to go straight home. There's something I want to look into."

Mary Aaron's face lit up with curiosity. "I'm not sure I like the sound of that," she teased.

Rachel pressed her lips together. "Let's talk in the car where there won't be any eavesdroppers."

"*Ya*. Sure." Mary Aaron slipped easily back into English. "Just as long as I'm home in time to help *Mam* with supper." She passed over a handful of one-dollar bills. "Very nice people you have staying here this week. That Jake *retts* up his room, makes his bed, and leaves on it every day a note and five dollars for the maid. Must have money, him."

"Or he's just a thoughtful person," Rachel replied. Tips were put in a box in the office and divided at the end of the month between all the staff, including the outside help. Ada refused to take her share, saying that she received fair wages for her cooking and didn't need Englisher handouts. The others gladly accepted the reward. "Funny, Jake Skinner doesn't give the impression of a man who would be so kind."

"*Ne*, he doesn't," Mary Aaron agreed. "But he's always polite to the staff."

"But not who you'd expect to come to a town like Stone Mill for a winter festival."

"So why *is* he here?" Mary Aaron asked. "I haven't seen him at the Dutch feast or at any of the events. But he was at the school gym on Saturday, so maybe he did come . . ." She left her thought unfinished. "He wasn't looking at any of the exhibits or the booths. And he didn't buy anything that I noticed. Most, I thought, he was looking for somebody."

"I agree," Rachel said.

They collected their coats and scarves, and after Rachel had changed back into proper clothing for visiting, they piled into her Jeep. Rachel didn't start the engine right away, but took the opportunity to explain about the hat she'd seen in the snow at Billingsly's house, the hat that had mysteriously vanished in the middle of the excitement. "I tried to tell Evan that something was strange about that," she said. "That Amish men don't lose their hats and walk away without them."

"*Ya.*" Mary Aaron fastened her seat belt. "Too much money they cost to be careless." She chuckled. "It would be like me accidently losing my *kapp* and not noticing. It would be . . . *indecent.* I can imagine what my mother would say if I walked into her kitchen without it." Mary Aaron considered for a moment and then looked sharply at her. "So, if it was there, you saw it in the snow, and then it was suddenly gone, who took it? Another of our people?" She nodded. "It would have to be. An Englisher with an Amish hat in his hands would be noticed."

"But not an Amish man," Rachel finished. "But Evan can't see how important it is."

Mary Aaron compressed her lips thoughtfully. "Maybe you should just remind him again and then stop asking questions. Let him do his job."

"I don't think I can. I'm on his list of suspects. He says he doesn't think for a minute that I'm guilty of killing Billingsly, but what if he's just saying that?"

"Why would he think you could do such an evil thing? Amish don't kill."

"A lot of people would say I'm not Amish anymore."

Her cousin tapped her heart. "In here, where it counts, you are. But you could not do murder, not even to save your own life from evil. It's not in you." She shrugged. "Me? I'm not so sure. Not to save my life, but . . ." She smiled mischievously. "Maybe to save yours. If we were in the backyard and a wild tiger came and was about to leap on you and make you his supper, then I—"

"There won't be any loose tigers in my backyard," Rachel said. "So I'm safe from tigercide." She turned the key, and switched on the heater. "Brrrr. Cold as a graveyard in here."

"In winter maybe. In spring a cemetery can be quite nice. Peaceful."

"Maybe it's what I need to do, find a peaceful graveyard where I can sit and think." Rachel looked away, staring out at the snow-covered yard. "Nothing between Evan and me can be easy now. I gave him his engagement ring back."

"You decided not to marry him?"

"We quarreled last night. At the ice rink, after I gave out the prizes." She wasn't ready to tell Mary Aaron everything, so she kept her explanation short. "I think maybe it was a mistake to ever agree to be his wife. We're so different. There are things about me that he'll never be able to understand."

"So you had an argument. This will blow over. I'm sure you both overreacted, said things you didn't mean."

"Maybe. But I made another mistake—that night. I was still angry with Billingsly over what he'd done to Annie and Joab. I went to his house."

"In the snowstorm?"

"Afraid so." Rachel grimaced. "But I never saw him. All the lights were on. There was a fire burning in the fireplace. I stood on his front porch, ready to knock and have it out with him, but I lost my nerve and went back home."

"And Evan knows you were there?" Mary Aaron asked.

"I told him. And that's what put me on his list of possible suspects." Rachel took a scarf from her coat pocket and tied it around her head. "So I've been asking around." In as few words as possible, she filled her cousin in on Blade's report of seeing the top-hack at Wagler's late Saturday evening. "I doubt if Evan will pay any more attention to that," she admitted. "So, I was hoping you could help me. How many top-hacks do you know of in the valley? No more than six, I think."

"*Ne*, not that many." Mary Aaron began silently counting on her fingers. "Five, no four. There were five, but Little John Miller's son took his to New York State when he moved to that big farm near the Canada border. Why he would go there, I don't know. A lot more snow than here. It would take a lot of hay to feed your livestock through those winters."

"Four top-hacks. That's less than I thought. And one I know belongs to Bishop Abner. So, I was hoping that you'd come with me today and we could go to each place and find out where they were Saturday night. I know one of them is Reuben Fisher's and I hoped you might know who the others belong to. We'd go around, talk to the owners, and try to find out who might have had their hack out late Saturday night. If we find out something substantial, then I can take it to Evan and he can handle it from there. So, are you willing to help me out, or not?"

Mary Aaron leaned back in the seat and sighed. "I suppose I'll come along, if only to keep you out of trouble. Honestly, Rae-Rae, I think you should have become a detective instead of running a guesthouse."

"I hear you." Rachel smiled, glad to have her cousin's support and common sense.

"You going to go by Bishop Abner's house first and ask him if he was at the tavern that night? Or maybe you should ask him if he murdered Billingsly?" Mary Aaron asked.

Rachel ignored the teasing. Mary Aaron was with her, and that was what was important. "What I'd really like is to get into Billingsly's house. Just to look around. See if there's anything the police missed."

"You mean anything that Evan missed?" Mary Aaron thrust her gloved hands into her coat pockets. "Aren't you always telling me what a great detective he'll make?"

"He is. He will. It's just that he's a man. You know how they are. Sometimes they can't see what's directly in front of them. Women have a different perspective. We don't miss much."

"So, if you want to go to the house, why not go now?" her cousin asked. "The yellow tape is gone, so the police must be finished there."

"I'd love to, but we just can't break into the house. That would be committing a crime."

"What crime? This is Elvie's day to clean his house. She'll be there. She won't care if we come in and look around."

"Do you think we could?"

Mary Aaron chuckled. "Only one way to find out."

Rachel drove out of her driveway and turned the Jeep toward Billingsly's Victorian.

# Chapter 10

Elvie opened the back door of Billingsly's house and smiled. "Mary Aaron, Rachel, nice to see you," she said in Deitsch as she stepped back to let them into the kitchen.

Petite Elvie was a childless widow in her midthirties who cleaned for some of the English families in town, as well as The George. She was wire-thin and bursting with energy behind a face framed with wispy dark hair and dominated by round, black-rimmed glasses that gave her an owlish appearance. "I was just taking these sheets down to the basement. Bill has a washer and dryer down there. He never wants me to hang the laundry out, not even in good weather." She shook her head. "Dryer sheets that are supposed to smell like roses. I can't understand why he wouldn't want the clean scent of sunshine and fresh air on his sheets, can you?"

Rachel glanced around the kitchen. Everything seemed in order. The counters were clean, the floor recently swept and no dirty dishes in the deep soapstone sink. Even the stainless steel cat dishes, filled with water and dry food, were shiny clean. The only thing that seemed out of place was a cast-iron frying pan sitting on the back burner of the stove. In the pan lay a thick, raw T-bone steak. No, it wasn't raw. There was no flame on under the pan, but there was a congealed grease puddle around the edges of the meat. Someone had cooked one side but not flipped it yet.

"Did we interrupt your lunch?" Rachel asked in Deitsch. Elvie had grown up in a much more isolated Amish community in Kentucky, and her English was sketchy at best.

"*Ne,*" Elvie said. "I never eat when I'm cleaning. I'll have my meal at home when I finish. That meat was on the stove when I came in. Bill must have been cooking it before . . . what happened. I always do the kitchen last. I start upstairs. Strip the bed and gather up the towels and any clothing in the hamper and start the washer. While the laundry is going, I clean the bedroom and the downstairs. Always the same. Bathrooms next, and finally kitchen. Bill doesn't use the dining room. Not much to do there but dust and vacuum. And he doesn't want me in his study. 'Never go in my study,' he says." Her face crumpled. "At least that's what he said. Poor Bill. Dead as last year's tomato plants."

Mary Aaron looked around and took a step closer to Elvie. "You didn't mind coming here after . . ." She grimaced. "After what happened?"

Elvie blinked behind her thick lenses. "It's Tuesday. I always clean on Tuesdays. First I go to the MacDonald house down the road, and then here. Bill leaves cash in an envelope with my name on it. On the mantel in the dining room. It's a big house, so I charge more. And the police made a mess. They tracked snow with their boots everywhere. I talked to that nice policeman of yours. He asked me about Bill. Asked me where I was Saturday night. He said I could clean."

"You're not afraid to be alone in the house after someone murdered him here?" Rachel asked.

Elvie blinked. Some thought her a little odd, but she had a sweet disposition and was a hard worker. "Bill wasn't killed in the house," she corrected. "It was outside on the porch. And the dead don't hurt you. Only the living." She rested her hands on her hips. "I really should get back to my cleaning. I can't take Bill's money if I don't do a good job." She sighed. "He leaves my money on the mantel. Four envelopes. One for each week. I don't know what will happen after the month is up. I suppose I'll have to look for another customer."

"Did the police know you were coming in?" Rachel asked. "To clean today?"

"*Ya.* I said. That nice friend of yours. He took down the yellow tape. He told me they were finished here."

"Do you mind if we stay a while?" Rachel asked. "Look around? We won't get in your way. I just wanted to do a little more checking . . . to see if there was anything that the English police missed."

Elvie nodded. "You help with finding the bad men. George told me. He is a nice man, too. Pays good for me to clean the bookstore. He told me that you brought one of our runaway girls home to her family. It's a good thing you're doing. But I don't think you will find anything here. Of course, I didn't go in Bill's study. He said not to, and I do as my customers ask. But other than the floors the Englisher policemen tracked up, it all looked the same to me." She hesitated. "Just one thing I did notice . . ."

"What's that?" Mary Aaron asked. Rachel saw that her cousin was studying the kitchen as well. She was glad that Mary Aaron had agreed to help. Often she would pick up on something out of place that Rachel missed.

Elvie motioned for them to follow her through the hall into the dining room and then into the living room, the same living room where Rachel had seen the fire burning in the fireplace Saturday night. Elvie led them to a maroon upholstered couch with ugly curved legs, and pointed. "Somebody left out Bill's nightclothes." She pursed her lips. "That's not right. Nightclothes belong to be put away, not left where anyone can see them. Bill keeps that on the back of the upstairs bathroom door."

Rachel inspected a red-plaid flannel bathrobe, folded precisely and left on a purple fringed pillow. Had the detectives done that? Or had Billingsly? Or was it his killer? Why hadn't Evan taken it for evidence? Elvie was right. The robe didn't belong in the living room, especially when Billingsly had ended up unclothed on his front porch.

Rachel glanced around. The high-ceilinged room was crowded with stiff Victorian furniture. It didn't have a single personal photograph or any other homey item. There were no books, no newspapers, no magazines, no coffee cup. Other than the cold fireplace littered with ashes, this might have been a room in a museum. Hardly somewhere you would expect a man to leave his bathrobe.

"It would make me nervous being here all alone," Mary Aaron said, glancing around uneasily. "How do you know the killer wasn't searching for something? That he won't come back?"

Elvie shrugged. "Not likely. If I was an evil man who could kill somebody by tying them outside to freeze to death, why would I come back? With all the police wandering about? I'll pray for Bill's soul, although I don't know how much good it will do. He was nice enough to me, but other people?" She shook her head. "He wasn't so nice. Those things he wrote in his newspaper." She shook her head again.

Mary Aaron wandered out of the room.

Elvie sighed. "I am not heartless. I hope you don't think it is wrong of me coming here, cleaning, but no one told me I shouldn't."

"I know you aren't a heartless person," Rachel said, looking around. Her gaze fell to the front door, and she remembered Evan saying it had been locked when the police arrived. All of the doors had been locked. "You must have a key to this house . . . so that you can get in to clean. Or did he leave the door unlocked for you?"

"*Ne.*" Elvie reached into her apron pocket and produced a key. "I have one. All of my clients give me keys to their houses."

"Do you know who else has one?"

"Bill had a key. It is his house."

Rachel fought hard to keep from smiling at that. Some

people said Elvie was slow. Rachel didn't think so; she just thought the woman was a little odd. "Anyone else, I mean?"

Elvie spread her hands, small fingers extended. "How would I know? We didn't talk. He was almost never here when I came to clean. I just clean for him. We're not friendly."

"Right," Rachel agreed. "Of course."

Elvie shifted her feet. The material in her cheap navy-blue sneakers was worn almost through, but spotlessly clean. "I should get those sheets into the washer machine. See you in church, Mary Aaron," she called. "And you, too, Rachel. It would please the bishop if you would come back to us."

Rachel offered a perfunctory smile. She wasn't going to get into this conversation right now. But as Elvie walked away, Rachel called to her, "I don't see the cat. Have you seen him? A big gray tabby."

Elvie stopped, turned back to her. "*Ne*, not today. Usually it is underfoot. I don't mind. Cats are useful. No vermin in a house with a good mouser." She lifted one slight shoulder beneath her plain blue dress. "But this is a big house. Lots of rooms. The cat could be anywhere. I'll keep my eye out. No one to take him. I'll take him home with me. I like cats." Without another word she turned on her heel and left.

Mary Aaron walked back into the living room.

"See anything unusual?" Rachel asked. When Mary Aaron shook her head, Rachel nodded. "When I was here Saturday night, there was a fire burning in here. Lights were on, inside and on the front porch. But when we arrived Sunday morning, there were no lights on anywhere."

"Odd," Mary Aaron remarked.

"Definitely," Rachel agreed. She frowned. "You didn't see a cat, did you? Billingsly had a gray cat."

"*Ne*. But it could have gotten outside when the police were here." Mary Aaron crossed to a marble-topped lamp table and picked up a bronze statue of a nymph rising from a pool of water. It was about fourteen inches high with a square stepped base. "Heavy," she said. "And she could have more clothes on." The female subject was swathed in bronze drapery that, while billowy, managed to reveal more of her naked body than it concealed. "Did they figure out what he was hit with? I think you could break a man's skull with this." She passed the sculpture to Rachel, who inspected it closely.

"They didn't. This isn't the right shape." She set it down. "George said he was hit with something narrow, thin. Like a stick, only not a stick. And the detectives would have checked that for evidence." Blood or hair, she was thinking, but it was best not to remind Mary Aaron of the gruesome details. "I guess it doesn't really matter. Technically, it wasn't the murder weapon. He died of exposure, not the blow to his head."

Mary Aaron's left brow lifted in a questioning expression. "Evan told you?"

"George."

"How did George know?"

"Someone from the medical examiner's office was talking, I guess." Rachel's gaze fell on the fireplace, with its iron grate and marble surround. A set of cast-iron fire tools stood to one side of the hearth. She walked over and picked up the long-handled shovel and tapped it on her palm. The shovel end wasn't the shape George had described, and neither was the ornate handle, but the middle of it certainly was. She lifted it in the air, imagining someone standing in front of her. It would make a good weapon. She lowered it, looking at it again. There was no blood on it. The police certainly would have noticed had there been evidence on it. Mulling that over in her head, she replaced it in the stand. It swung ever so slightly, hitting the brush next to it. Her eyes widened. "Look," she said. "The poker is missing."

Reuben Fisher pointed to a top-hack minus a front wheel sitting on blocks in an open shed. "Not going far in that buggy. See. Been meaning to get that repaired, but I've got some cracked floorboards in the bed and with the bad weather this winter, I just haven't had time to get to it."

Rachel had gotten out of the Jeep to inspect the damage. From the cobwebs adhering to the cement blocks and the bottom of the buggy, she guessed it had been out of commission for weeks, if not months. She looked up at him. "Well, I thank you for your time."

"That was a long ride for nothing," Mary Aaron remarked as they drove down the long, stony lane.

"It wasn't for nothing," Rachel said. "That's one eliminated. Who's next?"

"Joe Paul Kurtz. He raises pigs and brings them to the sale regularly. Nice people. I think they have eight or nine children."

"They live near Mose Bender's place, don't they?"

"Across the road and down one farm. There's a sign at the end of the driveway for eggs for sale. It's maybe seven miles from here. Turn left at the next crossroads."

When they reached the Kurtz farm, there was no one home and no sign of a top-hack in the yard or carriage shed. "I guess we can't cross this one off our list," Mary Aaron asked as they drove away.

"No, we can't," Rachel answered. "Joe Paul could have driven it someplace. We'll have to try back later this afternoon." She frowned. "I'm beginning to think this is a wasted trip."

"At least at Billingsly's, you got a lead, the possible murder weapon."

"The absence of something isn't necessarily a lead, but I guess it's something," Rachel agreed. "Detective work is more careful elimination than startling revelations like you see on TV murder mysteries."

Her cousin giggled, and Rachel grimaced and joined in on her amusement. "I guess you don't watch much TV. All right, I'll admit it. I can be a dunce sometimes."

"You're forgiven. I'd still rather be riding around with you than be home. There, I'd just be scrubbing floors or sewing patches on my brothers' trousers. I hate mending boys' clothes. It's the same thing over and over, and then they just tear their pants on something else the next day. Last week, Jesse and some of his buddies were jumping off a windmill into a snowbank. He caught the seat of his trousers on a nail and ripped a hole you could have driven a hay wagon through."

"Get used to it. Once you and Timothy are married, you'll probably have a dozen boys to sew for," Rachel teased. She slowed the Jeep at a spot where melting snow had flooded a section of the road.

"*If* we get married. I don't know, maybe I'll decide to be an old maid. Wait until I'm forty and then marry an old man with a big farm and grown sons and daughters to do most of the work."

Rachel laughed. "Where to next, Sherlock?"

"Ira Esh's place. I know his top-hack is in good shape because he was at Russell's Emporium on Monday afternoon. I saw him and his brother. They had been to the feed and grain because they had bags of feed in the back of the hack."

Twenty minutes later, the two climbed out of the Jeep at a dairy farm at the far end of the valley. Rachel didn't know Ira's family, but Mary Aaron was acquainted with Ira's oldest daughter, Agnes. A middle-aged woman, two teenage girls, and a boy of about ten came out of the house to stare at the red vehicle. Mary Aaron went to the house and spoke with the woman, then returned to Rachel. "She says her husband's mending the pound fence." The sound of hammering coming from beyond the barn confirmed Mary Aaron's statement.

Rachel and Mary Aaron made their way around the corral, better known in the valley as a pound, past a dozen curious Holstein milk cows and several heifers. The woman, the boy, and one of the girls trailed after them. A red-bearded man paused in setting a nail in a board and nodded a greeting. Again, Mary Aaron, who knew the family better, offered the first general greeting and an explanation of why they had come.

"I know your father well," Ira said to Mary Aaron. "Fair man. He sold me a driving horse not long ago. You tell him that I sold him on to a man from Lancaster and made a good profit. Any more stock he has to sell, tell him to come to me first."

"*Ya,*" Mary Aaron replied. "I'm sure *Dat* will be pleased to hear that."

*Not,* Rachel thought. Uncle Aaron never liked to be bested in horse trading. He was a good man, but a shrewd one and a man who watched his pennies.

"Heard you came up with the idea for the Winter Frolic," Ira said to Rachel. "My brother sold some of his rocking chairs there this week. The family appreciates it."

Rachel smiled at him. Ira made no mention of her unorthodox Plain attire or her abandonment of her church community to go over to the English world. Mary Aaron had already offered up all the small talk and explanations, so she asked about his top-hack and if he'd driven it to Stone Mill over the weekend.

"Not likely," Ira said. "Laid up with the croup."

"He's still got a cough," the woman offered, coming to stand beside Mary Aaron. "I told him he shouldn't be out here in the wind, but he's a man and he's got his own mind."

"Don't you have a nearly grown son?" Mary Aaron asked. "Lemuel?"

"Could Lemuel have taken the buggy into town Saturday night?" Rachel added.

"He's running-around age, isn't he?" Mary Aaron continued. "No chance he could have taken it in?"

Ira snorted and let out a laugh so loud and deep that he began coughing. "Lem? I don't think so. Not unless he has wings. Lem's in Ohio with his *Grossdaddi* Zook. Miriam's father's putting up a new barn this week and he needed Lem's help. *Ne,* this top-hack set right there in the barn until Monday, when I went for feed."

"Thank you," Rachel said. "I appreciate your help. There's

just one more question I have, and then I'll leave you good folks in peace to get on with your chores." She smiled at the mother. "Mary Aaron said you have another son."

"David. Fifteen. But I don't let him take the buggies out by himself. He near lamed one of our driving horses last fall in the buggy," Ira explained.

"None of your men are missing a hat, are they?" Mary Aaron asked. "A black go-to-church hat?"

Now it was the mother who answered firmly. "Indeed not. Any man here, young or old, who came home without his hat would be in big trouble with me."

"Now what?" Mary Aaron asked as they left the Esh farm. "The only one left that I know is Bishop Abner, and I hardly think that he's your killer."

Rachel concentrated on the road ahead of her. They had seen little traffic all afternoon: a dozen or so cars, a few pickup trucks, a few buggies, and an Amish youth leading a cow. The tourists who'd come to spend time in quaint Stone Mill were obviously not driving these backcountry roads, which was just as well because they were narrow and icy. Some had never been plowed. That didn't prevent the Amish from getting around. The design of the buggy, with its high wheels, meant that snow or high water rarely stopped it.

"We are going to Abner and Naamah's, aren't we?" Mary Aaron asked. "You're going to question Bishop Abner just like the others. Why? When you know he can't be guilty?"

"It's just standard practice for an investigation. I don't get to decide what's important and what's not. And just as Evan has to consider me a possible suspect, I can't rule out Bishop Abner's buggy just because I like him. What if it was stolen?"

Mary Aaron scoffed. "If his buggy had been stolen, the news would be all over the valley by now. You know how the Amish telegraph works. Once one person knows something, the story just takes on a life of its own and spreads like hot butter on a biscuit."

"The whole notion of the top-hack being a clue in the case might be erroneous. Blade could have been mistaken. He could have misremembered or he could have lied," Rachel told her cousin. "People don't always tell the truth. And they make errors in judgment. Humans make mistakes. But we started this and we have to finish. We need to talk to Bishop Abner, we need to go back to the Kurtzes', and we need to find out if there are any other working buggies like that in the valley. Once we've eliminated everyone, then we know that the buggy is a false lead and we can go on to something else."

A huge orange tour bus came around a curve ahead of them, and Rachel squeezed over to let it pass. "Besides, Bishop Abner's isn't far from your place. We'll stop in there, ask a few quick questions, and get you home in time to help make supper. Aunt Hannah will be happy and you'll stop finding fault with my investigation."

"I'm not finding fault. I'm helping. You would have forgotten to ask the Esh family about the hat if it wasn't for me," Mary Aaron reminded her.

"No, I wouldn't have."

"Would, too."

"Probably," Rachel agreed with a chuckle. "What would I do without you?"

"Probably get into more trouble than you do now. I still can't believe you went out at night in that storm and walked to a man's house. What would your mother think if she knew?"

"I don't want to imagine," Rachel admitted. "It wouldn't be pretty."

Less than twenty minutes later, they were sitting in Naamah's kitchen, drinking freshly made coffee and eating lemon pound cake with Naamah, Bishop Abner, and Naamah's nephew Sammy.

"What a nice surprise to have you stop by," Naamah said. "We like to have a little bite in late afternoon. The bishop doesn't like to eat his supper until after evening chores, and we all need something to tide us over. And our treat tastes twice as good when we have friends to share it."

Bishop Abner finished his cup of coffee and held out his mug for a refill. Mary Aaron got up, took his cup, and carried it to the gas range. Using a dishcloth to protect her hand from the hot coffeepot, she filled the cup to the brim.

"Two. That's your limit," Naamah warned her husband cheerfully. "Too much caffeine and he won't sleep a wink tonight."

"I haven't had that many today," he said with a wink at Rachel. "Hardly enough to wet my whistle."

"He had twenty cups," Sammy declared as he finished his second slice of cake. "I had a hundred."

Bishop Abner chuckled. "Six, maybe, but hardly twenty," he said. Smiling at his wife, he said, "Naamah makes the best lemon cake in the valley. Uses real lemons. She had me grating the rind for an hour."

"Don't believe a word of it," Naamah protested. "That's Sammy's job. He's my cake helper. He helps and then he gets to lick the bowl when the cake goes into the oven."

"I made the cake," Sammy said. "I put ninety-nine eggs and five hundred lemons in it."

"Don't forget the sugar," the bishop teased.

"And five pounds of sugar," Sammy said. "And a zillion Little Debbies. I like Little Debbies. Chocolate ones."

"Hush now," Naamah chided. "Let the grown-ups talk, Sammy. And stop making up stories. You know there are no chocolate Little Debbies in this lemon cake." She gave the bishop an amused glance. "And don't you egg him on. He's bad enough as it is."

"You were saying, about the buggy," Mary Aaron said.

"*Ya*, about my top-hack." Bishop Abner took another bite of the rich yellow cake. "Once we got home from the Winter Frolic, we were in all night, weren't we, wife? All that snow and the wind. You couldn't have tempted me out on a night like that."

Rachel nodded. It would have been more sensible if she'd done the same. She ate her cake slowly, savoring every bite. Somehow, she'd forgotten to eat lunch today and now she was starving. This cake was scrumptious. It would rival Ada's best.

"I took the buggy," Sammy proclaimed. "I drove it to the store in the snow and I bought a hundred Little Debbies. I put them in the cake. I did." He pushed his empty plate toward his aunt. "Can I have another piece?"

Naamah frowned. "You cannot have more cake. And you just hush. What did I tell you about making up such tales?" She flushed and let out a long sigh. "Sometimes I'm at my wit's end with this boy."

Rachel smiled in understanding and turned to the bishop. "This is going to sound like an odd question, but do you know of any Amish man who's misplaced his hat? One of your parishoners, maybe? A black one."

"I don't." Abner shook his head. "Not something that happens often. You hear of anyone losing a hat, Naamah?"

"Certainly not," Naamah declared. "Why do you ask?"

Rachel gave a wave. "It's probably nothing."

"I lost my hat!" Sammy declared loudly. "I lost twenty-seven hats. I lost twenty-seven hundred hats."

Naamah glanced at her nephew and frowned. "Put your coat and your hat on and go feed your cat; I told you he won't stay around the barn if you don't feed him there. Then go gather the eggs. And be careful. Don't drop any."

"But I got the eggs already. A thousand eggs."

"Abner." She gave her husband the *look*.

"Go on, boy," he said quietly. "Do as your aunt says. See if there are any more eggs in the henhouse." He watched as Sammy rose from the table. "That's a good boy."

Naamah refilled Mary Aaron's cup. No one spoke until Sammy put on his coat and left the kitchen.

"You'll have to forgive him for his wild talk." Naamah handed Mary Aaron her second cup of coffee. "Those crazy stories of his. His mother just couldn't deal with them. He starts in and gets worse and worse until you have to get firm with him. It's why she sent him to us. He's a sweet boy. One of the Lord's children, but he can be a trial. Sometimes I wonder if I will be able to do any better than my poor sister."

"You will," Bishop Abner assured her. "You've already done wonders with him. Love and patience. That's what it takes with young things. As the Bible tells us, 'Bend a tree in the way it will go.' I don't have the slightest doubt. You'll be the making of Sammy."

# Chapter 11

An hour later, they were at the Hostetler farm. "See you to-morrow," Mary Aaron called as she waved from her mother's back step.

Rachel backed the Jeep up carefully, not wanting to get stuck in the snow. She rolled her window down and called after Mary Aaron. "Thanks. Give your mother my love."

Jesse appeared at the corner of the house and heaved a snowball in Rachel's direction. She laughed as it splattered on the windshield. As usual, Uncle Aaron's farmyard was a hodgepodge of disordered activity. An assortment of dogs barked; a long-eared donkey, head hanging over a gate, brayed; and a gaggle of white Emden geese hissed and flapped their wings at the shrieking, running children. The children were so heavily bundled against the cold that Rachel couldn't tell if they were boys or girls. A goat had scaled the peak of a stack of straw bales, and its bleating intermingled with the rusty creak of the windmill blades.

Rachel braked hard to avoid a lean tomcat that strolled leisurely out of the barn, green eyes gleaming, the limp body of a rat dangling from its mouth. This cat was tawny yellow with one ragged ear and a stump of a tail, but it brought Billingsly's missing cat to mind. She hated to think of the animal alone and hungry in the rambling house or shut outside in the cold. If the cat was inside, she would have to make certain someone took charge of it.

Many people in the English world lived such solitary lives that when they died their pets were often left to fend for themselves or ended up in the back of an animal control officer's truck. Not so with the Amish. There were always family, friends, and neighbors to care for the old or infirm, to pick up the shattered threads of life after a tragedy, and to take in the livestock and four-legged creatures left behind.

Many outsiders looking at the aging Hostetler farmhouse, with its patched roof, sagging doors, and mismatched windows, might mistake frugality for poverty and miss the strength of love and faith that held this family together in good times and bad. No stray cat tossed from a passing car window or footsore dog was ever turned away, and each of the round dozen babies born to her aunt and uncle had been welcomed as if he or she were the first and only child. Her uncle might be stern, but he was fair, always ready to lend his back to lift a neighbor's burden or carry firewood or food to someone without, Amish or English.

"Rachel!" John Hannah shouted.

She rolled down her Jeep window as her cousin came out of the wood shop carrying a three-legged stool.

He grinned at her. "It's finished. What do you think?"

Rachel nodded admiringly. The milking stool was carved from the limbs of a fallen black cherry tree that John Hannah and his brother Alan had cut up near the river two years back. The lumber had been drying and seasoning on racks in the shop since. John Hannah had carved, sanded, and oiled the irregular seat and gnarled legs, fitting the joints together and fastening them with glue. The finished stool was one of a kind, as much an object of art as it was utilitarian, fit for either a child's seat or an extra chair for a dinner table. John Hannah was saving for his own driving horse and buggy, and he hoped to begin selling small items of furniture in her gift shop in the B&B.

"Do you think it's good enough?" he asked. "Will the English like it?" He was a nice-looking boy, almost a carbon copy of Mary Aaron. Both had their mother's sweet smile.

She nodded, thinking, *If someone doesn't snap it up quick, I'll buy it myself.* The stool was beautiful, the swirls of grain and the glowing hue of the rich cherry so amazing that she longed to run her fingers over the smooth surface. "I'll sell it," she promised. "And for three times the amount we talked about. It's a piece to be proud of, cousin."

He grinned. "Don't let *Dat* hear you say that. He couldn't find fault with it, other than that the seat wasn't round, but he doesn't think any Englisher will want it. He says it's an old-time milking stool, and any English farmer that still has cows uses electric milkers. They don't milk by hand."

"I can guarantee that this stool will never go near a barn again," Rachel said with a chuckle. "Put it in the back of the Jeep." She got out and walked around the vehicle. "I was wondering. Do you happen to know the Esh boys, Lem and David? Lemuel's a little older than you. David's fifteen, I think."

"*Ya.* I know them. Lem played softball with us last summer. He's not much at pitching, but he can hit good." Carefully, he placed the stool in the cargo area and shut the back of the Jeep. "What about them?"

"Are either of them run-arounds? You know, do they hang with the fast boys? Get into any trouble?"

"Like what?"

"John Hannah!" Uncle Aaron's voice boomed from the interior of the wood shop. "I need you to hold this board."

"Coming, *Dat*." He shared a conspiratorial smile with her. "Why you asking about Lem and David? Are you playing detective again?"

"You're too smart for your own good, John Hannah," she retorted. "I was just wondering. You don't know if either of them drink alcohol, do you? I'm just asking some questions, clearing up a few inconsistencies. I know their father owns a top-hack, and one was parked Saturday night in Wagler's parking lot after hours. I wondered if maybe one of the boys had used it to sneak into the Black Horse."

"Lem Esh? Whoever told you that Lem could be in a tavern is pulling your leg. He's a goody-goody. Clean as a whistle. You'd be more likely to find me there. Not that I would. That's not a practice I want to start. And don't tell my father I made a joke about it. But no *rumspringa* for Lem. He's baptized. He'll be a deacon or a preacher one of these days. Besides, he's in Ohio. His girlfriend, Bertha, told me that at the ice rink last night."

"And what about Lem's brother David?"

"John Hannah! Are you coming?" her uncle called.

"Got to run," her cousin said. "But it couldn't be David. He's a little runt, looks closer to twelve than fifteen. No one would let him in the Black Horse."

Rachel laid a hand on his arm. "Who else do you know who has a top-hack in the valley? I checked out Reuben Fisher. Nobody was home at Joe Paul Kurtz's. And then I talked to Ira Esh."

"I think Israel Yeoder used to own one, but he sold it last fall to a man who was moving to Virginia. I don't know of anybody else," John Hannah said. "They're handy. I'd love to have one, but first I've got to get up money for a courting buggy."

"Planning on courting anybody soon?" she asked. John Hannah was only twenty, far too young to get serious with any young woman as far as Rachel was concerned.

"Not me. I just want something to drive the girls home from singing and frolics." He started to walk away. "Of course, you know Bishop Abner has one. But I don't think he's who you're looking for."

Rachel chuckled. "No. Besides, he was at home with his wife."

He turned back to her. "Not Saturday night."

"*Ya*, Saturday. After the festival, he and Naamah went home and stayed there all night."

He shook his head slowly. "You must have gotten something mixed up, Rae-Rae. I was out pretty late myself. Over at the Peacheys'. Martha and her brother had a singing. Saw no reason to cancel it for the snow as long as we were all walking. I saw Bishop Abner on the road."

"Where?"

"I couldn't say for sure. But it was him. I know his horse. It was snowing and you could hardly see the mare for the snow coming down."

Rachel was still thinking about what John Hannah had said about seeing Abner as she pulled out onto the blacktop. She had every intention of going home, but she knew that the inconsistency would nag at her. Better to stop by Abner's, speak to him again, and get it straightened out.

She found the bishop coming out of his barn with a bucket of milk. He looked up in surprise as she pulled up beside him and then smiled. "Rachel. Back so soon?"

"I'm sorry to bother you again. I know that it must be time for your supper, but I think I must have misunderstood something you said."

He rested the bucket in the soft snow. "And what is that, child?"

"I thought that you'd told me that you came home from the Winter Frolic and then stayed in all night. But I heard that someone in the community passed you later on the road."

Bishop Abner looked up at the sky and stroked his beard. "Warming wind coming. Do you smell it? This snow will be melting soon."

The back door of the house opened, and Sammy stepped out onto the stoop. "Aunt Naamah says soup's on."

"I won't keep you," Rachel said. "Maybe the people who thought they saw your buggy were wrong."

He moved closer to the Jeep and placed an ungloved hand on the window frame. "*Ne,* they weren't mistaken. I misled you. I was out after I brought Sammy and Naamah home. But I can't tell you where or why."

She couldn't see his eyes under the wide brim of his hat, but she could feel guilt congeal in the pit of her stomach. What right did she have to question the word of an elder of the church? There had to be a reason for his deception.

"You counseling someone?" she asked. Counseling was private. No bishop worth his salt would ever share private information with another. It would be a breach of the faith. No one would trust a bishop with their secrets or deep concerns if he gossiped about his members' spiritual or personal matters.

Bishop Abner's wrinkled fingers tightened on the window frame. He smiled and spoke gently. "You are a good girl, and what you have done for Stone Mill and the valley can't easily be counted. But this nosing around the community asking questions could cause harm you don't wish. It could alienate people who can't understand why you left your faith and family."

"I'm only trying to help," she said.

He nodded again. "I believe that your motives—like mine when I led you to believe that I was home that night—are for the best. But I was wrong to have told an untruth, and you are wrong now. Let your Evan Parks do his job. He is a wise man. I can't think that he would approve of your snooping. The death of the newspaper editor was a terrible crime, but you won't find his killer among the Plain folk. And seeking him here may muddy the water to find the real evil one."

"But—" she began.

He cut her off firmly. "Hear me, Rachel. You have always been different. Always pushing against the rules of community and our society. But you cannot change that you have been born to a woman's place. Not better than a man or less.

But a woman's place and not the place of a man. Push too hard and the line will break. You may lose more than you imagine."

Startled to hear him speak so, Rachel opened her mouth to reply but instantly bit back her retort.

"I'm sorry if my words cause you distress," the bishop said. "But someone had to tell you. You are too impulsive, child, and I don't want to see you hurt." He stepped back and picked up his milk bucket. A little milk splashed over the rim and ran down into the muddy snow. Through the open window, Rachel caught the familiar smell of warm raw milk, earthy and sweet. "Come again whenever you like," Bishop Abner said cheerfully. "You're always welcome at our table and at our worship service."

Still confused and smarting from Bishop Abner's admonition, Rachel had every intention of returning to the house and catching up on her office work. But as she pulled into her driveway, she noticed that the only light on next door at the Schenfelds' was coming from Hulda's study. On impulse, she decided to pay her neighbor a visit. She parked her Jeep, entered the B&B's kitchen, turning on lights as she went, and walked through to the dining room, where fresh, home-baked cookies were available for her guests. Gathering a little plate of cookies and a carafe of steaming coffee, she went out the front doors and across to Hulda's and rang the bell.

Two minutes later, a smiling Hulda was leading her into her private sanctuary. "What a wonderful surprise," Hulda said. "They've all gone somewhere, thankfully. You know I cherish my family, but sometimes I find them all rather silly."

So far as Rachel knew, none of Hulda's sons or grandsons or extended family was ever admitted to the study, a grand chamber that Rachel thought exuded both the aura of a nineteenth-century Russian archduchess's suite and an upscale San Francisco bordello of the same time period.

Crimson velvet drapes, illuminated by a crystal chandelier, swathed the floor-to-ceiling windows. Gilt mirrors and oil portraits of long-dead Austrian noblewomen in revealing gowns, powdered wigs, and too much jewelry lined the walls. The antique furniture was dark and equally authentic, and the polished hardwood floors could hardly be seen for the thick Turkish carpets. Scattered around the room, crowding the surfaces of shelves, tables, a mahogany secretary, and a Hepplewhite sideboard, were dozens of black-and-white family portraits in silver frames. Lying open on a Lincoln-green chaise lounge was a MacBook Air laptop, a fantasy game paused in midplay. A tray with a half-eaten bowl of what appeared to be tomato soup and three crackers stood on a low, upholstered stool.

"Come in, come in. Find a seat," Hulda said. "Just move those books onto the floor. They'll end up there anyhow."

"I'm sorry to interrupt your supper," Rachel said, making room for herself on the couch. "I thought maybe you'd like coffee and—"

"Something fattening that Ada baked, I hope," Hulda interrupted. "Excellent. And you're not interrupting anything. That soup is that low-salt stuff that the doctor recommended for my grandson. They put a picture of vine-ripe tomatoes on the can and pass it off as healthy. Nonsense, if you ask me. No salt, no flavor. I wouldn't serve it to a goat."

Hulda didn't elaborate on which grandson. As far as Rachel was concerned, there wasn't much difference between them. None of Hulda's offspring showed much intelligence or inclination to work in the family business. They seemed more interested in speculating on when Hulda would die and leave them her fortune.

"You are a lifesaver. Literally. Another move and I would have plunged into the *pit of despair*. Three weeks to reach level nine, and I fall prey to a shape-shifting troll and waste my last magic acorn on a dragon key that led to a blank wall." She chuckled, clicked a few keys on her Mac, and closed the laptop. "Now, my dear. What can I do for you?"

Rachel accepted a linen napkin and spread it on her lap. She poured a cup of coffee for Hulda, slipped off her shoes, and curled her feet up under her. As it had been the last time she'd been in Hulda's study, the air was heavy with incense and her hostess's perfume, an exotic floral. "I've been trying to clear up a few questions regarding some inconsistencies that occurred the night Billingsly died," she said.

Hulda used silver tongs to drop a single lump of sugar into her coffee. "Delicious," she said after taking a sip. "Reminds me of the coffee we had on our honeymoon. A little guest-house near the harbor on Santorini. Have you ever been to Greece?"

Rachel shook her head. "Never. But from the pictures I've seen, it's beautiful."

"Words can't express it. You and your Evan should go there on your honeymoon." She nibbled a chocolate-chip-and-pecan cookie. "I could make a supper of these." She looked up at Rachel. "I gather your investigation isn't going well."

"You could say that. I think I was just dressed down by Bishop Abner. Apparently, I'm forgetting my place—as a woman. He thinks I should leave the questions to the police."

Hulda considered. She was dressed in a pale lavender-and-white ski sweater and gray yoga pants. On her small feet she wore a pair of gray Uggs. Her white hair was stylishly cut, her manicure and makeup perfect. She wore no jewelry other than a heavy gold wedding ring and tiny diamond chips in her ears. Rachel doubted she would ever appear so elegant when and if she reached her nineties.

"It's been my experience that men say that sort of thing when they feel threatened," Hulda offered. "But you didn't do so shabbily last time you played detective, so I wouldn't pay too much attention. Abner Chupp is a lovely little man, but he is only a man." Hulda leaned forward. "What is it that you're trying to track down?"

Rachel explained the report about the buggy at Wagler's Saturday night and the bishop's refusal to tell her his whereabouts that evening. "First he told me that he was home with Naamah all evening and then he changed his story. I know that an important part of his position as bishop is counseling his members, and I think that's where he was that night. Of course, he would never say where. But Bishop Abner does drive a top-hack, and Wagler's Grocery isn't that far from Billingsly's home."

Hulda looked at her, faded eyes shrewd. "So you believe it may have been the bishop's buggy in the parking lot?"

"Maybe. I'm not sure," Rachel admitted. She set her cup down, the coffee untasted. "This is going to sound pretty farfetched, but . . . I know that Billingsly had a reputation for being a womanizer. You don't suppose that he was involved with an Amish woman, do you?"

"With an Amish woman?" Hulda frowned. "I doubt it. I've never heard of one of your people in a romantic affair with an English man."

"No, neither have I." Remembering that she was still wearing her *almost* Plain attire, Rachel removed her scarf and folded it into a small, tight square. "But I got the bishop to admit he was out Saturday night. I think he must have been counseling someone, but couldn't say so."

"I see."

"If Billingsly had been having an affair with an Amish woman, Bishop Abner might have been counseling him. And he certainly wouldn't want anyone to know that was why he was there. Or that he was there at all." She hesitated. "I know it sounds far-fetched, but anything is possible, right?"

"You know I'm a fan of mystery novels," Hulda said. "And of true crime books. And from those, I gather that most murders are committed for either financial gain or passion. But Billingsly wasn't the type to be interested in a Plain woman, and if he had been, your bishop would have been praying with the woman, not her seducer. And if the bishop had gone to Billingsly's, he would have been armed with words, not a weapon." Her mouth firmed. "No one knows of anything valuable missing from Billingsly's home? Did the house appear as if it had been tossed?"

Rachel smiled at Hulda's choice of words. "No, not at all. That's another odd thing. Everything was in perfect order, as though he had just stepped out. There was a half-cooked steak still on the stove top. How does someone break into a house, commit murder, and leave everything tidy?"

"What does your detective think?"

"Evan's not talking, at least not to me." She looked down at her hands. "I was still angry with Billingsly after the argument we had at the festival, and I went to his house Saturday night to have it out with him." She grimaced. "I told Evan I'd been there. I never saw Billingsly because I thought better of it, but he wasn't on the porch when I was there."

"And you being there the night of the killing makes you a suspect?"

"Exactly." She wanted to tell Hulda that Billingsly had been flirting with blackmail, given who knows how many people a grudge against him, but sharing that was too close to telling Hulda that the editor was about to expose her criminal record. She couldn't bring herself to do that. "You've lived in Stone Mill most of your life," Rachel continued. "And you don't miss much. I thought that if Billingsly had become involved with someone in the Amish community—"

"I'd know about it." Hulda chuckled. "I must have quite the reputation as a busybody. No." She raised a small palm. "Don't apologize. I know that I've always been interested in my neighbors' activities. Wasn't it Jane Austen who wrote something about that very subject in her *Pride and Prejudice*? It's human nature. But to answer your question, I could give you the names of several of the town's respectable ladies who have sewn a few wild oats in that quarter, but not one of them was Amish. Now in the other direction, that's a different story. There've been more than a few Amish men who've wandered from the farmyard, if you get my meaning. It's not common, but it happens. And as you say, I've lived here a long time. Men are men, Amish, English, or what have you."

"I've never heard of it here in the valley," Rachel admitted.

"Then you've lived a sheltered life." Hulda finished her cookie and carefully gathered the crumbs in her napkin. "And you were away for years."

Rachel moved closer to her. "Now you have to tell me. Who?"

Hulda lifted her gaze. "Are you certain you want to know?"

"What if it will help me unravel what happened Saturday night?"

"I doubt that it will be of much help. It happened years ago, but . . ." Hulda said. "But since you ask." She took a breath. "You know that this is a second marriage for your Bishop Abner. His first wife passed away after a long illness, and he reportedly took it quite hard. It must have been a love match because most Amish widowers don't remain single long. Abner was the exception. It was a while before he married Naamah. Between his two marriages, he was intimately involved with a *married* woman here in town. An English woman."

Rachel's jaw dropped. *Bishop Abner?* Maybe she was naïve, but that was the last thing she'd expected. "I never heard anything about him . . . not that sort of thing."

"It would have been the worst sort of scandal if it had become general knowledge, costing Abner his position in the community and the woman her marriage. But like most irregular affairs of the heart, it blew over. He made his peace with his church, met and married Naamah, and the English woman divorced her husband. They'd been separated at the time, her here in Stone Mill, him working elsewhere."

"It's difficult for me to believe," Rachel said. "Is it possible it was just idle gossip?"

"I'm afraid not," Hulda insisted. "It was more than a rumor, Rachel. I know that it was true because I caught them in a most compromising situation. He ran like a scared rabbit, and she broke down and spilled the entire story."

"Can you tell me who it was?"

Hulda thought for a moment. "That would seem too much like gossip." She shook her head. "And with the child—"

# Chapter 12

Rachel stiffened. "What do you mean *with the child?*" She swallowed. "You're not saying—"

"I shouldn't be saying anything." Hulda placed her cup and napkin on a gilt-edged end table. "I'm a foolish old woman," she sputtered. "Forget I said anything about your bishop."

"Please," Rachel said. "This could be important. And he isn't my bishop. Although he is a friend." She uncurled her legs and placed her feet on the rug. "You aren't foolish."

"Then I'm at least a meddling gossip." Hulda sighed and made a dismissive gesture with one hand. "It was a long time ago. Abner was single. She was legally separated and in the process of getting a divorce. I suppose they didn't think they'd harm anyone." Hulda straightened herself and dropped her hands into her lap, threading her fingers together. "I promised that I'd keep the secret, and I've broken that promise. And who am I to pass judgment on anyone? They certainly didn't expect to bring a child into the world. And for what it's worth, I don't believe it was just lust. I honestly think they were in love. If they hadn't come from different worlds, she might have married Abner."

"But it was impossible."

"Exactly."

Rachel tried to get her thoughts around Bishop Abner and an English woman. No matter how difficult it was to process,

Rachel believed every word Hulda said. She might know everything that went on in Stone Mill, but she was no idle gossip. And what she did confide was genuine. "Who was the woman?"

Hulda shook her head. "I've said too much already."

"Was the child a boy or girl?"

"With a few math skills and a little detective work, you should be able to figure that one out yourself," Hulda said. "But please don't try to question the mother. She and Abner seem to have put the past behind them. We're all human, Rachel. And humans tend to make mistakes." Hulda's mouth twisted into a wry smile. "And the older you get, the more mistakes you add to your collection. This is mine for the month and maybe for the year." She looked pensive. "I always did speak too quickly."

"How did you discover them?"

Hulda shrugged. "I'll only say that the two of them showed a great disregard for common sense one afternoon. I was where I had every right to be, and I came upon them quite by accident."

"Did you fire her?"

It was a shot in the dark, and to her shame, Hulda didn't see the trap until it was too late.

"Fire her? Certainly not. She was in enough trouble without me making it worse for her. She still works for me." Hulda's face flushed. "Oh, dear. Rachel, that was unfair."

"I know, and I'm sorry. But a man is dead. And if someone doesn't happen to find the real culprit soon, I'm going to have Evan reading me my rights." Rachel's heartbeat quickened. Sandy Millman came to mind. Sandy, plump and sweet-natured, attended the Methodist church and had worked at Russell's Emporium since she'd graduated from high school. She had only one child, Eddie, who delivered the town newspaper and had been one of the first ones to discover Billingsly's body. "I won't tell anyone what you shared with me," Rachel promised.

It had to be Sandy, although Rachel couldn't think of anyone less likely to be carrying on an affair with an Amish preacher. Rachel tried to think if Eddie bore any resemblance to Bishop Abner, but it was impossible to compare a slight, ordinary-looking twelve-year-old English boy with a sixty-something, bearded Amish man. "I promise I won't tell anyone what you've shared with me."

Hulda's brow wrinkled. "You're too clever by half for your own good. And I can see that I'll have to be far more careful what I tell you."

"Please don't be angry with me, Hulda." Rachel moved to put her arms around her neighbor. "I'd never do anything to hurt any of them."

Hulda's eyes clouded with emotion. "You can't promise that," she said. "Not when you're investigating a murder. None of us can."

"If the woman and her husband were separated, why wasn't her pregnancy a matter of town gossip?"

"I arranged for her to work for a friend in New Jersey. She left town after telling everyone that she and her husband were trying to reconcile. But there was no fixing that marriage. They'd married too young, and there were the usual problems: financial struggles, his infidelity, and his inability to hold a position more than a few months. When she came back to Stone Mill with the baby, no one paid much attention. But she's a good person and an excellent employee. She's been through enough, Rachel. No need to drag up old heartaches."

But that was exactly what Billingsly had done with his tattle-tale column, Rachel thought as she cut across the driveway, headed home. He dragged up old scandals to sell newspapers. Was it possible that he'd learned about Abner's fall from grace and intended to use it to smear his good name? *Amish bishop involved in sex scandal.* That would titillate readers, not just in Stone Mill but all over the country. The story might be enough to generate the type of dirty publicity that poor Beth Glick's murder had done. She shivered as a finger of cold apprehension traced her spine. And what if Billingsly's death could be linked to the Amish community? She could see the headlines now: *Bishop's love child shocks Plain community!*

Inside the back door, Rachel set the coffee carafe on the floor and shrugged out of her coat. As she lifted it to place it on a hook, she heard her keys jingle. She'd be looking in all her pockets tomorrow for them. Fishing them out of her pocket, she reached out to drop them in the basket on the wall that held keys and assorted junk. As she did, she caught a glimpse of a yellow paper tag . . . with *BB back door* written on it in her own handwriting.

As Rachel picked up the key, she felt slightly nauseated. BB. Bill Billingsly. It was the key to his back door. He'd given it to her over a year ago when she'd agreed to check on his cat while he was out of town. A peace offering that obviously hadn't amounted to anything. The missing cat.

She thought about what Evan had said about all the doors being locked in Billingsly's house when they'd found him. She was the one who had suggested someone else might have a key.

She dropped the key into the basket and wondered if it was time to start thinking about an attorney.

An hour later Rachel was just getting out of the shower when her cell phone rang. Wrapping a robe around herself, she hurried to the bed and retrieved it from her purse.

"Hey, Rache." Evan's voice came deep and familiar. "Is this a bad time?"

"*Ne.*" She smiled and settled into a deep rocker. "I'd hoped you'd call."

"Long day," he said.

"How's it going?"

"Slow. But I have every reason to believe we'll get him," Evan replied. "I've been thinking about you."

"Me, too," she admitted. "About you. Us. I'm sorry—"

His "I'm sorry" came at the same instant. "I shouldn't have been so—"

"Me either. I said things. . . ."

"We both said things that we shouldn't have."

Her throat constricted. "We need to talk, Evan."

"We do. I've got this engagement ring. . . ."

She thought about the key in the basket downstairs. "I didn't kill Billingsly," she said, her voice surprisingly emotional.

"I never thought you did. It was . . . the other thing. You should have told me."

"I should have."

"I want to make this work, Rache. I love you. No matter what happened, no matter what you did, I still love you."

"I love you, too." She hesitated. "Do you want me to tell you what happened?"

"Can I come in?"

She glanced at the dark window, her forehead creasing. "Where are you?"

"Outside."

She smiled again. "You'll have to wait while I get dressed." She shrugged off her robe and went to her dresser for sweatpants and a sweatshirt. "Can you give me a minute? I was in the shower."

"Actually, I need to talk to Skinner again. I see his rental is parked in the back. Is he there, or should I go to the Black Horse?"

"I think he's here. The light was on under his door when I came up. He could be out, but I think I heard him. Let yourself in. The kitchen door's open. You want me to send him down?"

"No. What's his room number?"

She gave Evan the room number. "Have time for coffee afterward?"

"Sure, and a sandwich if it's not too much trouble. No fuss. Grilled cheese will do. Haven't had time to eat today."

"I'm sure there's something more substantial than that in the fridge," she promised. "See you in a few minutes."

Fifteen minutes later, as Rachel came down the stairs, she heard Skinner's raised voice coming from the front entrance hallway. "I didn't kill him and I'm leaving Friday, so if you want to arrest me, you'll need to do it soon. Either that or come find me in Colorado."

Evan said something in response, but she couldn't make out his words. Then came the distinct sound of the front door closing. Hard. From the second-floor landing, she saw Evan standing under the chandelier in the front hall, making a notation in his notebook.

"Everything all right?" she called softly to him.

Evan looked up, his features set and unreadable. When their gazes met, he offered a half-smile and a shrug. "I think Mr. Skinner thinks I'm becoming a pest."

She smiled. "You want to eat in here?" She gestured toward the dining table.

He shook his head. "You know me. I'm a kitchen-table kind of guy."

"Me, too," she agreed. "Girl . . . woman." She waved her hand. "Whatever. I've got chicken salad, but there's got to be something I can heat up, if you want something hot."

"Chicken salad sounds perfect," he said, following her into the kitchen. "I'm starving." He washed his hands at the sink and dried them with the towel she offered. At the table, he unfolded his big frame into a chair and watched as she set the table for them.

Once the simple fare was out, Rachel sat down across from him at the little table. "I take it that that interview didn't go well."

"You smell good." He reached up to touch a stray lock of

hair that had sprung loose from her hastily secured ponytail. "And you look good, too."

"Really?" She'd pulled on clean sweats when he'd said he was coming in. As usual, she wore no makeup. But his saying she looked nice made her cheeks grow warm. Evan was such a sweet guy, and she cared for him deeply. She truly did. "Thank you," she murmured, wondering if they had a chance. Could they get through this rough patch and find a future together, or would what she'd done and the differences between them make it impossible? "My mother wouldn't approve," she added. "Not of what I'm wearing or me sharing a late supper with you."

"Unchaperoned?" He shook his head. "It's not as though we're alone in the house. You've got, what, a dozen guests upstairs?" He paused to take a bite of the chicken salad on thick wheat bread. "Delicious," he murmured.

"To begin with, I'm not wearing a prayer *kapp*." She glanced down at her oversized super-comfy pink sweatpants and chuckled. "I think it's all downhill from there." She passed the macaroni salad, rich with chunks of ham and egg. "Help yourself. Ada just made it this morning. Come to think of it . . ." She went back to the fridge and returned with a covered dish of deviled eggs. She knew they were Evan's favorites. "Milk?" She loved watching him eat. He had good manners. He wasn't sloppy, but he always ate with enthusiasm, like a man who hadn't tasted anything so good in ages.

"I think I'd rather have hot tea," he asked between bites. "Aren't you eating?"

"Sure." She smiled. "I'll put the kettle on." She got mugs and tea bags from the cupboard. "Why did you want to talk to Skinner again?" she asked as she returned to her chair.

"Because he lied to me about knowing Billingsly, and when you lie about one thing, that suggests you could be lying about something else. I confronted him with it, and he all but admitted that he hadn't been honest with me. But you can't arrest everybody who lies to you in an investigation. It happens more than you'd think. Some people lie to you on purpose, but others just can't recall the facts correctly. In Skinner's case, he flat-out lied."

She paused, a forkful of the macaroni salad halfway to her mouth. Evan seemed so shocked. "Isn't that what I told you? Billingsly was obviously disturbed by Skinner's appearance at the school. I told you that they knew each other and there was some kind of problem between them. You could see it on Billingsly's face." She put her fork down and leaned forward. "So you think Skinner might be a viable suspect for Billingsly's murder?"

"I haven't made up my mind. What I have so far is only circumstantial evidence and suspicions. I don't have anything that puts him at the murder scene. I don't even have a motive."

"You said he had a police record for battery. Does that have any weight in the case?"

"Not really. It was years ago. A bar fight." He took another bite of sandwich. "I did a little research on him on the Internet this afternoon. He's known in all of the Vietnam vet circles. He had an impressive record and campaigns for vets' rights. He did three tours in Vietnam. Decorated for bravery under fire. Honorable discharge."

She nodded. "Doesn't sound like a guy who would murder someone by tying him to his front porch to freeze to death, does it?"

Evan shook his head. "No, but you never know. People do crazy things. The way I found out that he knew Billingsly for sure was on a veterans' blog. The two of them have been having a heated debate online."

"What about?"

"Apparently over national legislation concerning psychiatric care for PTSD—post-traumatic stress disorder—for veterans. Skinner doesn't think the government does enough for vets once they come home from war. Billingsly disagreed. He was full of facts and figures, taking the position that we're already spending millions on mental care for these men. And you know Billingsly. He wields that pen like a sword."

Rachel got up from the table, went to her office, and returned with her laptop. The teakettle had started to whistle, and she turned off the flame under it. "What's the name of the site?"

When he didn't answer, she stared at him as she set the laptop on the table and opened it. "You know I'll find it anyway."

He exhaled, obviously not happy with her. "You should just let me handle this, Rache. You're not in a position to be interfering with a police investigation."

She ignored him and started to type Skinner's name into the search bar.

Evan exhaled again and told her the name of the site.

While he finished eating, she read the exchange between Skinner and Billingsly. After a few minutes, she paused and looked up. "This isn't just a disagreement over politics," she said. "It's personal. There's bad blood between the two of them."

Evan pushed his plate back. "How do you figure that? They just didn't agree on a health care funding issue. Arguments about money can get heated."

Rachel resisted the urge to roll her eyes. *Men.* They never read between the lines. Even the smartest of them. "You need to take a closer look at what they're saying, Evan. For whatever reason, Skinner had a grudge against Billingsly. He was angry with him and resentful. How angry is hard to say."

"I think you're jumping to conclusions." Evan wiped his mouth with his cloth napkin. "And you need to rein in your emotions and let me do my job."

Stung by his words, Rachel closed her laptop. "I'm just saying that—"

"Well, don't." His tone became terse. "You're jumping to conclusions again. Women's intuition or whatever it is that sends you off on these tangents is more hindrance than help in real police work. *Evidence* is what we need. Hard facts.

That's what I have to base my case on. Not conjecture or hunches, but facts."

She bit back several retorts that sprang to mind, most of which pertained to past murders in the town that she'd solved when the police couldn't. She closed her laptop. "So what hard evidence have you come up with today? Any new directions?"

Evan's shoulders slumped. When he spoke again, he'd tempered his voice. "Nothing. Which is why I keep coming back to the same persons of interest." He glanced up at her, clearly feeling guilty.

She went with her *women's intuition*. "Including me?"

He met her gaze and then glanced away. "Nothing turned up in the autopsy that wasn't apparent at first glance. No evidence to speak of at the crime scene. No fingerprints, and we did a second sweep."

"You see a cat when you were in the house? A gray tabby?"

He shook his head. "No cat. And no murder weapon. I think that whatever the killer hit Billingsly on the head with, he took it with him when he left."

She went to the stove and poured cups of tea, carried them to the table, and then went to the counter and lifted a cake cover. "Have room for a slice of German chocolate?"

"Always."

She cut a generous slice and put it on a plate. "I still say that Jake Skinner came here for a specific reason, and it wasn't for shoofly pie." She slid the cake toward Evan. "And now you know that he lied to you."

Evan shrugged. "Well, he's not the only one. Blade claimed to be at a book club meeting Saturday night, but he wasn't. I found out today that the meeting was canceled due to the storm. I'm going back to question him again in the morning."

She pinched the tea bag tag dangling in her mug and worked the tea bag up and down. "So you're left where?"

"I have to keep going back to the circumstantial evidence

because that's all I have." He hesitated. "I'm going to be honest with you, Rachel. Unfortunately, you're at the top of my list. You admit being at Billingsly's house around the time of his death, and he had something on you. Something that could have been potentially devastating to you if he'd published it."

She suddenly felt a little sick to her stomach. She let go of the tea bag and sat back in her chair, crossing her arms over her chest. "That isn't funny."

"It wasn't supposed to be." He leaned forward on the table. "Look, you didn't do it. I know that, but you have to admit that to someone who doesn't know you, it doesn't look good. Being there at his house after having a public fight with him. Over something serious. Talk about being at the wrong place at the wrong time. It wasn't the smartest thing you've ever done, Rache."

"I suppose not." Suddenly she was annoyed with him. She only hesitated a second before she said, "If you're looking for circumstantial evidence, I might as well give you more."

"What do you mean?"

She got up and went to the small basket on the wall in the entryway. She picked up the key with the tattered yellow cardboard tag hanging from it. She tossed it across the table to him.

"What's that?" He picked it up and read the tag.

"Bill Billingsly's back-door key," she told him. "You said that Billingsly's doors were all locked and that you wondered if the person who killed him had a key to his house. I've had it more than a year. I fed his cat when he went to some conference in New Mexico." She folded her arms over her chest. "So maybe you'd better save time looking for hard evidence and read me my rights."

# Chapter 13

By ten the following morning, Rachel was at the high school gym to check on the day's scheduled activities. Her fiancé, whom she wasn't even sure she was still engaged to, hadn't arrested her the previous night, despite her encouragement. Or baiting, depending on whose point of view one saw. But the evening hadn't ended well. They'd parted frustrated, if not angry, with each other, agreeing, tight-lipped, to talk later. Rachel refused to allow herself to stew on the matter, though. She truly believed that if they were meant to be together, they'd work it out, and if they weren't meant to marry, it was better if it ended now.

Still, she wasn't in the best of moods when she arrived at the gym. It was busier than it had been on Monday or Tuesday because the Amish lunch-basket auction and winter picnic were scheduled. The best Amish cooks prepared their best dishes and tucked the lunch food into beautiful handmade baskets. Those who successfully won the bidding had their choice of eating the lunch in a special picnic area of the gym, outside on tables surrounding the ice rink, or in one of several Amish one-room schoolhouses throughout the valley. Competition was fierce, and bids often went higher than fifty dollars per basket, with the entire proceeds going to refill the shelves at the Stone Mill Food Bank, which served all the residents of the valley.

Because of the auction, there were more booths open than the previous day. Most of the newcomers were the most frugal Amish, who'd chosen to rent booths for the busiest day rather than the entire week. As Rachel entered the busy room, friends and neighbors called out to one another and to her, seemingly caught up in the cheerful atmosphere of the Winter Frolic. White prayer *kapps* and broad-brimmed black hats mingled with fur hoods and stylish cloches. And everywhere there were children, Amish and English, riding in strollers, toddling behind mothers and fathers, and playing uninhibitedly in the special roped-off area full of blocks, wooden toys, wagons, and supervised activities. None of the children seemed to notice one another's strange clothing or language as Amish and English preschoolers eagerly joined in playing hopscotch, finger painting, listening to stories, and watching a puppet show. Even the mood of the adults seemed lighter today, almost as if tragedy hadn't struck their small town just a few days before.

*Life goes on*, Rachel thought, then wondered if she'd grown callous. Sunday morning she'd witnessed something that she hoped never to see again in her life, and already she was going hours without thinking of Billingsly's murder or how close her shameful secret had come to being publicly exposed. She hoped she wasn't becoming inured to crime. She had prayed for the deceased last night when she went to bed and again this morning. Her compassion was genuine. Billingsly had been a despicable person, but he didn't deserve what had happened to him. And it was important to find out who was responsible and bring him to justice.

Two laughing Amish boys, six or seven years old, blond and blue-eyed, as alike as two peas in a pod, dashed in front of her, wide-brimmed straw hats barely held in place as they darted around the booths in a reckless game of tag, barely avoiding colliding with shoppers and merchants. "Slow down," Rachel cautioned in Deitsch. "You'll get in trouble with your *dat* and *mam*."

School was in session for the English children, but many

Amish kids were present. Technically speaking, the Amish children were supposed to be in class today, but their one-room schools had been thrown open to visitors for the lunch-basket festivities, and many of the kids had come to help their parents with the booths. For the Amish, all education was a preparation for work, and selling crafts, honey, cheese, and baked goods contributed to the family and the community. Rachel was torn between the traditional outlook and wanting to see the Amish youngsters get as much from their school years as possible. But, in the end, it was parents who made the decisions and her opinion didn't really count.

It was heartening to see the throngs of shoppers adding to the community's financial well-being, and Rachel couldn't have been more pleased to see that the Amish craftsmanship was so appreciated by outsiders. At midweek, her own booth had already sold almost all her stock from the gift store at Stone Mill House. Life was often hard for Plain people, and she was happy to help add to their income in any way she could. She took a percentage of each sale, but she'd never intended the shop to be a moneymaker for the B&B. It was her way of giving back to the people she still considered her own.

The running boys made her think again of the hat she'd seen in the snow outside Billingsly's house. Even Amish children knew better than to be careless with their hats. So why had someone, some Amish man, left his at the scene of a murder? Or was Evan right? Had the wind snatched it off some innocent's head and deposited it there, causing her to search for clues where there were none?

"Miss Mast?" A young woman in a dark business suit and heels came toward her, a cameraman trailing her. The woman's jacket bore an ID giving her name and title and a TV station's call letters. "I'm Elaine Dorsey." She extended a well-manicured hand. "We have an appointment later today to film a piece for tonight's broadcast?"

"Yes, of course." Rachel had almost forgotten. She'd agreed to the station's request for a brief clip of her and Evan in the

Amish horse-drawn sleigh. Rachel wondered if Evan remembered. She guessed she'd have to call and remind him. Awkward.

Elaine Dorsey flashed a professional smile. Her perfect teeth were small and model white. "A little bird told me that you and Detective Parks have recently become engaged. I'm sure our viewers will find the sled ride romantic," she simpered. "I just wanted to confirm for three o'clock at the sled staging area behind the school's main parking lot."

Rachel winced inwardly. If her betrothal became public knowledge, she'd have to tell her parents. But if the reporter asked Evan today about their engagement, what would he say? "Three o'clock. We'll be there. Wouldn't miss it." The truth was, she wished she could skip the whole thing, but the publicity for the Winter Frolic was too important to pass up. There were still four more days of festival events before they wrapped up Saturday afternoon with a cook-off. She'd made a commitment to the community, and she had to fulfill her promise. A successful week would do a lot toward putting Stone Mill on the map for future tourist trade and maybe even population growth. Her real goal and the goal of the town committee was to increase the financial opportunities for all of the valley's residents, Amish and English alike, to bring much-needed jobs and to improve the quality of education for all the children.

Rachel didn't like to be dishonest, but she wondered if she could find some way to cancel Evan's appearance that afternoon. That way, there need be no mention of their engagement. She could always give the excuse that he was too busy with the ongoing murder investigation. "Don't miss the lunch-basket auction," Rachel suggested to the newswoman. "This is the first year of the Winter Frolic, but the lunch-basket fundraiser has been an annual event for the past two years. It's a lot of fun," she added. "We have an Amish woman auctioneer, and she can be really funny. Everyone enjoys her jokes."

"A woman?" Elaine's interest was immediately piqued. "That surprises me. I thought that Amish women rarely spoke up in public. Aren't they supposed to center their lives around the home and let the men do the talking?"

Rachel chuckled. "You can't believe everything you hear about the Amish. And I certainly wouldn't consider Rhody Miller to be shy and retiring. Amish women may dress differently, but they are as resourceful and independent in their own way as English women."

"I notice you speak of *English* women. By that, you mean non-Amish?"

"Exactly," Rachel agreed. "I grew up in a traditional Amish household, and in some ways, I suppose, many of my expressions and thoughts remain with my heritage. I know I have a strong respect for the culture." She smiled at the reporter. "And if the two of you haven't packed a lunch from home, I'd strongly advise you to bid on a basket at the auction. You won't regret it. The food is fantastic."

They exchanged a few more pleasantries, and Rachel excused herself, saying that she had committee obligations to see to. Elaine Dorsey seemed nice enough, but Rachel had a natural wariness when it came to the press. Somehow whatever you said to a reporter always came out differently than what you intended. And there was always the possibility of the conversation veering to Billingsly's murder, and the town certainly didn't need more of that kind of publicity.

Once Elaine and the cameraman disappeared into the crowd, Rachel made her way to Coyote's pottery booth. She was hoping to catch Blade alone. She couldn't tell him that Evan intended to meet with him today; that wouldn't be right. But maybe now that Blade had had a chance to calm down, he'd realize that she wasn't his enemy and tell her where he'd been Saturday night. She was only trying to get to the truth and find out who else might have been at Billingsly's that night before her position as chief suspect became set in stone.

But as she approached the pottery stall, she saw not Blade but a red-cheeked Amish girl, Martha Swartzentruber, at the register. Martha, sixteen, blond, and blue-eyed, was cheerfully wrapping a purchase for a customer. As Rachel drew nearer, she saw Coyote seated in a rocking chair at the back of the booth with a Peruvian poncho thrown over her. Her little girls were busily engaged with a dollhouse, miniature furnishings, and an array of brightly colored pottery horses on a rag rug at Coyote's feet while Remi sat in his wheelchair at one end of the booth, bent over his iPad. Coyote's poncho stirred and gave off a decided burp, and Rachel quickly realized that her friend must be nursing her baby. "Hi," she called. "How's it going?"

"Come on in." Coyote motioned her to come around to the back, through the opening between tables. "Good to see you." She patted the baby's back, made a few adjustments to her smock, and pushed the poncho onto her lap. The baby, as blond as his mother and sisters, gurgled happily as Coyote held him up. "He probably needs a change."

Rachel took the baby, put him on her shoulder, and patted his back. Again he burped. He was warm, cuddly, and as squirmy as a puppy. "Sweet baby boy," she murmured, sniffing the baby's neck. "He's getting heavier by the day." She hugged him again, and for a second, thoughts of a baby in her own future teased the far corners of her mind. She wanted children. She knew she did. She just wasn't certain if she wanted them *now*. And what if she and Evan couldn't make their relationship work? She knew that many women chose to have children without a husband, but that wasn't the life for her. For her, children would be only in marriage. "He's adorable." She passed the baby back to his mother. "Where's Blade? Don't tell me that he left you on your own today?" she went on, trying not to sound like she had come looking for him. "Basket-auction day is crazy busy."

Coyote settled her son on her knee. He was dressed in a blue-plaid flannel shirt and denim overalls with a yellow honeybee hand-embroidered on the bib. On his tiny feet were a pair of soft, beaded deerskin moccasins. Coyote's outfit matched the baby's, except that instead of overalls, she wore a calf-length denim dress over knee-high leather moccasins. *My hippie artist friend,* Rachel thought. Coyote's hair hung to her waist like a sheet of rippling water, allowing only glimpses of her dangling silver earrings. As always, she was gorgeous without a stitch of makeup.

One of the girls snatched a toy horse from her sister, and the older child wailed. "Play nice," Coyote warned softly. "Share, or the horses go back in their box." She directed a motherly gaze of disapproval in the direction of the transgressor. "And tell your sister you're sorry."

"Sorry," came the response.

Peace restored among the girls, Coyote turned her attention back to Rachel. "Yup, we're all alone here today, but I have Martha. She's a treasure."

Rachel waited, hoping her friend would volunteer her husband's whereabouts. If he was at the house, she might have time to stop by there to speak to him before Evan found him. But when Coyote didn't offer any more information, she asked, "He stayed home today?"

"No." Coyote smiled. "He drove to Willingsburgh to pick up a supply of slip for me. For the redware, I used up the last of what I had, and I've been buying it from the same source for six months. It's a good ways from here, five hours in decent weather, not a drive I look forward to in winter with the baby."

"That was nice of him to offer," Rachel said, still fishing for more information.

"He should be back by eight," Coyote continued. The baby started to fuss and she located a pacifier. "It *was* sweet of him to go for me, but then, I think being locked up all day in this weather was getting to him. He's been on edge the last few days. Ten hours alone in the car with Bob Dylan music should set him right. He can be moody, but it never lasts. He's a terrific guy. I couldn't ask for better."

"He certainly seems to think a lot of his kids. Not many men take such a hands-on interest in their children."

"It's what drew me to him from the first day I met him," Coyote confided. "Find a man who likes dogs and kids and you can't go wrong."

"Excuse me," Martha said, turning to Coyote. "This lady has a question about the blue-and-gray mixing bowl."

"Certainly." Coyote rose to her feet. "I'd be glad to talk with her." She glanced back at Rachel. "Sorry."

"Go ahead." Rachel waved her away. "I have to run, anyway. I'm supposed to pick up Mary Aaron at her house and I'm going to be late, and I have a casserole in my Jeep I need to drop off at my parents' house."

Why Ada was sending food to the Mast kitchen, Rachel couldn't imagine. There was always a ton of food at her mother's house. Ada and her mother knew each other, of course, but they'd never been close friends. Weird or not, though, it was best to do what she was told when it came to her often eccentric cook. Without Ada she couldn't imagine how she would manage to keep her guests provided with such wonderful fare or how she would keep her cleaning staff on time and on task. Ada might be prickly, but she was invaluable.

When Rachel stepped out of the gym, she found that it was snowing again. Big, lazy flakes fell on her as she crossed the parking lot. The snow didn't seem to worry the festival visitors. Dozens of people, bundled in coats, mufflers, gloves, and hats, were noisily making their way toward the building. She reached the Jeep and started to open the door, then noticed a sheet of paper affixed to the windshield by the left wiper. She pulled the paper free and slid into the front seat.

Starting the Jeep first, she then unfolded the single sheet of cheap, lined paper. Her heart skipped a beat as she stared at the hand-printed message, written in pencil in plain block letters.

**IF YOU KNOW WHAT IS GOOD FOR YOU RACHEL MAST YOU WILL STOP ASKING NOSY QUESTIONS. MIND YOUR OWN BEESWAX OR YOU WILL BE SORRY.**

The threatening note felt like it was burning a hole in Rachel's pocket all the way to Mary Aaron's. Who would write such a thing? Was it the killer, or someone who simply resented her questions? Was she a nosy busybody doing more harm than good in the community? Traditionally, the Amish liked to keep their lives private and didn't appreciate anyone prying into their affairs.

By the same token, who did? Certainly not Blade. He'd been angry with her. But Blade was out of town. And the wording on the warning had been odd, stilted. Who would write *Mind your own beeswax?*

She wondered if she needed to tell Evan about the note. Was the note evidence? Of course, if she did share it, she'd have to admit that she was doing what he'd explicitly told her not to do. She was still trying to track down clues that might lead to Billingsly's killer. Telling him that she'd disregarded his request would only make things worse between them and might push their relationship to the breaking point.

Did she tell Mary Aaron? By the time she pulled into her cousin's barnyard, she'd decided she'd sit on it for a little while. Think it over.

"I have this casserole to deliver to my mother," Rachel explained to Mary Aaron as the two made their way down her uncle's snow-clogged lane. "And then I think we've got time to drive back to Joe Paul Kurtz's place and ask him about the top-hack buggy. See if he or some of his family drove it to town on Saturday night."

"No need," Mary Aaron replied. "I've been asking around, and Alan says Joe Paul drove his top-hack into a ditch and broke the axle Saturday morning. Alan knows because he helped him get his groceries and grain home. They tied the horse to the back of Alan's buggy and left Joe Paul's buggy at Shorty Beachy's place until they can get another axle."

Rachel frowned. "Alan was sure the top-hack couldn't be driven?"

"Positive. You know how long it takes to get replacement parts and put them on."

Rachel concentrated on steering the Jeep down the lane. Some of the snow had melted, leaving deep puddles, and some had drifted across the drive so that she had to put the vehicle into second gear and then first to get through without getting stuck. "Which brings us back to Bishop Abner's buggy."

Mary Aaron folded her gloved hands in her lap. "Maybe Blade was mistaken. He must have been." When Rachel didn't say anything, Mary Aaron gazed out the window. "Why is Ada sending food for your mother?"

Mary Aaron looked cute today in a new sky blue dress and matching wool head scarf. As usual, Rachel felt like the poor cousin in her worn denim jumper and thick black stockings. Both wore almost identical navy coats; Rachel never wore her white parka when visiting Amish family or friends. The plain coats were thick, with lining against the cold, but where Mary Aaron's coat was neatly stitched and fit her perfectly, Rachel's own coat had seen better days. There was a three-cornered tear and a dark stain on the sleeve where one of the goats had chewed it, and some of the hem in the back was coming out. She supposed that she'd have to ask one of her sisters to mend it again, or maybe she could bargain with her brother Paul's wife, Miriam, to sew her a new one. Miriam's skill with a needle was legendary in a community where most women learned to sew well as children. *Another of my character flaws,* Rachel mused. *Not only do I not mind my own beeswax, but I will be a failure if my future husband needs a button sewn on.*

"I have no idea why Ada made it. But you know how she is."

"Right." Mary Aaron laughed. "You just do what she says. The fewer questions, the better."

"I'm just going to run in the casserole," Rachel said when she pulled into her father's farmyard. "Who knows? If *Mam*'s alone in the kitchen, she might be forced to speak to me."

Mary Aaron looked dubious. "Doubt it," she replied. "Your mother is as stubborn as my father, and you know how far you got when you tried to talk him into doing something he didn't want to do." Mary Aaron's father was her mother's favorite brother, and the two shared a lot of characteristics.

Rachel opened the door to get out, and her brother Moses came out of the house and down the back step. With him was her brother Levi. Rachel called out to them and the two waved. Moses lived on his father-in-law's farm nearby. "Is *Mam* in the kitchen?" she asked.

Moses pointed to the woodshed and said something that Rachel couldn't make out to Levi, then walked over to the car. Levi waved to her and headed for the shed.

"*Mam* and the girls went to the basket auction at the English school," Moses said. "House is empty."

Mary Aaron greeted the boys and then said to Rachel, "I'll take the casserole in."

"Thanks." Rachel turned her attention back to her brother. "Why aren't you at the school? Who's driving the horses and sleigh? Remember, I told you about the TV crew filming a piece on the Winter Frolic today at three. Evan and I promised to be in it. They want to feature the horse-drawn sleigh."

"John Hannah's filling in for me today." He rubbed at his beard. "I don't want my picture on the television. And you know John Hannah. He's not strict about having his photo taken. He'll probably show off for the camera. I'll go in after supper with a fresh team. That was a good idea of yours, to give sleigh rides to the tourists. They pay a lot to ride behind a horse, them Englishers." He grinned. "Lucky it's been cold enough so the snow hasn't melted."

"I'm glad it's a success," Rachel said. "How's Ruth? Is she well?"

"Right as rain. I've got some news you haven't heard," Moses told Rachel proudly. "Ruth and I will be welcoming a new member to the family by harvest."

"Wonderful," Rachel exclaimed, clapping her mittened hands together. "You both must be thrilled." She knew that her brother and his wife had been praying for a baby ever since they'd married several years earlier.

"We're really happy about it," he admitted shyly. "Ruth's parents are beside themselves. Naturally, her father is hoping for a boy. As for me and Ruthie, all we pray for is that the baby be born healthy." He quickly added, "Of course, we'll love it, no matter what."

Levi came back out of the woodshed carrying an armload of kindling.

"Two more trips," Moses ordered their younger brother. "And make the next two bigger pieces of wood. There's no excuse for *Mam*'s wood box to be empty." He returned his attention to Rachel. "Levi will get out of chores if you let him. Always has his nose stuck in a book. Just because he's the youngest boy is no excuse for not pulling his weight."

"And I suppose you never goofed off?"

"I liked playing well enough. Remember the time Paul and I tried to put a saddle on the bull?"

"Let's hope your baby has more sense than that," Rachel teased.

Levi came back out of the house and started to walk toward them, but Moses pointed to the woodshed. "More wood."

Feet dragging, Levi went for another load.

Moses grinned proudly. "You know how Ruthie loves babies. She's hoping for a round dozen. She was just saying last night . . ." Moses, being the most garrulous of her brothers, chatted on.

Rachel smiled and nodded. While big families were the custom among her people, her own wishes were more modest. Two or maybe three children would be fine with her, providing she ever married.

When Moses paused for a breath, she jumped in. As much as she would hate to admit it, her mind had wandered a bit while her brother had been talking about babies. "I know this is going to sound odd, *Mosey*, but do you know of any men who have recently lost a hat?" She deliberately used the childhood nickname that he'd favored when he was Levi's age. "Not a straw hat," she elaborated, "but a black dress one? Maybe someone mentioned it in passing?"

"A hat?" He removed his own navy stocking cap, ran his fingers through his hair, replaced the knit hat, and pulled it down over his ears. Moses's hair was a decent dark brown, but his close-cropped curly beard and sideburns were a bright auburn.

"*Ne*. How would anybody lose his hat? Maybe mislay it in the house, but it's not like you take it off unless you're in church or eating at someone's table." He shrugged. "You're right. It is a strange question. Why do you ask?"

"You talking about Sammy's hat?" Levi approached the Jeep from the passenger's side, his arms full of log sections.

"Sammy's hat?" Rachel repeated, confused.

Levi flashed a mischievous grin and shifted the weight in his arms. "Sure. There was one in the snow by the house where the dead man was. I picked it up and gave it back to Sammy."

Rachel's mouth gaped. "But I sent you and Danny back to the house. How could you—"

Levi made a face. "We went, but I wanted another look at the body. I saw the hat, and I picked it up."

"How did you know the hat belonged to Sammy?"

"Easy." Levi's grin widened. "He's really forgetful. Always leaving his hat somewhere. He does it so often that Naamah sewed his name into it."

# Chapter 14

*✦✦✦*

"What time this afternoon did you say you and Evan are doing the piece for the television station?" Mary Aaron asked as they left Rachel's parents' house.

"Three." She glanced in the rearview mirror. "I was thinking about running by Abner's on the way back to town."

"But you *are* going home to change before you meet the film crew, right?" Mary Aaron asked. "Because you can't be seen on TV in that getup." She indicated Rachel's skirt and scarf. "Not much of a hotel-owner look." She chuckled. "And certainly not Amish. You'll give us a bad name."

Rachel moved to the center of the blacktop and passed a mail truck pulled over, putting mail in her parents' neighbors' mailbox. "I keep thinking about what happened with Billingsly."

"Of course you do. Everybody's talking about you questioning people, about the buggy and the hat. *Mam* is worried about you. It's awful that such a thing could happen in Stone Mill, but you don't have to be the one to find the murderer. Not this time. That's the job of the policemen and Evan. Evan especially."

"Whose side are you on, Mary Aaron?"

"So there are sides now? It should never be that way." Mary Aaron's tone became more serious. "I'm here, right? But I'm not going to hold my tongue. I'll tell you if I think you're going too far. I care about you, and I don't want to see you make enemies in the valley."

"You don't understand." Rachel threw her a long look.

A deer leaped over the fence just ahead of them, touched down once, and then gave another big leap and vanished into the woods on the far side of the blacktop. Rachel braked.

"Good reflexes." Mary Aaron glanced at Rachel again. "So why are we going to Bishop Abner's again?"

Rachel lowered her voice. "Because of something Levi told me back at the house. The missing hat. I found out who it belonged to. It was Sammy Zook's."

"Sammy's?" Mary Aaron frowned. "I'm surprised Bishop Abner would have taken his wife and nephew to Billingsly's house."

Rachel shook her head. "I don't know that he did. I didn't see them there. And when I saw the hat at Billingsly's house, it was half buried in the snow. It looked as if it had been there at least a good part of the night. Turns out," she said, all in a rush, "it was our Levi who took it. He and Danny followed me to Billingsly's. I told them to go home, but at some point, Levi picked up the hat, saw Sammy's name sewn in the inside, and took it with him. Levi told me that he dropped it off at the Chupps' on his way home."

"On Sunday?" Mary Aaron asked.

"Yes. But remember when I asked Naamah and Bishop Abner about the hat, neither of them said a word about Sammy having lost his. Isn't that strange?"

Mary Aaron sighed. "Not really. Sammy's always leaving his hat somewhere. He left it under the bench at services last week and at the feed mill the week before. And you asked about a man's hat."

"Sammy's hat *is* a man's hat." Rachel tightened her grip on the steering wheel. She didn't like the idea that Bishop Abner could have been involved in the murder of Billingsly any more than Mary Aaron did, but if there was one thing she'd learned after the murder of Willy O'Day, it was that you never know what a person might do when he feels as if he's been pushed to the brink. "It wasn't snowing on Sunday morning. Sammy had to have lost it Saturday or sometime in the night."

"So Sammy Zook's hat was in the yard. So what? That doesn't prove anything. It doesn't prove he was there. Maybe the wind blew it there. It was a snowstorm," Mary Aaron reminded. "Lots of wind that night. Sammy might have lost it at the ice rink or the school, anywhere, and it blew there."

"And the hat happened to end up in the yard of a man who was murdered?" When her cousin didn't answer, Rachel said, "It's considered circumstantial evidence."

"I don't think this *circumstantial evidence* means anything. Circumstantial evidence says *you* could have killed Billingsly."

"But we know I didn't," Rachel insisted, "which means we have to look at what other directions the evidence points us."

Mary Aaron rolled her eyes. "You think that Sammy Zook went to Billingsly's house—an Englishman he doesn't know—dragged him outside, tied him up, and poured water on him so that he froze to death? And then turned out all the lights in the house and locked the doors on his way out? That's *lecherich*. Ridiculous. Sammy wouldn't hurt a flea. And honestly, if he wanted to hurt a flea, he wouldn't know to tie it to a front porch and pour water over it." She reached out and touched Rachel's shoulder. "I wish you hadn't seen that dead body. You're usually so sensible, but I—"

"I don't think Sammy killed Billingsly," Rachel interrupted, not liking her cousin's tone. She wasn't being irrational; she was being the opposite. She wasn't letting the fact that she liked Bishop Abner, practically adored him, get in the way of the facts. "Mary Aaron, I think Billingsly's murder was very personal. Someone hated him enough or was afraid of him enough to do that to him." She stared at the road ahead of her. "Maybe Sammy was there. He might have witnessed the murder."

"And what would Sammy be doing out at night alone? You know Naamah and Bishop Abner watch over him like he was a little child—which, for the most part, he is. Naamah says he's afraid of the dark. He won't sleep without a light in his room. Which worries her because he wants a lamp on at night."

"My point exactly," Rachel insisted. "Sammy wouldn't have been there alone. If he was there, someone he knew and was comfortable with took him there."

Mary Aaron's eyes widened. "No, you can't think that. . . . You've known Abner all your life, Rachel. You know what a good and wise man he is. How kind. You can't really think that he could be involved in murder."

Rachel lifted her foot off the gas as they approached a patch of ice on the road. This time of year, the snowplows came by more than once a day. It was good that they cleared the snow, but it sometimes resulted in sheets of ice on the pavement that were more dangerous than the snow. It was at times like this that she was glad that after she lost her old Jeep to the depths of the rock quarry the summer before, she'd made the decision to buy the same four-wheel-drive vehicle, despite its hefty price.

Clear of the ice, she slowly accelerated and glanced at her cousin. "Have you ever heard any rumors about Abner and an English woman? It would be some time ago, twelve, thirteen years? Someone told me that after his first wife died, there was a scandal involving him and—"

"An Englisher woman? *Ne,* I never heard such a thing. Bishop Abner is a man of God. He would never—"

"My source, a reliable one, told me that he did. And that Abner and this woman had a baby together."

"Why would you listen to such malicious gossip about our bishop?" Mary Aaron asked, clearly angry. She took a breath and put her hand on Rachel's forearm. When she spoke again, the anger was gone. "I don't want to exchange harsh words with you. Maybe you should take me home. Maybe this isn't a good time for us."

"This isn't easy for me either, Mary Aaron. Abner is my friend, has been my friend. But the person who shared this with me is no idle gossip."

"Hulda." Mary Aaron sat back on the seat, crossing her arms. "But why would she say such a thing?"

"Maybe because it's true. Billingsly was an evil man. He hurt a lot of people. Look what he did to the Herschbergers. He ruined their lives. Maybe Billingsly found out about Abner and the Englishwoman and threatened to tell everyone. Think what it would do to the bishop's reputation . . . and what Englishers would say about the Amish."

"But . . . if such a thing did happen, why wouldn't I have heard it? Never. Not a word."

"Think about it, Mary Aaron. You were in school then. You weren't keeping company with the mothers and young wives and older women, circles where it might have been discussed. No one would have said anything about the bishop's misdeeds to a schoolgirl."

"*Ya*," Mary Aaron admitted. "That's true." She shook her head. "But I still don't know if I believe it."

"I've always thought that Abner was one of the best men I've ever known, but he's human," Rachel said softly. "Humans make mistakes."

"I really don't think this is your business, Rachel. All this prying, it's not good for anyone. You might hurt someone by falsely accusing them. I'm sure there is a good reason for Sammy's hat being there. And it doesn't prove anything. I think you need to worry about yourself." Mary Aaron hesitated. "I didn't tell you, but . . . yesterday, at the B&B, when you were at Coyote and Blade's house, Evan called me there."

"You spoke to Evan?"

"*Ya*. He's worried about you, too." Mary Aaron sighed.

"He told me that he didn't think you were taking the matter of Billingsly's murder and your whereabouts at the time seriously. He's afraid he's going to have to take you in for questioning. Officially. He's concerned about how that will look for the festival. And the whole town. He's worried about your reputation."

"So Evan told you he thinks I might be the murderer?" She didn't really believe it, but her feelings were ruffled, too, and the thought that he'd discussed her with Mary Aaron didn't make her any happier.

"*Ne,* you know better than that. Of course he doesn't think you killed Billingsly. Evan loves you."

"I'm not so sure about that." Rachel chewed on her lower lip. "Things are not so good between us right now."

"Which will pass. No one is themself in the town right now." Mary Aaron's gaze met hers. "There is a lot of responsibility on Evan's shoulders. It is his job to find this killer, not yours. And I think he feels you don't trust him to do it."

Rachel took a deep breath. She'd had no intention of talking about this with Mary Aaron, but she needed her to understand that Evan was telling the truth when he said the evidence pointed to her. She needed her cousin to understand why it was important that she find out who did this to Billingsly. And quickly.

She signaled and pulled over into a driveway and put her Jeep in park. "There's more to this than you realize," she said, turning to face her cousin. "I've got something in my past, something I did while I was away . . . something I never wanted anyone to know. But Billingsly found out, and he threatened to expose me. He was going to write about it in his nasty gossip column in the paper. He said it would ruin my name in the community, ruin my business. I was very angry with him Saturday night when I went to his house."

"You were not angry enough to kill him." Mary Aaron unbuckled her seat belt, slid over, and put her arms around Rachel. She hugged her. "You don't have to tell me. I'll pray for you, that this burden is eased in your heart. But you don't have to say any more; I don't need to know, cousin. You are a good person, and nothing you could tell me would ever make me stop loving you."

A lump rose in Rachel's throat, and she blinked against the rising moisture in her eyes that threatened to cloud her vision. "What would I do without you?" she murmured, hugging Mary Aaron.

"Or me without you. You know you are closer to me than my blood sisters." She grew firm again. "But I'm serious about this. You need to back off and let the police ask the questions."

"You and Evan aren't the only ones who think so." When Mary Aaron gave her a quizzical look, Rachel pulled the note out of her coat pocket and handed it to her. "I found this on the windshield of my Jeep this morning."

"In your yard?"

Rachel shook her head. "At the school parking lot. Someone left the message where I would be sure to find it when I came out of the gym."

Mary Aaron lips moved as she silently read the note again. "This scares me, Rae-Rae. You need to show Evan this."

"I intend to. Just not yet. Like you said, I still don't have any real evidence. I really want to try and straighten this out with Abner, to find out where Sammy was Saturday night and why. I have some questions for Sammy, too."

"Now who's being stubborn? And you talk about your mother. I can see the apple doesn't fall far from the tree," Mary Aaron fussed. "If I had any sense, I would make you let me out of the Jeep. I've just started my baptism classes, and I'm going to get in so much trouble for doing this with you again."

Rachel glanced at her in surprise. "You're taking lessons? You're going to be baptized into the church?"

"You know there was never any question about that. I just haven't decided when yet. But I may as well do the studies. They run for months, and I'll have to do it before I marry."

"And Timothy? Does he want you to attend this year's sessions?"

"*Ya*, he does. He's already told his family that he's ready. You know *Mam* and *Dat* want me to make the commitment, to the church and Timothy. They say it's time I quit running around and grow up." She gave a little smile as she slid back over and buckled her seat belt. "I think they think you're a bad influence on me."

"Maybe I am," Rachel agreed. "I don't want to be. And I do hope I'm mistaken about Bishop Abner. But he didn't tell me the truth about staying home on Saturday night, and when people aren't truthful, you can't help but be suspicious." She offered her cousin a smile. "Besides, we did some good work last summer, didn't we? When we went to New Orleans looking for Hannah Verkler?" She looked both ways and pulled out onto the road again.

"I suppose, but no one was threatening you then. And I wasn't risking accusing the bishop of murder."

"You aren't doing that now," Rachel soothed. "You're just riding in the Jeep with me."

Mary Aaron cut her eyes at Rachel. "And why is that?"

"For moral support. And for protection. If someone comes after me, they'll have two of us to get the better of. The odds are all in our favor."

"Gambling odds, maybe. And you know that gambling is a sin. Or have you forgotten everything you learned in church?"

"Not everything. I promise. And I won't accuse anyone of anything, least of all Bishop Abner. Not unless there are solid facts to back me up."

"Why doesn't that make me feel any less worried?"

Neither one of them said any more until they reached the Chupp farm. Rachel pulled up into the yard beside the barn and was disappointed to see that the spot where the family buggy usually stood in the carriage shed was vacant. In fact, no one seemed to be around.

"They're away," Mary Aaron said. "See, this wasn't meant to be."

"Go up to the house and knock on the door."

Mary Aaron shook her head. "Nobody's home. If you want to walk through all this mud and slush in the yard, *you* go knock on the door."

Rachel grimaced, climbed out, and made her way to the back step. Melting water and mud oozed up over her shoes and soaked her stockings. She rapped hard several times, with no answer.

Mary Aaron put down her window and called out, "Told you so."

"Know-it-all," Rachel called back, stuffing her hands in her pockets for warmth.

Rachel was halfway back to the Jeep when she heard a deep male voice call, "Kucha, Kucha, Kucha."

"Sammy? Is that you?" Rachel called. A moment later, Sammy's red face appeared in a barn window. He looked as though he might be in distress.

"Sammy, is something wrong?" She continued on to the freshly painted Dutch door on the side of the barn. "Sammy, it's Rachel."

Sammy trudged out of the shadows. "Can't find Kucha," he mumbled.

"Your cake? You've lost your cake?" she asked in Deitsch. And then, "Is the bishop here?"

"*Ne.*" His nose was running and both eyes were red. "Can't find Kucha. He's hiding."

"Maybe I can help," she suggested. "But I don't know Kucha. What is he?"

"My new *katz*, silly. He got lost."

"Oh." She smiled at the realization that he'd named his cat Kucha, the Amish word for cake. "Does he live in the barn with the other cats?" Rachel asked. The last time she was here, she'd seen lots of cats. Most farmers kept them to keep down the rat population.

"*Ne*. Kucha lives in a tree." Sammy giggled. "In the windmill." More chuckling. "In the buggy."

"Is he a real *katz* or make-believe?" Rachel asked.

Sammy giggled. "Make-believe. He can fly."

"Oh." She smiled. "Then why are you crying?"

"Not crying." He rubbed his eyes again.

She studied the big man for a moment; he definitely looked as if he'd been crying. "Will the bishop be home soon?"

"*Ya*. Soon."

She glanced at the house, thinking it odd that they had left Sammy at home alone. "Did Naamah go, too, Sammy?"

He shook his head and put a big finger to his lips. "Shhhh. Sleeping. Don't wake her unless there's fire or blood. That's what she says."

Rachel had to smile. Her mother used to say the same thing. Her mother used to grab a catnap sometimes, too, or at least lie down for a couple of minutes on busy days. "Sammy," she began softly, "can I ask you something? Did you lose your hat on Saturday? Maybe you left it at the frolic? Or at the ice rink?"

"*Ne*. Aunt Naamah says, 'Don't forget your hat, Sammy.'" He grinned at her. "Kucha stole it. But it's too big. Silly Kucha."

Rachel tried not to feel impatient; she knew Sammy couldn't help how he was. "Sammy, did you go to town on Sunday morning? It would have been visiting day. Did you see the dead Englisher on the porch?"

"Saw a goat. Two goats. And a pig. Sunday is church. No goats in church." He wagged a finger at her. "Don't leave your hat in church."

"You don't remember if you lost your hat? And my brother brought it back to you?"

"I have my hat." He pulled the hand-knit black wool beanie down tightly over his ears. "I didn't lose my hat. Got it right here." He frowned. "But I can't find Kucha."

Rachel knew when she was beaten and she sighed. "I hope you find your cat," she said, walking back to the Jeep. "I'm sure he's here somewhere, playing with the other cats. He'll be back at milking time." As she got in on the driver's side, she wondered if Sammy would tell the bishop that she'd come to the farm and asked him questions. And if he did, how would Abner react? An innocent man would probably think nothing of it, but what about a man with something to hide?

Rachel started the engine. "I talked to Sammy," she told Mary Aaron. "Abner's out. Naamah is in the house napping."

"And did you learn anything about the hat from Sammy?"

"What do you think?" Rachel put the Jeep into reverse and slowly backed up to turn around. And as she did, she noticed the movement of a white curtain on the second floor. For just an instant, she thought she glimpsed a face behind the glass. But then it was gone, leaving her to wonder if it had been just her imagination.

At two fifty, Rachel was at the horse-drawn sleigh staging area. Elaine Dorsey and her cameraman hadn't arrived yet, but as Moses had predicted, John Hannah was putting on his best performance for the other reporters and the tourists. There was also a cluster of giggly Amish teenage girls whispering in Deitsch and admiring the roan and white horses and their driver. Evan was nowhere in sight. She'd sent him several text messages, none of which he'd answered. She hoped he hadn't forgotten the event because if he didn't show, she was going to feel foolish.

"Miss Mast?"

It was a reporter from one of the Harrisburg newspapers, a baby-faced man who'd written a particularly explicit piece about a tragic buggy-and-truck collision the previous fall. She ignored him and checked her phone again. *Come on, Evan,* she urged silently. *Don't let me down.* If he'd been too busy to keep the commitment, the least he could have done was to let her know so that she could make a respectable excuse. She quickly sent yet another text.

**WHERE ARE YOU?**

Evan's text messages were always in lowercase. He hated it when people used all caps. Another news crew showed up. The minutes ticked by. She turned to the horses and stroked their broad heads and soft, velvety faces. Rachel heard the faint whir of a camera. John Hannah struck a pose and grinned for the evening news. "Show-off," she teased in Deitsch. He chuckled and spoke soothingly to the team.

Rachel glanced at her phone again. What if Evan had gotten her messages and simply decided to ignore them? Was he completely fed up with her? She sighed to herself. Maybe things really were over between them and she just wasn't seeing it yet. But if he really didn't want to be with her anymore, would he come out and say it? It would only be fair. But how fairly had she been treating him? He was right; she should have told him about the conviction before their relationship had gotten this far.

She needed to tell him exactly what had happened . . . why she had pled no contest to the charge of insider trading. She owed him that much. Even if their engagement was permanently off, she valued his friendship. It would be better to have no more secrets between them.

She needed to find the right time to tell him, though, and right now didn't seem like the right time. Not now, when he was already so stressed about this murder case. The same went for the note. She'd tell him, but maybe not tonight. Because honestly, what would be the point? It was not as if he was going to haul every man and woman who had been in the gym today to the troop for a handwriting analysis.

There was a flurry of motion in the gathering of onlookers. The group parted, and Elaine and her cameraman hurried toward the sleigh and team. A third man followed close on the cameraman's heels, carrying a light on the end of a pole.

"Rachel!" Elaine called. "Sorry to be late. Where is . . ." She glanced around and then beamed. "There's our Detective Parks."

Rachel saw Evan's sturdy form striding from the direction of the ice rink and gave a sigh of relief. He hadn't left her alone at the mercy of the wolves. She looked back at John Hannah and said in Deitsch, "Here he comes. We can get this dog and pony show rolling."

John Hannah only grinned and gathered up the reins in a gloved hand.

"Detective!" Baby-Face blocked Evan's path, raised a small camera, and snapped off a quick shot. "Any progress on the William Billingsly murder?"

Evan threw up a hand to shield his face. "No comment," he said brusquely.

"Any new leads?" another reporter asked. Two more closed in on him. "The public has a right to know what our police—"

"I said, no comment." Evan looked up and met Rachel's gaze, his expression grim.

Rachel took a step toward him.

"Detective—" someone else shouted.

"Our public information officer will make a statement at a later time, as yet to be announced," Evan said. "Until that time, this is an active investigation, and I'm not at liberty to discuss it."

"But Detective Parks—" It was Baby-Face again, pressing through the throng, raising his camera for another photo.

"Nothing more at this time," Evan declared.

# Chapter 15

"I was afraid you weren't coming," Rachel whispered to Evan when they were settled into the backseat of the sleigh. She tucked a royal blue blanket up around them and smiled at Elaine as her cameraman and lighting tech adjusted their equipment.

"Thought about it," Evan admitted, keeping his voice down so no one could hear him but Rachel. Not even John Hannah. "No time for this stuff. Too many reporters here to suit me. I wouldn't have come if I'd known I was going to get grilled about the Billingsly investigation."

Rachel leaned close and turned her face away from the by-standers and toward him. "I wasn't expecting it either. I'm so sorry. It was just supposed to be a fluffy publicity piece for the festival." When he didn't answer, she asked, "Are you doing okay?"

His face was expressionless. "Not particularly."

Elaine approached the side of the sled, her white dress boots splashing through the slush. "I understand congratulations are in order," she said to Evan. "Have the two of you set a date?"

Evan glanced at Rachel and then at Elaine. "I'm afraid that's another *no comment*, Ms. Dorsey. We're still in the planning stages. And I'd appreciate it if you'd keep that information about our engagement confidential." He bestowed his most charming look on her. "We haven't shared the news with our families yet, and we wouldn't want any hurt feelings."

Elaine returned his smile. "I understand, Detective Parks. And with the investigation ongoing, I'm sure you have a good deal on your mind." The cameraman said something to her that Rachel couldn't make out, and then Elaine said, "We're hoping to get this first part in one take. We thought maybe you could take the sleigh out and we could get the shot as you ride back in. Then we can do the actual interview. Does that work for you?"

"Of course," Rachel agreed. "Whatever you think works best."

Elaine motioned to John Hannah and then toward the snow-covered athletic fields. "Could you drive the horses out into the field and then bring the sleigh back again?"

"*Ya.*" John Hannah nodded. "I can do that." He tugged his hat down, exchanged glances with his admiring Amish contingency, and took the leathers in hand. Pulling back on the reins, he got the big horses' heads up and then guided them in a tight circle to the approving comments of the crowd.

The powerful animals pulled the light sleigh easily, quickly passing through the slush of the immediate area and out onto the open field and the expanse of pristine snow. Beyond stretched the valley, stone fences, and the encircling mountains. Normally, Rachel would have been thrilled by the beauty of the moment, but not today. The unpleasant tension between her and Evan was so strong she could almost taste it. Worse, she didn't know how to fix it.

Once the sleigh and horses were well away from the cameras, Evan, who obviously felt as uneasy as she did, slid a few inches away on the seat. "I went to see Blade Finch this afternoon," he said, his voice low. "Apparently, he had to leave town on an *important* errand. His wife says he won't be home until this evening." He glanced at her, held her gaze for a moment, and then frowned. "But you already knew that, didn't you?" He exhaled, shaking his head, and looked away. "Rachel." He sounded so . . . disappointed in her.

She felt bad and she didn't even know why. "I *did* know, but only because I saw Coyote at the gym this morning and she told me."

She wondered if she should rethink showing him the note she'd found on her windshield that morning. Would it be better to tell him for the sake of not withholding any more information, or would it be better to try and find out who had left it first? Whoever left the message on her car wanted her to stop asking questions, but that didn't mean the murderer had left it. Mary Aaron had said the Amish were talking about her asking questions about the buggy that had been parked at Wagler's and about the missing hat. Anyone could have left it, even a prankster.

"I don't know what to say, Rachel," Evan continued. "I've asked you not to interfere in the case, but clearly you've chosen to ignore me." He exhaled. "This isn't a game. A man died, and if we don't find who killed him . . ."

He left the rest unfinished as John Hannah swung the team in a giant arc and urged them into a high-stepping gait.

"You think I don't know a man died?" she whispered. "Remember, I was there that morning. I saw what was left of him." She shuddered at the thought.

Again, Evan was silent. The sleigh bells jingled, the air was crisp on Rachel's cheeks, and snow crunched under the sleigh runners. Elaine Dorsey was right. It probably made a romantic picture for the TV cameras, but Rachel's heart was anything but light. She forced herself to appear as though she were having the time of her life, when she wanted to cry. "I'm so sorry, Evan. I'm not trying to interfere."

"Aren't you? Because that's how it looks to me. We were supposed to be a team, Rache, but it seems like you want to be out front. And where does that leave me? If you're going to disregard a simple request—"

"I know we need to talk. But not here, and not in front of the cameras. We need to straighten out these misunderstandings. Miscommunications."

"I thought we'd done that at your kitchen table last night, but we keep hitting the same wall."

She didn't say anything. She didn't know what to say. He was right. She was right. They were both right. And both wrong, she surmised.

"I'll call you tonight if I can." Taking out his cell phone, he glanced down at it, scrolling through his messages.

"Promise?" she asked.

"No, I'm not going to promise. I've got a meeting at the troop with my superiors in half an hour. It might be a long night. But I'll try to call." He slid closer and put an arm around her shoulders as John Hannah brought the team back to the starting point. Evan brushed her cheek with his lips, climbed down, and strode off, paying no attention to the reporters calling questions.

Fifteen minutes later she was done with the interview, which was a good thing because John Hannah had a line of visitors waiting to take a ride on the horse-drawn sleigh.

One couple, a Mr. and Mrs. Washington from Richmond, waved to her. Elaine noticed them and beckoned them over and asked if she could ask them a few questions for the evening news. They heartily agreed, and when she inquired about their interest in Stone Mill and the festival, Mr. Washington gave a sterling review of both the town and Rachel's B&B. "We've loved it," he pronounced. "We'll certainly recommend this as a destination for our friends. I wish we'd brought our girls. We don't have Amish near our home, and this has been a wonderful opportunity to get to learn about the history and the culture."

"Not to mention the shopping," his wife added.

Elaine wrapped up the piece with another shot of children waving from the sleigh and waited for her cameraman and technicians to pack up. "I won't say a word about your coming nuptials," she said to Rachel. "But I'd appreciate a heads-up on the murder investigation, once an arrest is made."

"I'll do what I can," Rachel promised. "Now, if you'll excuse me, I have some other commitments. Our cook-off is coming up on Saturday, and we're flooded with entries."

"The piece should air on the ten o'clock evening news," Elaine said. "And again tomorrow morning and again at noon if we're lucky. Good luck with your cook-off."

Rachel thanked her and hurried away, all too grateful to escape before something else went wrong.

Inside the gym, things were humming. Rachel collected her clipboard from the information desk, checked in with her assistant in charge of her booth, and began making the rounds of the other stalls to see if anyone needed anything. There were several small snags that needed unraveling, one ruffled mother who'd misplaced her twins, and some overflowing trash cans that she emptied herself rather than tracking down one of the two Amish teens she'd hired for cleanup.

Before Rachel knew it, nearly two hours had passed, and she needed to get home in time to feed the goats and chickens. Some days her brothers were able to help, but Wednesdays, Fridays, and Sundays, she was on her own with the evening chores. There were lights in the barn, but she liked to get the livestock cared for before dusk. When she was growing up, her father had taught her it was only right to feed others, including animals, before sitting down to eat yourself.

The afternoon light was fading when Rachel crossed the parking lot and spotted Abner Chupp standing next to her Jeep. She wondered how long he'd been waiting in the cold for her; his nose was bright red. "Bishop Abner," she said in an attempt to smooth over what she was sure was going to be another unpleasant interlude. "I stopped to see you this afternoon, but you were—"

"What's gotten into you, Rachel?" he cut her off harshly. "What do you think you're doing? Where are your manners?

I know you know better. I know your parents taught you better." He shook a gloved finger accusingly in her face.

She couldn't remember the last time she'd seen Abner lose his temper, but he was angry now. And he was obviously angry with her. "I . . ." she began, but he rushed on.

"You can't come to my home and question Sammy about me and where I am. What were you thinking? You know how Sammy is. He doesn't know what he should and shouldn't say."

Now Rachel was taken aback by the bishop's words and behavior. They seemed over-the-top for what she'd done. After all, she'd only asked Sammy where he was. He could have been at the blacksmith's. She hadn't meant to pry into the private business of his parishioners. "Bishop Abner—"

"I'm not done," he interrupted. "Not only did you ask for information that isn't any of your business, but you've upset my wife terribly. You know how protective she is of Sammy. She's very disappointed in you, and so am I."

Rachel glanced around, hoping that no one was near enough to hear what Abner was saying. She didn't think anyone was, but across the parking lot, an Amish family was looking their way. No one had to hear the words to know that Abner was unhappy. His body language showed that plainly.

"You know very well," Abner continued his tirade, "that much of what a bishop does in our community is private. No one should ask where I'm going or when I will be home. Not even my wife. Naamah and I have befriended you when many of our people thought you should be cut out of our community. I have defended you for your worldly ways, and this is how you repay us?" He shook his head in disgust. "Naamah is beside herself. Sammy was quite upset by whatever you said to him. In tears, she said."

"I didn't mean to upset Sammy . . . or Naamah," Rachel protested. "I stopped to speak to you, but Sammy said you were gone. That was all he said. And Naamah was in the house. I never spoke to her at all. And I didn't make Sammy cry. He couldn't find his cat. That's why he was upset."

"*Ne*. No excuses. I know what you are doing. You are playing a game of policeman with your English boyfriend. Three times you come to my house, questioning my integrity, demanding to know personal information." Again, he raised his finger to her. "I won't have it. It's not acceptable for a member of my church, and even less for you who have left your faith for the world."

"What I'm doing is for our community. I'm not accusing anyone of anything, least of all you. And all I did was ask Sammy—"

"What? You expect a boy touched by God to give you answers about an evil crime? An innocent who cannot remember what boot goes on what foot? You expect a sensible answer from Sammy?" Bishop Abner was so irate and standing so close that tiny beads of spittle sprayed her face.

The injustice of his fury, however, had the opposite effect of what the bishop expected. Instead of breaking into tears, Rachel's own anger rose. If Abner was already this furious with her, what harm could it do to ask him the answer to the question she'd come seeking in the first place? "I understand that you once were involved with an English woman in this town. Are you still seeing her, Bishop Abner? Is that what you're hiding?"

The older man's face twisted. "You have no right to ask such a question of me," he said. "Didn't our Lord say, 'Let he who is without sin cast the first stone'?" He stepped back away from her, hands splayed. "I must be honest with you. I am concerned for your soul, Rachel Mast." His voice dropped to a harsh whisper. "You are always welcome in my church or in my home, but you may never, *ever* speak to me in such a disrespectful manner again."

That night when Evan called, after ten, Rachel was still going over in her head the conversation she'd had with Abner. She couldn't figure out if the conversation was exactly what it had appeared to be, that she really had stepped over the line, or if the good bishop really did have something to hide.

"Evan. Hi."

She waited for his familiar "Rache," but it didn't come. Instead, after a pause, he said, "Finch didn't come home. I just spoke to his wife. She said he was *delayed*. Now she doesn't expect him until late tomorrow. Did you already know that, too?"

"No. I assumed he was home." Rachel sat up, swinging her bare feet over the edge of the bed. She'd been just drifting off, and she wasn't completely awake. "Did she say why?"

"A delay at the shop he went to. Then bad weather. He decided to stay the night somewhere. It sounded flimsy," Evan admitted. "And he won't return my calls to his cell. What if Coyote's covering for him and he's on the run? He could be halfway across the country by morning. Our Mr. Finch has a record of being a tough customer. He'll have connections."

"Don't assume that Blade's deceiving you," she said. "It could all be true. I know this family, Evan. I can't imagine that he'd ever leave her and the children, and I don't see him as a killer."

"Not even when you know that he killed before?"

"People change, Evan. I don't think that Blade's the man he was before he met Coyote . . . before he opened his heart to God. He might be capable of violence to protect his wife and children, but not over money."

"I hope you're right. But don't be too quick to overlook Blade's past. He wouldn't be the first jailhouse convert to religion. I know sometimes it sticks, but you'd be naïve not to realize that sometimes it doesn't."

"He's not like that," she insisted.

"I have to go with the evidence, Rachel." He was quiet for a second. "Is Skinner still at your place?"

She sighed. She'd seen him that evening on her way up to bed. He'd tipped his hat to her. "He is still here, but there's something about him . . . I still think he's hiding something."

"Isn't everyone?" Evan asked.

Again, she thought about the note, the paper now lying only an arm's reach away on her nightstand. "I guess by that you mean me," she said.

"You should have told me you had a record."

Guilt suffused her, and she bit her lower lip. "It was wrong of me," she said. "You're absolutely right. I should have told you. But when? At first, we were friends, and then . . . then things started to get serious between us. I was afraid that if you knew what I'd done, you wouldn't give me a chance. It's like I said about Blade. People change. I don't pretend I haven't done things that I'm ashamed of, but I've grown up. I think I understand more about what's right and wrong. I'm not that foolish young woman anymore."

There was silence on his end.

She hesitated. She really didn't want to lose Evan. It had taken her a long time to realize that, but she really did love him. "Can you come over, Evan? I want to tell you what happened, but not on the phone. It shouldn't be over the phone," she said softly.

Again, he was quiet for a moment. "Not tonight, Rachel. I just can't. I've got a lot to finish up here before the start of shift in the morning. I—" He stopped and started again. "I think we should table this discussion until the Billingsly case is solved. The truth is, Rache, I'm getting pressure from higher-ups to bring my primary suspects in for questioning. You may want to think about getting legal representation."

Her mouth went dry. "Me? You think I need a lawyer?"

"I think you'd be a fool not to have one if I do have to bring you in. And you're no fool."

"Are you going to say the same to Blade?"

Evan sighed. "If he can't give me a reliable alibi for Saturday night, yes. Like it or not, you, Blade Finch, and Jake Skinner are my only persons of interest right now. I can't bring them in without treating you the same way. There's already been talk of pulling me off the case because of my conflict of interest."

She felt light-headed. If Evan took her in to the troop, if she was questioned, people would find out. How long would it be before her past record became public knowledge? People wouldn't understand. Something like this could ruin her reputation in Stone Mill. She felt like she was about to burst into tears. "I didn't kill him, Evan."

"How many times do I have to tell you I believe you?" he asked. "Have you not heard anything I've been saying? I don't believe you killed Billingsly, but I have to follow the evidence, and the evidence suggests that you could have murdered him."

She could hear the emotion in his voice, almost see the pained expression on his face. *He's a good man,* she thought. *If I lose him, I may never meet anyone to match him.* But maybe it wasn't up to her anymore. Maybe she'd already lost him. The words *I love you* formed on her lips, but she couldn't say them. Again, this wasn't the right time.

"So let's table this for now because I'm not ready to give up on us yet and I don't think you are either. But I have this investigation," he said. "You have the rest of the frolic to attend to. We're both carrying a heavy load, and neither of us is at our best. There will be time later to work this out between us."

"I want to," she said.

"Me, too."

She rose from the bed and padded across the cold floor in her bare feet. Finding her slippers, she slid her feet into them. "This probably isn't the right time for this, but I have to ask you. I know you went through Billingsly's files, the stuff he was intending to run in his column. Did you find anything about an affair between an Amish man from the community and an English woman?"

Evan's reply was firm. "I couldn't tell you if I had and you know it."

She sighed. She had expected him to say that. In fact, she would probably have been disappointed if he'd answered otherwise. "I've found out something about an old scandal involving an important member of the Amish—"

"Rachel, isn't that what we've been arguing about? You trying to do my job."

"I didn't realize we were arguing."

"Right. Maybe that's the real problem. We're not speaking the same language."

"I only thought that it might be—"

"You don't give up, do you?" He stopped and started again. "This isn't getting us anywhere. We're going in circles. I'm tired; you're tired. I need to go. How about if we see what tomorrow brings? But I'm serious about the attorney. If I do have to take you in, don't say anything more to me or to anyone until you've hired a lawyer. Okay?"

"Okay," she repeated.

His tone softened. "Good night, kiddo. Talk to you tomorrow."

"Good night, Evan . . . I love you." But her last words were too late. He'd already disconnected. "I do," she murmured. "I love you, and I'm so, so sorry."

Sleep wouldn't come. Another hot shower didn't help and neither did two cups of warm, honey-sweetened herbal tea. She finally drifted off into dreams sometime after three a.m.

The incessant ring of the house phone cut through her muddled fantasies. She forced her eyes open, and light rushed in. What time was it? She tried to think. Was that her landline? She recovered her cell phone from the nightstand. Two missed calls? From a number she didn't recognize. She climbed unsteadily out of bed and made her way to the table where her landline phone stood.

"Stone Mill B&B," she said groggily.

It was Mary Aaron's hoarse voice on the other end. "Rae-Rae. I've been trying to reach you."

"What's wrong?" Rachel could hear the panic in Mary

Aaron's tone. "Where are you calling from?" Rachel wondered again what time it was. She must have overslept.

"A friend's cell. Rachel, you have to get over to Bishop Abner's house right away. There's been a terrible accident."

"Who? Wha—"

Mary Aaron cut her off. "It's bad. Really bad. Hurry, Rachel. We need you!"

# Chapter 16

By the time Rachel arrived at the Chupps' home, the road leading to the bishop's house was already lined with buggies. Two Amish men crossed a snowy field and climbed through a fence as she watched, and more Plain folk were walking toward the house. Rather than adding more confusion to the barnyard, Rachel parked at the edge of the road and hurried up the lane that led to the house. An ambulance and a single state police car stood in the yard. She caught a glimpse of uniforms amid the throng of black Amish clothing. Rachel didn't need to have been told that something dreadful had happened here this morning. The air seemed to smell of sorrow and tragedy.

A familiar figure broke from the crowd in front of the barn and ran toward her. "Rachel!" Mary Aaron threw herself into Rachel's arms and the two embraced. Her cousin's face was strained and damp with tears, her eyes bloodshot and swollen. "It's terrible," she managed.

"What happened?" Rachel peered over Mary Aaron's shoulder, attempting to see. Through the milling group she saw a stretcher and someone lying prone on the snow-covered slush, a sheet covering the whole body. Emergency responders only covered the faces of dead people. Her first thought was that Abner had committed suicide. He had realized Rachel had too much evidence against him and ended his life. "Tell me," she whispered, looking into Mary Aaron's teary eyes.

"Sammy," Mary Aaron choked. "He fell out of the hayloft and broke his neck. He's dead, Rae-Rae. Sammy Zook is dead."

Rachel frowned, struggling to understand. "But that doesn't make any sense. Sammy would never go up into the hayloft. He was terrified of heights. Are they sure that's what happened?"

Mary Aaron pulled away from her and wiped her nose with a handkerchief. "Of course, that's what happened. They found him dead right there under the open door." She pointed to the swinging door high on the second floor, through which bales of hay and straw were loaded.

Rachel stared up at the red door that was flung open, then down at Sammy's body covered with the white sheet. "What was he doing up there?" Something wasn't right. Rachel knew it immediately. Something didn't ring true. Why would Sammy climb up in the loft and open the loft door? It had to be a good fifteen feet off the ground. And to fall out, Sammy would have had to venture right to the doorsill. It wasn't logical.

"What difference does it make why he was up there?" Mary Aaron said. "We all knew that Sammy wasn't smart." She twisted the handkerchief in her hands. "Naamah and Bishop Abner are devastated. How are they going to tell Sammy's mother?" Fresh tears ran down her cheeks.

Rachel heard the metallic click of the ambulance door opening. An English woman's authoritarian voice cut through the murmur of conversations. "Can we get everyone to move back, please?" They were putting his body on the stretcher now, to take away in the ambulance.

Mary Aaron turned toward the house. "They need someone to take Naamah to Sammy's parents'. The policewoman offered, but Naamah says she won't get into the car. I called you because I was hoping you could take her."

As the two of them reached the back step, Rachel glanced back to see the medics loading Sammy's body into the vehicle. The door closed, and the men got in. The driver slowly turned the ambulance around. As they pulled away out of the yard, there was only the crunch of snow and ice under the tires. They didn't bother to use the siren.

"Miss Mast?" A tall female trooper crossed the yard to the back door.

Rachel recognized her. Lucy Mars, who'd responded to the Billingsly death. And now this. Her face was pale, and lines around her eyes etched deep into her face. Rachel felt a wave of pity for her. This wasn't a good week for Trooper Mars.

"I understand that Mrs. Chupp wants someone to drive her to the boy's family to notify them," the policewoman explained. "It's really my job to notify the next of kin, but . . ."

"I can do it," Rachel offered. "Naamah and the Zooks will be more at ease if I drive her."

"I'll have to accompany you in my own car," Trooper Mars said. "I can be ready in a few minutes, if that suits. I have a few details to finish up here first."

"No problem," Rachel answered. She put her hand on the doorknob. "You can follow in your police car. Just keep it as low-key as you can." Trooper Mars nodded, obviously glad to have someone else sharing the onerous task of bringing the worst kind of news to the Zook family. Rachel hesitated, stepping aside so that Mary Aaron could go into the house ahead of her. She looked into the trooper's face. "Can you tell me exactly what happened to Sammy?"

Trooper Mars met her gaze. "Such a shame, these farming accidents. The victim fell from the loft window. He landed wrong. There will be an autopsy, naturally, but I assume he simply broke his neck." An expression of slight discomfort passed over her features. "Am I correct in assuming that Mr. Zook had some sort of learning challenges?"

"Yes, that's correct. Do you know what he was doing in the loft?"

"Bishop Chupp stated that Sammy went out before breakfast looking for his cat," the trooper replied. "It was just an accident."

"Yes, it must have been," Rachel agreed. She offered a tight smile to the trooper, then followed Mary Aaron into Naamah's kitchen. Through the archway, Rachel could see the men in the parlor. Again, as always, the menfolk were clustered together in one area and women in another.

The kitchen was packed with women of all ages, young children, and babies. Already pies, cakes, and platters of cooked ham were beginning to line the counters and fill up the table and stove top. Where had the food come from? Rachel wondered. Surely no one had time to cook before rushing over to comfort the grieving Chupps.

But this was the tradition, the way it had always been. In times of loss, neighbors and friends brought baked goods, casseroles, and meat so that those who were suffering would not be further burdened by kitchen chores. Likewise, men and boys would show up unbidden to milk the cows, tend the horses, feed the chickens, and gather the eggs. Visitors would come and remain with the family, staying to help lay out the deceased and then sit watch over the body. They would share memories and prayers, and they would help to fill the void that death brought until the dead were placed into the ground, passing on from the trials of this world to the comfort of the next. It was the Amish way, one that had not changed in Rachel's lifetime, in that of her mother, or her grandmother, customs that she strongly suspected would not be altered in another three hundred years.

Naamah sat woodenly at the table, tears running down her stunned face, surrounded by women, mutely accepting their sympathy and whispered words of comfort. Bits and pieces of conversation drifted over the heads of the gathering.

". . . God's will."

". . . A good boy, a credit to his family."

"One of the Lord's special children."

"Such a loss for his mother."

"And for you and the bishop."

". . . Praying for you."

Aunt Hannah was at the sink making a fresh pot of coffee. Cups clinked. Milk was poured for children, space made for a nursing mother to feed her infant. Someone placed a cup of tea into Rachel's hand, and she realized with a start that it was her sister Annie. "Such a shame," Annie murmured.

Rachel nodded. "Is *Mam* here?" She'd been certain she'd heard her father's voice in the farmyard. She hadn't seen him, but she was sure that it had been him.

"*Ne,*" Annie answered. "*Dat* and Amanda and I came over together. *Mam* wasn't feeling good this morning. *Dat* told her to stay home and keep warm and he'd bring her over later."

"Annie? Can you get those cinnamon twists out of the oven?" Aunt Hannah called.

"*Ya.*" Annie glanced back at Rachel, taking in the denim skirt. "You'll need a proper dress for the funeral. That's pretty awful."

"I know," Rachel murmured. "But it's all I could find in a hurry."

"Come by the house," Annie said. "We're about the same size. I'll give you one of mine."

Mary Aaron signaled to her, and Rachel saw her opportunity to speak to Naamah. "I'm so sorry," Rachel said, approaching her.

"I wanted him to have his breakfast," Naamah was saying. "A cold morning. He needed his breakfast. I made him scrapple. But he ran out the door. He was looking for his cat, that gray cat. He left before . . ." Her lower lip quivered. "Didn't even stop to put on his hat. Poor Sammy. So young. And now I have to tell his mother that . . ." A sob wracked her body, and she covered her face with her broad, work-worn hands.

Rachel hugged her. "I'm so sorry," she said. "I'll be glad to drive you to your sister's farm so you can tell her that her boy's gone to heaven."

"It would be a kindness," Naamah said. "I would appreciate it." She glanced around, seeming disoriented. "When should we go?"

"Whenever you feel up to it," Rachel assured her. "You've had a shock."

"Where are the extra mugs?" someone called.

"Naamah keeps them in the pantry," Aunt Hannah said. "You can't miss them." And then to Rachel, she said, "Could you take coffee to the bishop?"

"Of course." Her aunt passed her a steaming mug of black coffee, and Rachel carefully made her way through the women. She saw Abner standing in the doorway, a hat in his hand.

"He wasn't my blood relative," Abner was telling one of his parishioners, "but I felt like he was." He looked down at the hat, turning it aimlessly between his hands. "If only I'd not taken so long at my morning prayers. Maybe I—" He glanced up, noticed Rachel, and hung the hat on the back of a chair. "Rachel. How good of you to come." He moved toward her. "Your father tells me that you've offered to take Naamah to Sammy's mother's. How can I thank you"—he lowered his voice— "especially after yesterday?" Abner's eyes were red and swollen, and Rachel felt a stab of guilt as she met his gaze.

She looked at the hat, wondering.

"*Ya*," Abner said. "That was his. Poor child. Poor lost lamb."

"But in the Lord's hands now," one of the men said.

Bishop Abner nodded. "I pray so."

"At least he didn't suffer." That was Rachel's father's voice. "We can be grateful for that much."

And the deacon's soft rasp: "God's will be done."

"I'm sorry if I seemed harsh yesterday," Bishop Abner began.

Rachel shook her head. "No need for that. I should never

have . . ." She trailed off, feeling terrible that she'd ever suspected this good man of committing the crime of murder. Maybe Mary Aaron was right. Maybe she was too suspicious. And maybe she should leave the investigation to Evan and the professionals. She handed Abner the cup, and he took it, careful not to spill the hot liquid.

"Thank you, Rachel," Bishop Abner said to her.

"If there's anything else I can do for you and Naamah . . ."

"Keep us and Sammy in your prayers," he replied.

"Always," she promised.

Several hours later, Rachel pulled her Jeep into the parking lot of Wagler's Grocery. It had been an awful morning, first the shock of Sammy's death and then the trip to the Zook farm. As promised, she'd driven Naamah and Abner to Sammy's parents' home and witnessed the family's grief. Rachel had expected that it would be just Naamah who would go to carry the tragic news, but Abner had insisted he go with her. And because of his position as a respected spiritual leader, he'd been able to support not only his wife but also Sammy's closest relatives.

Although she was no longer a part of the Old Order Amish church, she couldn't help being touched by the way that Naamah, Abner, and Sammy's parents and brothers and sisters relied on the strength of their religion and their absolute acceptance that Sammy was safe in heaven. In spite of his own grief, Abner seemed to search in his heart for exactly the right words that would provide solace and use them to soothe the pain his wife and the others were experiencing.

Seeing Bishop Abner's steadfastness and faith, hearing his words of hope and the promise that they would be with Sammy again in a better place, made her feel intense shame that she'd suspected him of evil. As Mary Aaron had said, Abner was a man of God, a truly good person, who couldn't possibly have killed Billingsly, no matter how much he deserved it. What kind of person was she that she could so misjudge Abner? How could she have been so wrong?

Yet in the midst of her self-castigation and waves of guilt, Rachel couldn't quite silence the small voice at the back of her mind. Something still didn't fit. Like a puzzle with a misshaped piece, the thought nagged her. Why would Sammy, terrified of heights, have climbed into the hayloft? And once there, even if he was searching for his lost cat, what would make him unhook the heavy iron latch and open the loft door? And if he did swing the door open, why would he have ventured to the opening?

Her cell buzzed and she picked up. Evan was on the other end.

"I just heard about Sammy Zook," he said. "I'm sorry, Rache. How terrible for the community." His voice conveyed the gentle compassion that had first drawn her to Evan, and she couldn't help wondering if she deserved him. She certainly hadn't acted like it lately. "I understand that you took Bishop Abner and his wife out to inform the boy's parents."

"Yes," she said. "It was awful."

"Not much worse than having to relay news like that," he agreed. "I've had to do it more times than I care to admit and it never gets easier."

She rolled down the window, hoping that a breath of fresh air would clear her head. She felt awful, and in another minute or two, she'd be in tears, and she didn't want to do that. "Were you able to meet with Blade?" she asked, changing the subject. "He did get back, didn't he?"

"He's not. And his calls are still going to voicemail. I don't like it. I know the Finches are friends of yours, but Skinner is still in town and Blade isn't. I don't know how long I can wait before I take it to the next step."

"Just hold off as long as you can," she begged him. "Give him just a little more time. I've got a feeling about this."

"No promises, Rache. Got to go. Call me later."

"I will. Just trust me on this, Evan. Blade didn't do this. I know he didn't."

"Hope you're right." The line went dead.

Rachel sat there for a minute or two, attempting to get her thoughts in order, then left the Jeep and entered the grocery. She'd offered to make a pot of soup to take to Naamah and Abner's. The female trooper had assured Sammy's family that the autopsy wouldn't take long. It was simply a routine procedure after an accident. Once the body was released, it would be laid out in the Chupps' parlor. Mourners would view the deceased and join the family in prayer, so there would be many people needing to be fed. After a day and a night, Sammy would be carried by horse and wagon to the Amish cemetery and there interred with a simple wooden marker to mark the spot.

Among the Amish, death was accepted as natural. Sammy, an innocent and a member of the faith, would go home to be with the Lord. Once he was buried, community life would go on. He would be remembered by those who loved him, but there would be little mention of his passing. This earthly experience was simply a forerunner to the greater life in heaven.

Rachel took a basket from the stack by the door. She wasn't much of a cook, but she could put together a hearty soup. And she wanted to do something to ease Naamah and Abner's burden. She kept thinking about Sammy's tearstained face the last time she'd seen him. His death seemed so senseless—an overgrown child looking for his pet. If the world were just, Sammy's cat would have come running and he would be helping Abner with the chores rather than lying on a slab in the morgue. It was so unfair.

What would she need for her soup? The pantry at Stone Mill House was enormous and well stocked, but she wanted quick-cooking barley and celery. On second thought, she traded her basket for a small grocery cart. She always thought that she could get by with the basket and ended up filling it so full that it was difficult to carry. She found purple cabbage and was

just leaving the produce area when she spotted Sandy Millman at the lunch-meat counter. Eddie's mother.

"If you could make up a cheese tray and then one of ham,
salami, and roast beef. Your largest size trays, please," she
was telling the girl behind the counter. "Hulda asked that it
be delivered to Abner Chupp's home as soon as possible. She
said you'd just put it on her tab."

"Sandy!" Rachel pushed her cart toward her.

Sandy Millman, a hearty fiftyish woman dressed more like
a lumberjack than the manager of a store, turned away from
the counter and came toward her. "I just heard about poor
Sammy Zook," she said, making no attempt to keep her husky
voice down. "Tragic, isn't it?" Sandy's graying hair was drawn
back into a severe ponytail, and her broad, freckled face was
windburned. "My heart goes out to the Chupps. And the
Zooks as well. I don't know them as well as I do Naamah
and Abner, but I understand they're lovely people."

"It's so awful." Rachel shook her head. "It's hard to believe.
To think that something like this can happen so quickly."

"I know, I know." Sandy motioned toward the deli. "I was
just ordering some lunch-meat trays for the wake for Hulda
from all of us at Russell's. You know . . . just to let the families know we were thinking of them."

Rachel ran a hand along the top of her cart. "I feel the
same way. I was thinking of making a pot of soup." She hesitated, then said, "I wondered . . . Do you have a minute? To
talk?"

Sandy's pleasant face creased with obvious curiosity. "Sure.
I don't have long. I'm on my break. I just walked over to order
the platter. I'll be happy to help you if I can. You've always
been so nice to Eddie. Buying all those greeting cards and
popcorn from the scouts. Not everybody is so kind."

"I'm glad to help in any way I can," Rachel said.

They stepped out of the way of another shopper pushing a
cart. "Eddie's not throwing your paper in the bushes again, is
he?" Sandy asked.

"No, no, Eddie's great. He's a fine boy. Best paperboy I've ever had." In fact, Eddie was the only paperboy she'd ever had. But what she had to ask Sandy had nothing to do with the newspaper delivery.

"I'm glad. You've been so nice to him, especially Sunday. Calling me and all when Eddie . . . Letting him wait in the house until I could come for him. It was such a shock, what happened to Mr. Billingsly. Not something any mother wants her child to see." She shook her head. "I can't believe it. Months go by without a death in Stone Mill, and then, this week, two tragedies in a matter of days." She waved. "I'm sorry. I'm babbling. What did you want to talk to me about?"

"I don't mean to intrude on your privacy, but I'd like to ask you something personal."

"Sure, Rachel. Anything."

Rachel glanced around; she knew most of the people in the store, shoppers and employees, which meant Sandy did, too. "Maybe we could step outside?"

"This sounds serious."

"How about my Jeep? Where it will be warmer? I can give you a ride back to Russell's, if you like."

"What about your groceries?"

Rachel gave the cart a little push. "I'll leave it right here and come back for it. This will only take a minute."

"You sure?"

"Positive."

The big woman zipped up her coat and pulled mittens out of her pockets. "Lead the way."

Feeling somewhat self-conscious, Rachel walked out of the store and to her Jeep and motioned for Sandy to get in. "You may have heard that I've been talking to people around town." Rachel started the engine and blasted the heat. "Since Billingsly's . . ."

"Murder. Yes." Sandy nodded. "But I don't understand why you would want to ask me anything. I didn't really know him."

Her bulk filled the front seat of the Jeep in a way that Mary

Aaron's petite form never did. No one could ever have called Sandy Millman pretty, but there was a cheerful kindness about her that radiated goodwill.

"There's no nice way to ask this, so I'll just come out with it," Rachel said. She held her hands out to a heating vent blowing warm air. "I understand that you and Abner Chupp knew each other well at one time."

Sandy's cheeks flushed a pale rose. "It's not much of a secret. If you're asking me, you probably already know that we . . ." She hesitated. "That we were *involved*." She licked her bottom lip nervously. "But that was a long time ago."

"How long?" Rachel pressed.

A hurt expression flooded over her face. "Abner and Naamah have been married for ten years. I'd never . . . He'd never . . . Did someone say I was playing footsies with Abner? Because if they did, they lied to you."

"I'm sorry for prying into your private life." Rachel dropped her hands to her lap. "Believe me, I wouldn't if it wasn't important."

Sandy's gray eyes glistened with moisture. "Hulda thinks of you like a daughter. I know you wouldn't ask me about Abner without good reason." She sighed. "What is it that you want to know?"

"Can you tell me a little bit about you and him?"

Sandy huddled in her parka, arms wrapped tightly around herself. "It was a bad time for me. My husband had walked out on me. I had nothing. No car, no money, not even firewood to heat the cottage. The rent was two months overdue, and the utilities had been shut off. I didn't know where to turn." She looked up. "I never knew who my own father was, and I wasn't good about picking men. I married Leon to get out of my uncle's house. Out of the frying pan and into the fire. Those old sayings, there's a lot to them. I didn't expect much from Leon, and I didn't get much."

"He was a bad husband?" Rachel suggested.

Sandy raised two fingers to stroke the crooked bump in

her nose. "He had a bad temper, and when he was angry, he lashed out. He used his fists on me, and sometimes his boots. Believe me when I tell you that Abner Chupp saved my life. He gave me hope when I didn't have any, and he taught me that not all men are brutal. Abner showed me that I had more strength inside than I knew."

"I imagine he was lonely, too," Rachel said. "He'd lost a wife that he loved."

"We were both hurting. I'm not proud of what we did, but I'm not ashamed either. He would have married me if it wasn't for Leon. But Abner's church doesn't recognize divorce."

"And would you have become Amish? If you were free to choose?"

Sandy's mouth twisted into a wry smile. "In a heartbeat. But it was impossible. So, long story short, when I got pregnant, Hulda helped me out. We told people I was trying to reconcile with my husband and I left town for a year. When I came back, everyone assumed Eddie was my husband's and that things just hadn't worked out. Abner and I . . . we never saw each other intimately after I left."

"But Abner knew about Eddie?"

"Yes. Abner knew. We agreed to end it and that it was time for us both to move on. He made his peace with his church. I urged him to. If we couldn't be together, then I wanted him to be happy. We had to let it go. . . ." She swallowed.

"Does Eddie know that Abner is his father?"

Sandy shook her head. "No, he thinks his father is dead. Leon wrapped himself around a tree when Eddie was in kindergarten. I know only because Leon's cousin contacted me, wanting me to pay for the funeral. Eddie only knows Abner as a family friend. I'll have to tell him sometime, I suppose, but not yet. I hate to do it, you know. What if he hates me? He's all I've got."

"I saw them together at the ice rink, Abner and Eddie. I think the bishop must be proud of him, the fine young man he's become. You've done a wonderful job with him."

"I've tried my best," Sandy said with a shy smile. "But I still don't understand. What does any of this have to do with why you're asking me questions now? I haven't been alone with Abner since Eddie was born."

"You know that column of Billingsly's, 'Over the Back Fence'? He was causing a lot of trouble for people in this town with his malicious gossip, digging up old heartbreaks, creating scandals."

"What's that have to do with us?"

"Is it possible that Billingsly could have threatened Abner? That he intended to expose the secret about Eddie's birth? You can imagine what that would do to Abner's reputation. And to the Amish in this valley. Are you certain that Abner never hinted that Billingsly might do such a thing?"

"You think he threatened Abner? And that Abner killed him to keep him quiet?" Sandy scoffed. "Not possible. Not the man I knew and loved. I don't know who killed Billingsly. Whoever it was, it wasn't Abner Chupp. I'd bet my life on it."

# Chapter 17

It was after eight that evening when Rachel reached Evan's house. After buying groceries and going home to make soup, she'd spent what remained of the day with the Chupps, and she was exhausted. She hadn't taken the time to change her clothing when she'd arrived home, but she'd elected to walk to Evan's place rather than drive. She needed to clear her head and try to shake the bad feeling that her dear friend Abner had done something terribly wrong. Evan had reached her by cell and invited her over for grilled cheese on rye and canned tomato soup, his standard go-to supper when he'd had a hard day at work. She'd been so tired that she'd thought of begging off, just going home and crawling into bed. But she couldn't. She needed to talk to Evan, to ease the distance between them, and she had to share her fear about Sammy's death.

The front door was unlocked and she went inside. She slipped off her boots and padded in her thick wool socks through the small ranch house and into the kitchen. Evan was stirring honey into two cups of tea. He put a mug into her hand and brushed her forehead with a tender kiss. "I get that you needed some air, but I'm driving you home. I don't like the idea of you walking around town at night. Not when we still don't have Billingsly's killer."

"Fine." She warmed her hands on the thick cup. "Have you heard from Blade?"

"No. I hate to do it, but I may put an APB out for him to-morrow if he doesn't show up." He returned to the stove and stirred the tomato soup. "How were things at the Chupps'? Was it as bad as you expected?" Evan asked.

"Worse." Sammy's body hadn't been released yet, but that hadn't prevented buggy after buggy of neighbors and friends from calling at the house. Rachel had lost count of the number of families who'd come to pay their respects and offer condolences. She took a long sip of the hot tea, letting the sweet liquid soothe the edges off the ragged day. "You'd think I'd be used to Plain mourning, but the older I get, the more it seems to affect me. And Sammy's death . . . it's just so sad."

"Yeah," he agreed. "I didn't know him, but he was too young to have something like that happen." His dark eyes radiated compassion. "Your dinner is ready. Want to eat in here or in front of the fireplace in the living room?"

"Fireplace."

He nodded. "I agree. It's a fireplace kind of night. Crackers? I've got those little oyster crackers you like."

"Mmm," she said, even though she wasn't very hungry. "That would be nice. Let me get the sandwiches."

"With a dill pickle," he said in an attempt to lighten the atmosphere. "The jar's in the refrigerator. I spare no expense when feeding my girl."

She stood in the doorway between the kitchen and the living room. "Am I?" she asked. "Still your girl?"

"Hope so."

In the living room, Rachel forced herself to eat the bowl of tomato soup and a handful of crackers. The grilled cheese was more of a challenge. She hadn't eaten all day, but just serving and handling all the food at Naamah and Abner's house had deadened her appetite.

Evan finished his sandwich and half of hers. "You may as

well say what's on your mind," he nudged. "I can see it about to bubble over."

She looked up at him. "Will you listen before you start telling me why I'm wrong?"

Looking contrite, he nodded.

She gazed into the fireplace and watched the flames for a moment. "I can't stop wondering why Sammy climbed up in that barn loft."

"I heard he went up looking for a cat."

She shook her head. "It doesn't make sense, Evan."

"Do accidents ever make sense? Farms can be dangerous places; things that shouldn't happen do. Remember, last summer, when that Peachey boy—"

"This is different." She turned to him and met his gaze. "I'd like you to have someone double-check the autopsy report. Maybe . . . talk to the medical examiner? Everyone assumes that Sammy's death was an accident. A mentally challenged young man fell out of the loft and broke his neck. The authorities assume that's what happened because that's what they were told. That's what it looked like. But what if that's not what happened? What if Sammy witnessed Billingsly's murder and the killer had to keep him from telling? Isn't it possible that he died of a broken neck, but didn't get it from falling out of the loft?"

"That might be difficult to prove," he said thoughtfully.

"Or," she suggested, "if Sammy did die in the fall, maybe someone lured him up into the loft so that they could push him out."

"That's a pretty far reach, Rache. And you base this theory on what? Your intuition? Not that I'm discounting it. You've got some pretty good instincts when it comes to solving—" Evan broke off as a vehicle pulled into his driveway, the headlights coming through his closed curtains in the living room.

"Were you expecting company?" she asked.

"No." He went to the front door and opened it.

Two minutes later Rachel tried not to show her surprise as Blade, Coyote, and Reverend Hayes, the Methodist minister, filed into Evan's living room. "Sorry for coming without calling," Coyote was saying as she came in the door. "But Blade wanted to straighten out what appears to be a misunderstanding. And we wanted to keep it as private as possible."

"Didn't know you'd have anybody here." Blade looked at Rachel. He, his wife, and the minister stood in a line just inside the door. No one had removed his or her coat. He glanced at the minister. "Would you rather—"

"I can leave." Rachel rose off the couch.

"Take my car." Evan reached into his pocket for his keys. "I'll get it tomorrow. I've got the police car to get to work."

"No need," Reverend Hayes said, looking from Rachel to Evan. "It's been six years. Maybe it's time this was all out in the open. My wife and I were just considering whether or not it was time to open up to the community."

Rachel and Evan just stood there, looking at them.

"You were right," Blade said to Rachel. "I did lie to you about being at the book club on Saturday night. And I lied to Coyote, too." He looked uncomfortable, but he reached out and grabbed Coyote's hand. "It wasn't my place to tell where I was."

"Don't you want to sit down?" Evan asked. "Let me take your coats?"

"No, thanks," Coyote said. "We can't stay. We need to get home to the kids. We've got a sitter, but she has school in the morning."

"I'm not sure where to start," Blade said, "but . . ." He shrugged. "It shouldn't be any secret that I'm carrying a lot of baggage from my life before I met Coyote. I served my time and I broke my chain of addiction. I've been clean for ten years, four months, and three weeks. But Narcotics Anonymous helps. I should have shared that with my wife, but I didn't want to worry her, have her think I needed the program to stay straight."

"So you're saying you were at an NA meeting Saturday night?" Rachel asked.

"Not exactly." Blade glanced at Reverend Hayes.

"My sponsor was out of town," the cleric said. "I was having a bad day Saturday, and I needed to talk to someone. I called Blade. We've been attending the same meeting in State College, on and off, for the last year." He threaded his fingers together almost as if in prayer. "Seven years ago, this week, I was involved in an automobile accident. Someone that I cared deeply about died, and I spent three weeks in intensive care. To make a long story short, I was in a lot of pain. Over the course of the next few months, I developed an addiction to prescription painkillers. It nearly cost me my career. I realized that I had to make changes, so I got the help I needed, and then took this position at the church here in Stone Mill. I've been sober for almost seven years, but I know I still need NA."

"Blade was with Reverend Hayes at Junior's Diner Saturday night," Coyote explained. "He couldn't tell me or you because it's just not something you do."

"Can you verify the time frame, Reverend?" Evan asked.

"I picked Blade up, down the street from his house, around seven thirty," Reverend Hayes continued. "We went directly to Junior's Diner out on the interstate and stayed there until ten thirty. I drove him back into town and dropped him off near Wagler's."

"And you walked straight home?" Evan asked.

"Blade came in at about eleven," Coyote said. "I noticed the time because he was usually home earlier than that, and I was concerned about the storm. Remi was having one of his bad nights. He suffers from asthma, and we were up with him until three a.m. And then we went to bed. Blade didn't go out again until late Sunday morning."

"And that crosses Blade Finch off my list," Evan told Rachel as he closed the door behind his surprise visitors a few minutes later.

"Aren't you glad you waited to put out that APB?" Rachel asked, sitting down in relief.

"Sure am." He dead-bolted the door and turned to her. "You were right. I'll concede. Your intuition was dead-on. He wasn't telling the truth, but for an entirely different reason than I suspected."

"Which leaves us with—"

"Skinner," Evan finished for her, gathering up the dirty dishes.

"And me." She met his gaze. "And maybe Bishop Abner."

"Abner Chupp? Why Abner?"

She grabbed the tea mugs and followed him into the kitchen. "Abner's been acting strange all week. There's something up with him; I get that impression every time I talk to him. I told you that Blade saw an Amish buggy, a top-hack, in Wagler's Grocery parking lot late Saturday evening. Abner has one. I checked. No one else in the valley had theirs out that night."

"Doesn't make him a murderer."

"Oh, there's more. I asked Bishop Abner if he was home all Saturday evening. He said he was, but then I found out that that wasn't true. He was seen on the road that night. When I confronted him with the evidence, he admitted he'd been out, but he wouldn't tell me where he'd been."

Evan stacked the dishes in the sink and began to run hot water over them. "People lie to me all the time. Sometimes it has nothing to do with a case. Blade is proof of that."

"Amish bishops don't lie. To a man like Abner Chupp, lying is a sin." She set the mugs on the stove. "It would trouble his conscience. And that's not the only untruth he told me. I told you about the hat I saw in the snow at Billingsly's house, the morning we found the body. I've been asking around among the Amish and—" She reached out and laid her hand on his arm. "I know you didn't want me involved in this investigation. But from the first, I've had a hunch that there was an Amish connection to this crime. And you know how difficult it is for an Englisher to learn anything about what goes on in the community. Like it or not, I'm still accepted among my family's people in a way you never will be. And I have a good reason for wanting to solve this crime, if I'm one of your main suspects. I need to clear my name."

He took her hand in his and squeezed it gently. "What were you going to say about the hat?"

"I asked the Chupps if they knew of any Amish man who'd lost a black hat. Abner said he didn't, but that was a falsehood. The hat in the snow belonged to Sammy. My brother Levi picked it up at the murder scene. It had Sammy's name sewn into it. And Levi told me that he returned the hat to the Chupps' farm the same day. Abner must have known."

Evan leaned against the counter, crossing his arms over his chest, thinking. "What you're suggesting . . ." He was quiet for a moment and then went on. "If the bishop had something to do with Billingsly's death, he'd have to have a motive. People don't commit this kind of murder without a motive."

She took a deep breath. He was listening. Not only was Evan listening to her, but he was considering what she was telling him, too. "Abner may have had a reason to want Billingsly silenced. When you were going through his files, did you find anything about an old scandal involving an Amish preacher and an English woman?"

Evan's mouth firmed. "Abner's a bishop, isn't he? Not a preacher."

"But he wasn't a bishop a dozen years ago when the affair took place; he was a preacher. He was chosen as bishop later, after he and Naamah wed. She's his second wife, but there was a relationship with another woman after his first wife died, before he met Naamah. A relationship that resulted in a child." She studied Evan's face. She had his attention. "Can you imagine the headlines that a scandal like that would make? Abner's position, his current marriage, and the life of the other woman would be drastically harmed. Not to mention what it would do to Abner's son. He's at such a vulnerable age. Is it possible that Abner killed Billingsly to protect his son?"

Evan rubbed his temples as if he was getting a headache. "It might be a motive, but . . ." He frowned. "Until you just shared that information, I had no knowledge of any of this. Spoken or written."

"So you found no reference to that affair in Billingsly's files?"

He shook his head and walked around her and back into the living room. "I can't say."

She followed him. "But not finding a column or notes doesn't prove anything, Evan. It doesn't prove that Billingsly hadn't threatened Abner in the same way he threatened me. What if Billingsly and Abner had an argument? What if the bishop was just smarter than me and made sure it wasn't public?"

"All conjecture." He sank onto the couch.

She sat on the edge of the recliner. "But you have to admit that it's a possibility. And trying to solve a crime is a process of checking out possibilities and eliminating them, one by one. Right?"

"So you want me to ask Abner where he was Saturday night?"

"I think you should also ask him if he and Billingsly spoke recently."

He leaned back on the couch. "Let me think about it. Maybe interviewing your bishop is a good idea, but I think I should wait until after Sammy's funeral. It seems heavy-handed to question him while they're trying to bury their nephew. You could be on to something, Rache, but you could be mistaken. I need to handle this carefully. Going after a respected religious leader wouldn't win me any fans in this town."

"Or me. I know it's all just circumstantial, but . . . what if it's all true, Evan?"

"Let me check with the medical examiner's office on Monday. And . . . maybe I will pay Bishop Abner a visit next week." He stared into the fireplace for a few minutes. "I'm going to talk to Skinner again. I don't have a motive, but if anyone appears capable of committing that kind of murder, I'd put Jake Skinner at the top of my list, certainly ahead of your Amish bishop. Just based on size and physical condition, an older man like Abner would have a hard time getting the best of someone like Billingsly."

"I hope I'm wrong," Rachel admitted, drawing her knees up so she could face Evan. "I'd rather Skinner is the perpetrator than Abner."

Evan crossed his arms over his chest and stared into the fire that was now beginning to die down. "So Abner Chupp had an affair with a non-Amish woman. Unbelievable. More secrets in this town than I suspected."

"Too many," Rachel agreed. She exhaled and stared at the flames for a moment before looking at him. "So maybe I should tell you what I've been hiding."

"I'm listening." He patted the spot on the sofa beside him. "It might be easier if you'd come over here."

Gratefully, she moved over to the couch. "It's not pretty, but all I ask is for you to hear me out before you form an opinion."

He nodded. "All right. I'll give it my best shot."

She took a deep breath, exhaled, and began. "There was a guy at the firm that I'd been dating. There was a fire at his apartment building. To make a long story short, I let him move in while his place was being renovated. Obviously it wasn't the best decision I ever made, but . . ."

"Were you in love with him?" Evan asked.

She grimaced. "You weren't supposed to ask questions yet."

"Sorry. But were you?"

"Looking back on it?" She shook her head. "No. No way. The firm was definitely high stress, and I never really got over the feeling that I was an imposter, pretending to be someone or something that I wasn't. I guess I was trying too hard to fit into the mold and I forgot what was really important."

"So you and this guy were lovers?"

"It wasn't like that, Evan." She pressed her lips together, determined not to cry. "We were dating, but it hadn't gone that far. I might have been stupid to let him stay at my place, but I wasn't dumb enough to fall into that kind of a relationship. This probably sounds silly in this day and time, but I'm not that kind of girl." She swallowed. "I don't expect you to believe me, but that's the truth. I knew within a week of him moving in that we didn't have a future together, but I felt bad that he had no place to live. And it would have been so awkward to have broken off things with him right then."

"Go on."

"I'd been working seventy, eighty hours a week on this particular merger between two fairly good-sized companies. I'm not making an excuse. What I did was wrong, but it never occurred to me at the time. I mentioned it in passing to him. It was late, and he'd ordered Chinese takeout, and I was too tired to think straight."

"So you told him about the coming merger?"

She nodded. "I told him about it, but not to give him insider information. We were just talking over dinner, you know? The next day, without telling me, he took out a loan and bought shares in the company being absorbed. Eventually he was investigated by the SEC, the Securities and Exchange Commission, because the purchase went through just days before the merger. When they questioned him, they discovered that we'd been dating at the time. They called me in, and naturally I admitted that I'd discussed the matter briefly with him. But I told them that I'd had no idea that he was going to try and profit from the information."

"But you didn't make any investment yourself?" Evan asked.

"No, absolutely not." She made herself look him in the eye. "I felt like such a fool; I knew better. I was guilty. I had given out privileged information. I hired an attorney, and she advised me to plead guilty and pay the fine rather than risk a trial and the loss of my reputation. So, I followed my attorney's advice. I thought maybe it might cost me my job, but my boss just laughed. It never even came up again. I worked for Baker, Crimmin, and Barrel for another three years before I left the firm."

"And the guy? What happened to him?"

"I have no idea. I believe he moved to another city. We broke up the week he moved back into his apartment, long before I learned about him purchasing that stock." She shrugged. "So that's it. That's my venture into the dark side. My first mistake was letting him into my home. My second was not guarding my words more carefully, and my third was trying to hide what I'd done from you when I found my way back to Stone Mill."

He brushed her cheek. "Not exactly a Sopranos-class crime, but you're right. You should have told me."

"I know." She looked at her hands in her lap. "But I was ashamed. And I knew how it would hurt my family if they'd known that I'd let a slimeball like that move into my home." She leaned against his shoulder. "I'm sorry, Evan. What more can I say? I was technically guilty of insider trading, but I didn't kill Billingsly to keep from being found out."

Evan exhaled. "I still might have to bring you in for questioning."

"I understand."

He reached out and covered her hand with his, and they sat there for a couple of minutes in silence, both lost in their own thoughts.

Beginning to feel sleepy, Rachel got up. "I can drive myself home in your car. Get it back to you tomorrow."

"It's not a problem." He offered a half-smile. "And if I drive you, I won't have to worry about you slipping on the ice and putting my new SUV in a ditch."

"Okay." She smiled back at him. "Deal."

It wasn't a fix, but it was the start of a fix, and she felt a little lighter as she zipped up her parka and followed him out to his vehicle. At least it was off her conscience, and she'd shared her concerns about Abner. Maybe Skinner would turn out to be the killer after all, and everything that had gone wrong in Stone Mill would start to go right again.

She hoped so.

# Chapter 18

Friday, when Rachel came downstairs, dressed for her morning barn chores, she found Jake Skinner waiting outside her office. He was wearing his customary fatigues: the faded military jacket and beret. A green canvas duffel leaned against the wainscoting at his feet.

"Good," he said when he saw her. "I wanted to check out, make sure I wasn't leaving owing you anything."

"You're leaving now?" she asked. Evan wouldn't be happy about that. She was sure that he hadn't had time to speak to Skinner the previous night. Stalling, she said, "I thought you wanted to extend your visit. I had your room reserved for two more nights. Is there anything I could do to change your mind and keep you from leaving this morning?" As far as she knew, there were no additional charges to his account. Skinner had secured his reservation with a credit card.

"No more reason for me to be here. Cops want me, they've got my location. Your friend Parks seems like a decent enough sort, but . . ." Skinner shrugged. "He's got that cop smell."

She must have shown a facial reaction because Skinner quickly added, "No offense intended."

She gave a wave, suggesting it was fine, and then pretended to yawn. "Sorry. I'm pretty useless until I've had my morning caffeine. Do you have time for coffee? There should be fresh-made in the pot. The timer starts it at six thirty."

"I'd rather have hot tea."

"Me, too. Do you like Earl Grey?" He nodded, and she hurried to say, "I can brew a pot in five minutes." She favored him with another smile. "Will you be flying straight back to Colorado?"

"Haven't decided yet. Got a buddy in West Virginia. Lives in a cabin at the back end of nowhere. I was thinking of stopping in to see how he's making out. So I might just keep the rental and drive home." He raised a bushy eyebrow. "Or Charlie and I might decide to go on walkabout. My plans are kind of loose."

Rachel wondered if there was any way she could get a text message to Evan without alerting Skinner. She was certain that he'd asked the veteran to remain in town until further notice, and Skinner was definitely planning otherwise. "I think there are some raisin cinnamon buns, or, if you like, I could fix you some breakfast," she offered.

"Just the tea." Skinner followed her into the dining room. She took the electric kettle into the kitchen to fill it with fresh water, hoping maybe he would take a seat at the dining table. Instead, he came to the doorway and stood watching her.

"I didn't off Billingsly," he said. "You don't need to be afraid of me. I'm kind of a John Wayne guy. I never hurt a woman in my life. Not even in 'Nam, and there were some pretty crazy babes there trying to see me blown away."

"I'm not afraid of you," she answered, hoping that putting the words out would make it so. "You've been a gentleman in my home and kind to my staff. And I can't say that about all of my male guests."

He pulled off his hat and tucked it into a jacket pocket. "Glad that I haven't been any trouble. This is a nice place. And I like you. You're a dame with good sense, and you know how nasty Billingsly was. So I wanted to tell you why I was here. You already figured out that it wasn't for the shoofly pie, although it's pretty darn tasty."

She returned with the kettle and took a tin of Earl Grey tea leaves from the antique pine corner cabinet. "I wouldn't have wished Billingsly dead," she said, "but I did wish him far away from my town."

Skinner grunted an agreement. "Like I said, a sensible dame." He hesitated, then went on. "I've been thinking about how the killer could be anybody. It's the quiet ones you don't suspect that are usually the ones you need to watch out for. I saw that in combat. The quietest guy, the one you'd think would be frightened of his own shadow, he could be the most lethal, if pushed far enough."

"So what you're saying is that Billingsly's killer could be someone we don't suspect?" Rachel asked, unable to keep herself from thinking about Bishop Abner.

"Yeah," Skinner agreed. "Take your cook. Now there's a formidable woman if I ever saw one. Prayer bonnet or not, I wouldn't want to get on her wrong side in a dark alley."

"Ada?" She chuckled. "You might be right about her. She terrifies me." Rachel poured the tea. "Would you like to go back to the parlor where you were with Detective Parks? We'd be less likely to be overheard there if what you want to tell me is confidential. Or . . ." She hesitated. "Was it what you just said about Mary Aaron?"

He gave her a long look. "You look like you were on your way out somewhere."

Rachel glanced down at her jeans, flannel shirt, and goose-down vest. "I was going to feed my dairy goats. Muck out their stalls. And tend to the chickens. It's one of my mornings to tend the animals. It's why I'm down early. But that can wait until we—"

"Naw, don't want to hold you up. I'll come out with you. I grew up on a ranch. Used to milk my pop's cows before school. I like barns. They're peaceful places, mostly." His gaze challenged her. "If you're being honest about not being afraid of me."

Rachel shook her head. "I think you're a trustworthy person. I'm not sure why, but I believe you are."

"My parish priest would be glad to hear that."

"You're a churchgoing man?"

He raised a shoulder. "Guilty."

That did surprise her. She offered him a tentative smile. "I've got an extra pitchfork if you're game."

"That's what I like," he said, cracking a smile again. "A dame with grit." He picked up his mug of tea. "Lead on, lady."

The goats greeted them eagerly as they entered the barn, bleating and crowding around as Rachel measured out the feed. Skinner took one of the forks and began to work through one of the stalls, cleaning out the dirty bedding.

"Before you say anything," she told him, walking over to turn the water on so she could fill the deep stone trough, "you should know that I know about your argument with Bill Billingsly on the veterans' website. It got pretty heated."

He lifted one brow.

"I Googled your names," she explained.

"Ah. Wonders of the Internet." Skinner leaned against his pitchfork. "That was a bit of a pissing contest, 'scuse my French. Politics. My real beef with him has been going on for a year."

Rachel watched water pour from a faucet into the stone trough.

"Billingsly's been making himself a name in veterans' circles, publishing stuff on various subjects. And not just for Vietnam vets, all vets: Gulf War, Afghanistan, Iraq, you name it. At the end of his pieces there's always one of those little blurbs about the author."

She nodded. "Right."

"Billingsly claimed to have been awarded a Legion of Merit for his service in 'Nam. But it was a lie; he was never awarded a Legion of Merit. I know because I fought with him. That honor went to a friend of mine, a guy by the name of Wally Minner. Wally was one of those guys who came back so fragile that he couldn't put the war in the past. He got tangled up in booze and pills and the wrong people. Died over ten years ago. Cirrhosis of the liver. I guess Billingsly decided to claim the honor, Wally being dead and not needing it." He stabbed a hunk of dirty straw and tossed it into a wheelbarrow. "I threatened to expose Billingsly for the jerk and liar he was if he didn't remove the award from his credentials and publically apologize to Wally."

"So you came here to confront Billingsly about his claim?" Rachel asked. "And he was afraid that his own reputation would be ruined?"

"I wasn't carrying a vendetta. Not even against the likes of Billingsly. All I wanted was for Billingsly to admit the truth. And if he'd refused, I'd have exposed him, but I certainly wouldn't have tried to kill him." He shook his head. "I guess it's a little late for Billingsly to apologize for claiming what was never his. But wherever Billingsly is now, maybe he'll still have a higher court to answer to."

"We can hope," Rachel agreed, going to shut off the water.

"You believe me?" Skinner asked. He'd set aside the pitchfork and was now spreading fresh straw.

"I do," she told him. Skinner was another example of what George O'Day liked to quote: "You can't judge a book by its cover." Underneath the rough exterior, Jake Skinner seemed a decent man who went out of his way to help others.

"Good." Skinner pulled his hat out of his pocket and over his head. "I'll be on my way now. You tell your cop friend what you want of this. If he wants to find me, I'll be back at my Colorado address by snowmelt, at latest. I never like to miss opening day of trout season. And tell him that I hope he finds Billingsly's killer."

A half an hour later Rachel watched from her bedroom

window as Jake Skinner's rental car pulled out of her driveway. She picked up her cell phone and texted Evan.

**Call me. Skinner didn't do it.**

**Can you give me the name of a good defense attorney?**

Just after noon, Rachel got a text back from Evan telling her that the authorities had released Sammy's body. He didn't mention the text she'd sent him or Skinner. She was attempting to reach him again when her brother Danny arrived at the house.

"*Dat* wants you to come and leave your Jeep at the house. He wants you to come with him and *Mam* in the buggy to Sammy's viewing," Danny explained. "So *Mam* says you'd best wear this." He dropped a black bag on the table. "She says you can keep it, and not to forget the head scarf."

Rachel opened the bag and removed a Lincoln-green dress with a faint pattern of apple blossoms in a lighter green. It had a modest neckline with no collar, three-quarter sleeves, and an A-line skirt that would fall to several inches below her knees. The material was soft against her fingers, and the stitching was fine. Folded carefully on top was a matching green scarf and a pair of high black stockings. "She sewed this dress for me?" Rachel asked.

Danny shrugged. "Guess. I don't know. Can you come right away? *Dat* didn't want to be out late, so we need to go to Bishop Abner's as soon as we can."

"Sure, I can come now. Wait and you can ride back to the house with me." She raced upstairs to change into the new dress. Every stitch in the dress had been sewn with thoughtful skill. Her *mam* must have worked on it for days. As she dressed, it occurred to her that she might be caught between the Amish world and the English, but she wasn't trapped so much as cradled. There was good in both worlds, and she was blessed to have the love of her family, her community, and a special man. Somehow, she had to find the balance to walk this uncertain path, because even though she wasn't going back to the old way, she wasn't running so far away that she forgot the strength and faith that had nurtured her and made her the person she was.

Two hours later, Rachel entered the Chupp home with her parents, brothers, and sisters. Sammy's body was already there. Naamah and his mother and sisters had dressed Sammy in funeral white and laid him out on a bier in the parlor. Rachel joined the line of mourners to view the remains and add her prayers to those of the Amish community. She wasn't sure what she'd expected, but she was grateful that there appeared to be no outward sign of the trauma that had killed him, or the autopsy. In death, Sammy appeared smaller and younger than he had in life, and once again, Rachel thought how senseless his passing was.

That evening, there was no formal service, no sermon, only quiet words of comfort and support for the survivors. Rachel, her mother, and her sisters soon made themselves useful preparing and serving food and helping with the children. Rachel and her parents remained at the Chupp house until after dark. Rachel's sisters and brothers had left earlier in a separate buggy so that they could do the chores.

Finally, her father found her in the kitchen and whispered that they would be leaving. Gratefully, Rachel made the rounds, saying her good-byes and promising to come tomorrow for the funeral. When they stepped out into the yard, it was bitterly cold and wind whipped sleet and freezing rain around them. Her *dat* had thrown a padded blanket over the driving horse, and brought a woolen lap robe from the back of the buggy for the three of them to put over their legs.

Neither of her parents had much to say when they first got in the buggy, but the whine of the wind and the sharp echo of the horse's hooves striking the road were oddly comforting. Sadness and grief for the community's loss had permeated the Chupp residence, but the sense that death was a natural part of life hovered above the mourning. Everything that could have been done for Sammy had been done. Now they had only to lay his body to rest in the Amish cemetery and go on, accepting God's will.

It was Rachel's father who broke the silence. "We're so glad you came with us today. We've been wanting to talk to you alone." He glanced at her sitting between him and her mother on the buggy seat. "I don't want you to be upset that we didn't share this with you sooner."

Rachel looked at one parent and then the other, suddenly apprehensive. She had no idea what he was about to say.

"Your mother and I had an important decision to make," her father continued. "We had to talk with each other and take advice from our good bishop. But most of all, we had to pray to try to learn God's will in this matter."

She clasped her gloved hands together under the lap robe. "Yes, *Dat?*"

"It is your mother's health," her father said. "She's not well."

"*Mam?*" Rachel reached for her mother's hand under the blanket and, finding it, squeezed it.

"A lump," her mother said, although if she was actually speaking to her, Rachel couldn't have said.

"Where?" she demanded. "Have you seen the doctor? You should see—"

"Of course she's seen a doctor. We are not so backward as that," her father said gently.

"A lump in my chest. Not large, no bigger than a grain of corn," her mother said, gripping her hand.

*Breast cancer.* Sweat broke out on the nape of Rachel's neck. Her mother's older sister and their mother had died of breast cancer. "Has there been a biopsy? Do you have a treatment plan?"

"Tell your daughter that it isn't as simple as that," her mother admonished.

Her father sighed. "It's a decision of faith for your mother. She wasn't sure if she should take the English doctor's treatments, or if she should leave it up to God's mercy."

"He has the power to heal," her mother pronounced. "I shouldn't have to tell anyone that. If it is His will that I live, why do I need to go to the hospital at all?"

"You see," Rachel's father went on, "we have two choices. Do as the doctor wishes *and* still pray for the Lord to heal her, or . . ."

"Or accept His plan for me," her mother said. "Tell your daughter, Samuel. This life is only a pale reflection of what awaits the faithful in heaven. Would you have me prove myself too weak to trust in Him?"

"*Mam,* you have to get the best medical treatment available. God gave the doctors the intelligence and the skill to treat disease. You can't simply do nothing. *Dat,* tell her—"

"That is what Bishop Abner says," her father soothed. "He believes that God sent these treatments and the knowledge, and that the miracle of doctors' healing is His work." He smiled grimly. "He's been wonderful. You know how stubborn your mother can be once she sets her mind to something. But she is wise enough to know that only a foolish person ignores the words of a good and pious man like our Abner."

"Bishop Abner's been counseling you?" Rachel asked.

"*Ya,*" her father said. "Almost every day he comes. Even in the midst of that terrible snowstorm, he was there for us."

Rachel turned suddenly to her father. "The night of the storm? Saturday night? Bishop Abner came to your house that night?"

"*Ya,*" her father confirmed. "So hard the snow was coming down by the time he was ready to go that I almost convinced him to stay the night with us and go home in the morning. But he feared to leave Naamah and Sammy alone in such weather."

He pulled back on the reins and the horse stopped. Rachel looked up to see that they were at her parents' back door. She turned to her mother. "Please promise me you're going to do what the doctors say, *Mam*." She took both her mother's hands in hers.

Esther Mast looked kindly into Rachel's eyes, holding her gaze as she spoke. "Tell your daughter to pray for me, Samuel. But she should not worry. I'll let the doctors put their poison into me and God will see me through this as He sees us through all our trials."

# Chapter 19

Rachel got as far as the end of her parents' lane before she stopped and allowed herself a good cry. How could she have gone so wrong? Not only had she not picked up on the fact that something serious was going on with her mother, but she'd also rushed to judgment, condemning a good man. How many people whom she loved and trusted had begged her not to interfere in Evan's investigation?

Not only had she thought Bishop Abner, her friend and her family's religious adviser, guilty of a horrendous murder, but she also had suspected that he'd been cruel enough to do away with his own innocent nephew to hide his crime. She'd let pride and a belief in her own intellect overrule common sense. Because she'd been able to help find Beth Glick's murderer and aid her uncle in a crisis, she'd thought herself smarter than the police, more competent than Evan. And the result? Her pride and recklessness had nearly done irrevocable damage to her community and Abner's reputation.

No wonder Evan had lost patience with her.

And now she'd have to tell him everything, explain how wrong she'd been, and try to undo the damage she'd caused. Hands trembling, she tried his cell again. *Pick up,* she urged. *Please, Evan, pick up.* She needed him, and she needed his forgiveness.

"Rache?"

At the sound of his voice, she burst into tears again.

"Rachel, what's wrong? Are you hurt?"

Her chin quivered and her breathing came in short gasps. "I need you to take me in to the troop," she managed.

"What?"

His one word said it all, shocking her back to reason. "No, it's not what you think," she blurted, realizing that now she must sound crazy to him. "I didn't kill Billingsly. But neither did Skinner. I left you a message. Several messages. And it wasn't Blade. And it wasn't Abner. I'm the only one left, Evan. You've got to take me in for questioning."

"Where are you?"

"At my parents'." She fumbled for a tissue, found a napkin from an infrequent stop at a fast-food place, and blew her nose. "In their driveway." She drew in another shuddering breath and swallowed. "My mother's sick. She has breast cancer. It runs in her family, and she's been contemplating getting medical treatment. Abner's been counseling her and my *dat*. It's where he was Saturday night."

"It doesn't sound as though you should be driving in this rotten weather. I'm on the turnpike. A bad accident. I got called in to help. I might be here most of the night, but I can send a trooper to drive you home."

"No, I'll be fine. I've got four-wheel drive, and there's no traffic on the road. I'm sorry to bother you tonight. I was just so sure that . . ." She blew her nose again. "I'm okay," she said. "Really. Just hearing about my mother threw me for a shock. Her sister died of breast cancer. And my grandmother."

"Don't think the worst. They're making headway treating breast cancer. But she needs to have it taken care of immediately."

"Luckily, they've already made that decision. With Abner's help. You know how stubborn my mother can be. But she's agreed to treatment."

"Good."

In the background, Rachel could hear hospital noises, the

clink of metal, footsteps, the whoosh of a sliding door, and, faintly, the wail of an ambulance. "I don't want to keep you on the phone," she said. "I don't want to jeopardize your job."

"You're not *jeopardizing my job*."

"With the investigation. You've stalled long enough in taking me in for questioning." Other than the lights from the instrument panels, her Jeep was dark. Wind rattled the windows. The wipers thumped monotonously back and forth, piling the heavy snow and depositing it in ever growing drifts on the hood. She should have felt terribly alone, but she didn't. Evan's strong voice filled the cold void, strengthening her resolve to make right what she'd done wrong.

"I'm certainly not having anyone bring you in tonight. Call the attorney Monday morning. I'll talk to my superior first thing Monday. If he thinks you need to come in, you can bring the attorney with you."

"It will be fine, Evan. I didn't do it. There's no evidence against me. Just circumstantial. I'm innocent. There can't be any of my fingerprints. No DNA. Because I wasn't inside the house."

"Maybe you should be the cop instead of me."

She managed the barest smile. "I'm so sorry about all of this. I'll do exactly what you've said. I'll get an attorney. I have faith in our justice system. There's not enough evidence to even reach a grand jury."

He chuckled. "Maybe I'm wrong about you being a police officer. Maybe you should consider law school instead of innkeeping."

"Right now I'm not doing too good of a job with either. I don't feel as though I've given my guests all the attention they should have had this week."

"Your festival finishes up tomorrow, right?"

"It does. With the cook-off. I don't know how many Amish will take part in that, though, because Sammy's funeral will be tomorrow."

"I'm off tomorrow. Promised to take my mother to that funeral in Harrisburg. But I never knew my great-aunt. Want me to cancel and come with you to Sammy's funeral?"

"That wouldn't be fair to your mother. I'll be fine. Call me tomorrow night if you can, when you get back from Harrisburg."

"You're sure? You'll be okay tomorrow?"

"My family will be there. And Mary Aaron."

"What time is Sammy's funeral?"

"Noon. I don't have to be back at the high school until four. Unless you think I should come in tomorrow to the troop."

"Monday afternoon if you can get legal representation by then." He hesitated. "If you do need to come in, you need to think about what your response will be if any reporters get ahold of it. Anyone who does a little digging is going to find your prior."

"I'm not advertising what I did, but I'm not going to hide it either." Her wipers groaned and skipped, and she turned up the speed. "Who knows, I might get lucky. It looks like our local paper might be taking a turn for the better." Her hand found the rolled-up newspaper on the car seat beside her. "I've got the latest edition here. The headline about the murder is in good taste. There's a lot of press on the festival, but then there's other local news, things that are important to local farmers, a good piece on the coming school board election. Billingsly's obituary was on page five, pretty low-key."

"Good." She could almost see the crease that appeared between Evan's brows when he was concentrating. "I did get your texts and your messages about Skinner," he said. "Excellent conclusions. He never looked like that promising a suspect to me to begin with. Too obvious. And information came in on his background. Jake Skinner is quite a powerhouse in his state for veterans' rights. He does a lot of volunteer work with injured soldiers. Raises money to buy power wheelchairs, arranges financing for service dogs, and spends a lot of time with soldiers, one-on-one. Not quite the sour apple he'd like to have us think he is."

"Another book I judged by the cover, I'm afraid," she admitted.

"Not your usual B&B guest, for certain. What about the TV thing the other night in the sleigh? Did the reporter say anything about our engagement?" he asked.

"No. Nothing. Ell recorded it for me. She watched it three times. It was short but good publicity for the town." She hesitated. "I guess that's still up in the air, isn't it? Our engagement?"

"We'll get through this thing with Billingsly and then we'll work things out between us."

"I want to, Evan. I do."

"Me, too. Look, I better go."

"Sure. Of course. My mother wants you to come to supper on Sunday evening. It's a church day, but she asked me to invite you back to the house."

"I'm off Sunday, but I've got a pile of stuff on my desk. I was thinking that I'd go in, at least for the morning. But I can probably come to dinner with you." Rachel heard someone call for Detective Parks, and then Evan said, "Text me when you get home so I'll know you got in safe. Don't forget. Or I will send a trooper looking you."

"I will. Take care."

"You, too."

She got out of the Jeep, brushed snow off the front and back windows with a little broom she kept in the backseat, and then got back in and fastened her seat belt. She felt a little better now. She shouldn't have. There was no telling what was going to happen with her mother's diagnosis. She had no idea who had killed Billingsly, and she didn't know whether she'd lost any chance of a happily-forever-after with Evan. Tomorrow was still the funeral of a sweet young man whose life had been cut all too short, and she would have to seek out Abner and tell him how sorry that she was for suspecting him of double murder. And to top it all off, by this time next week, the past she'd tried to hide might be common knowledge.

"God help me," she murmured. "I am still a work in progress." She sighed and shifted the Jeep into drive. She would go home, say her prayers, and crawl into bed. And then she would get up in the morning and attempt to set her life back on the right track again.

Saturday was cloudy and cold. The sun was high overhead as a preacher from Sammy's district finished the graveside service for Sammy and the mourners began to make their way slowly back to the line of black buggies waiting on the dirt road. The Amish cemetery spread across a gentle hillside and was surrounded by a fieldstone wall and simple wooden gate. In spring, violets and daffodils would spring up over the resting place of so many generations, and even now the cemetery seemed more a peaceful resting place to Rachel than an ominous location.

Among the dark-clad women, Naamah and her sister stood close together, black bonnets almost touching, reddened faces wet with tears. People came to them, singly and in couples, to offer their condolences. Rachel saw Abner, shoulders hunched against the cold wind, surrounded by the older men, talking to the preacher who'd delivered the words of comfort and led the prayers. Small children clustered close to the sides of mothers, aunts, and grandmothers, while older boys and girls walked quietly to the gate and waited for their parents.

Rachel had driven out from Stone Mill House in her Jeep rather than come with her parents. Among the rows of buggies were the vehicles of English and Mennonites, all come to remember Sammy and perhaps take away the preacher's words of hope and resurrection. Many of the attendees were close relatives and friends of Rachel's, including her mother and father, Aunt Hannah and Uncle Aaron, her brothers and sisters, Mary Aaron, and more cousins than she could easily count. Counted among the non-Amish were prominent members of the community: George O'Day, Polly Wagler, Coyote Finch, Hulda Schenfeld with her middle son, and Sandy Millman. Trooper Mars and another officer in uniform were on the road directing traffic and keeping sightseers from disturbing the services.

"Will I see you back at the house?" Mary Aaron's deep purple dress and black coat and bonnet echoed those of many of the matrons, but her freckled face was just as youthful and alert as normal. "At the Chupps'?"

Rachel shook her head. Once again, people had been invited to pay their respects at the Chupps' home, where a meal would be served and those from out of town could be properly welcomed and thanked for their concern. Also, chores for both the Chupp household and that of Sammy's parents would be quietly apportioned out to volunteers for the coming week so that those who mourned him most would be free of responsibilities for rest and prayer. "*Ne.*" Rachel explained. "The festival . . . I've got things that have to be wrapped up and the cook-off—"

"I understand," Mary Aaron said. "I'll try to get away and come in to see if there's any help I can give you with the cook-off. *Mam* and *Dat* are going back to the Chupps'. I don't think there's any need for me to accompany them. I'll just see the kids are situated at home, and then I'll come to town in the wagon."

"Thanks," Rachel said. "I appreciate it."

Her cousin's beau, Timothy, standing among the younger men near the stone wall, caught Mary Aaron's glance and smiled at her. He reached up and tugged at his hat. She nodded, and he said something to his friends and walked toward her.

"Excuse me," Rachel said, brushing her cousin's arm as she spotted Abner taking leave of the group of men. "I need to speak to Bishop Abner for a moment."

"*Ya,* you go on," Mary Aaron said. "See you later." She

stood waiting as Timothy approached and spoke quietly to her. Rachel wondered if the two were officially walking out together yet. They might be. Mary Aaron could be close-mouthed when it came to her relationship with Tim. But he was a good man with a promising future, and if she did choose him for a husband, Rachel was sure that they would get on well together.

The elders were moving away from the grave site now. A few families had already gotten into their buggies, the Englishers were walking to their cars, and soon the cemetery would begin to empty out. Rachel knew that this wasn't the place to try and apologize to Abner, but she couldn't stand it. She had to tell him how wrong she'd been and how sorry she was that she'd misjudged him.

Abner lingered alone by Sammy's grave. Rachel hesitated for a few seconds and then hurried toward him. "Bishop Abner! Could I speak with you? Just for a moment."

He raised sad eyes to her. "Of course." The deacon of Abner's church, a tall, angular man with a sweet face, started coming in Abner's direction, but Abner motioned toward the line of buggies and the deacon nodded and turned away. Rachel kept walking until she reached the graveside.

"I'm so sorry," she said.

"He was a good boy," Abner agreed.

"Not just about Sammy," she answered. "Bishop Abner, I've made a terrible mistake. My mother told me—"

He touched her shoulder lightly. "You know about her health."

"Yes, and how you've been counseling them. I can't thank you enough. You've been so good to them. And I . . ." She sucked in a deep breath and shook her head. "I thought that you . . . I thought that you might have been the one who killed Billingsly," she blurted. "Because he'd found out about Sandy and Eddie and was going to tell everyone. And, God forgive me, but I even suspected that Sammy's death was no accident. That you—"

His eyes closed for a second, and his lips moved. And then he finished for her. "You thought that I had killed Sammy?"

She nodded. "It all started with your top-hack. Blade thought he saw one in Stone Mill late that night. And you were out when you originally said you were home. But . . ." She shrugged. "He was probably wrong. He's an Englisher. What does Blade know about Amish buggies?"

Abner didn't answer, so she went on.

"And Sammy's lost hat. It was at Billingsly's house the morning they found the body. And because you told me that you were home when really you weren't . . . And then Sandy and Eddie." She took a breath and went on. "I'm so sorry, Bishop Abner. In my pride, I was so sure I could solve this murder like I did the other ones. I jumped to conclusions. I've been such a fool."

"I'm not without sin, Rachel. Who of us is? What Sandy and I did, that was wrong. We wouldn't have wanted it known because we've thought that our son is too young to carry such a burden. Someday we will tell him the truth, but we've thought it best to wait until he is a man." He shrugged. "And who knows if that's the right thing to do? But to kill a man to hide my sin? No, I would not have done that. As for Sammy . . . I loved him. His death was an accident, nothing more. We're human, Rachel. Humans are frail. We are easily hurt. But our Sammy was one of God's own. He is safe. As much as we would want him to remain here with us, it should comfort us to know that he is in a better place."

"I don't expect you to forgive me or to forget," she said. "I only want you to know how deeply I regret my suspicions of you."

"What suspicions?" Naamah asked, coming up behind her.

Rachel turned to her. "Naamah," she said, "I was just telling Bishop Abner how much I appreciate his kindness to my parents and, of course, how sorry I am about Sammy's passing."

"What suspicions?" Naamah repeated, looking to Abner.

He took one of his wife's hands in his. "We can talk later. We should go. Folks will be arriving at our house."

Naamah turned to Rachel. "You're coming back to the house, aren't you?"

"*Ya,* you must," Bishop Abner said. "You are one of our family."

Rachel looked him in the eyes. "After everything I've told you? You'd still welcome me into your home?"

Abner smiled sadly. "Of course, child. It would sadden us if you didn't come."

"You must come and eat something," Naamah insisted. "All that food. It will go to waste if no one comes."

Promising that she would stop for a few minutes, Rachel said her good-byes and returned to her Jeep. It was only mid-day, but it felt as though she'd been up for hours. She had to get through the rest of the festival and then hopefully talk to Evan. Abner had let her off far easier than he had any reason to. He might have forgiven her, but how could she ever forgive herself?

She tried not to think about the question that hovered in the shadowy corners of her mind, but it would not be stilled. If all of their suspects had been proven innocent, who had killed Billingsly? And would he kill again?

# Chapter 20

The snow crunched under Rachel's boots as she crossed her yard to the barn Sunday morning. It was early; the sun was barely up, and the roosters hadn't started to crow yet, but she needed a good half hour to care for the animals and still have time to shower and dress for church. She and Evan had talked on the phone the previous night until well after midnight, and if their differences weren't entirely mended, they'd certainly been smoothed over. After she'd told him about her apology to Abner and the guilt she felt at suspecting the bishop of murdering both Billingsly and Sammy, they'd dropped the subject of the investigation by mutual agreement. Instead, she and Evan chatted about ordinary things: the success of the festival, the possibility of more snow, and his daylong excruciating expedition with his mother. His mother was high maintenance, and he was the dutiful only son, which sometimes called for more patience than he possessed.

After she had listened to Evan's humorous retelling of his ordeal and made the appropriate sympathetic responses, Rachel confided how relieved she was that the Winter Frolic had wrapped up on a high note. The cook-off that George and most of the town business people had feared would be a flop had produced so many Amish entries that extra prizes had to be awarded. The winner, with a traditional Pennsylvania Dutch apple strudel topped with Granny Smith home-churned ice cream, had been Lucy Mose Troyer, age seventy-nine. Before Evan hung up, he'd promised he'd try to join her at the morning worship service. But if he couldn't, he wouldn't forget that he was expected at Rachel's parents' for supper at six.

After getting off the phone with Evan, Rachel had thought that she was so keyed up from the day that she'd lie awake half the night. She hadn't. She'd fallen into a deep slumber, and if she hadn't thought to set her alarm, she wouldn't have awakened early enough to do her chores before church.

Rachel clapped her gloved hands together to warm them as she approached the refurbished barn. She'd bundled up well against the cold, but the wind sweeping down from Canada was still a shock after the warmth of the house. She shivered inside her North Face parka. "Morning, girls," she called to her goats as she pushed open the heavy door. The hinges groaned, a sound that made her wince, reminding her that Danny had told her the hinges needed oiling. On a farm, even one as small as hers, there were always more waiting chores than time to do them.

The goats bleated a greeting, and three curious faces peered through the railings of the pen. "Poor babies," she sympathized. "You hate winter, don't you?" The nanny reared on her hind legs and capered about in agreement while the two younger females jostled for a favored spot closest to the feed bin. Rachel had acquired the three dairy goats, mother and daughters, by accident, but she had become quite fond of them. "Don't worry. Spring will come, and then you can romp in the clover again," she soothed as she went to the faucet and turned it on.

She waited as the ancient pipes gurgled and huffed, and then, when she'd almost decided that the plumbing had frozen again, a blast of clean, cold water gushed out of the faucet and into the old stone trough. Running water in the barn was a luxury and a constant source of delight to Rachel. Growing up, she'd carried hundreds of buckets of water for the livestock in both freezing weather and the heat of summer. Here, with the magic of electricity and modern plumbing, all it took was a turn of the faucet handle and water flowed out.

The good thing about the old soapstone trough was that it was deep and held a lot of water. The bad thing about it was that it was deep and held a lot of water, and had to be drained often in summer and scrubbed to keep out mold. But the massive trough had stood here as long as the barn had, and Rachel loved it. When she'd cleaned up the barn and rebuilt the stalls for the goats, she'd spent half a day cleaning decades of spiderwebs, trash, and rodent droppings out of the trough. Her labor had been rewarded by knowledge that, with proper care, the trough would continue to provide a clean source of fresh water for the animals for decades to come, and because of the way that the stall dividers had been repositioned, the water could be freely accessed from both sides.

Humming to herself, Rachel climbed up the ladder into the loft, her mind drifting, against her will, to thoughts of the following morning. She'd have to call the attorney's office. A formality, she told herself. The interview with the police would go fine. She didn't do it, and the police would realize that soon enough. But still, the idea of being questioned by police was upsetting.

She rolled a bale of hay to the opening in the floor of the loft where the ladder came through and went back for another.

Of course, if she didn't kill Bill Billingsly, and Abner didn't do it, and Blade didn't do it, and Skinner didn't do it, the obvious question was, who did? As she lifted a bale of hay onto its side, she thought about Sammy's hat in Billingsly's yard. How had it gotten there? And what about the top-hack? She'd been so upset about her mother's diagnosis and her own false conclusion that Abner had killed Billingsly that she hadn't really sorted out the clues . . . which had not changed. Rachel had told Abner, the previous day, that Blade must have been mistaken about the top-hack parked at Wagler's Saturday night. But that didn't make sense. Blade had seemed so certain. And she considered him a reliable witness.

The hair on the back of Rachel's neck suddenly stood up, and she felt a shiver that ran deeper than any cold winter morning could ever produce.

What if the top-hack *had* been Abner's? What if someone *else* had driven it to town that night?

She'd never asked Abner which buggy he'd taken when he went to her parents' place that night.

Reaching the hole in the floor, Rachel upended the bale of hay and gave it a shove. It tumbled to the barn floor, breaking one string in the fall so that the bale divided and fell into sections. She pushed the second bale through the hole, her thoughts coming faster.

What if Sammy really *had* been at Billingsly's that night?

What if Sammy's accident really *hadn't* been an accident?

She needed to call Evan. *Now.*

As Rachel made her way down the ladder, all three goats ran to the far end of the stall and went on alert, peering between the rails, flicking their tails. Her back to the door, she felt a blast of wind and heard the squeak of the barn door. For a second, she assumed that she'd not closed it properly and it had blown open, but then the nanny bleated loudly, a sure sign that she'd spotted someone who might be a new source of apples or sugar lumps.

"Levi?" Rachel called, coming down the ladder as quickly as possible. The banging door hadn't spooked just the goats.

"Danny? Is that you?" It was a church Sunday. Her brothers shouldn't have been there this morning. They should be at home making ready for the long worship service. A furry gray streak zipped past the goats to vanish in the recesses of the barn as her feet touched the ground. A cat.

But not one of her cats . . .

Rachel turned to see a large cloaked figure in the doorway, outlined in the glare from the snowy barnyard.

The door banged shut, and it grew darker inside the barn again. And suddenly Rachel knew who was standing there. "Naamah?" she murmured, her unease turning to fear.

It was a church morning; a bishop's wife was never anywhere but at his side.

Naamah stepped out of the gloom, a stick or something in one gloved hand. She strode toward Rachel, chin thrust forward, large and imposing in her black go-to-meeting dress, sturdy black lace-up boots, black coat, and black bonnet. She moved quickly for such a big woman, rushing to enfold Rachel in her arms. "This isn't my doing, *kuchen*," she murmured in Deitsch. "I'm so sorry."

Rachel caught a whiff of starch and sage mingled with damp wool, then saw a flash of movement. Before she could react, a heavy object struck the side of her head. Stunned, Rachel staggered back and pulled her wool knit hat off. The inside of the hat was stained with blood. "Naamah?" She stared in disbelief, trying to fathom what had just happened. It wasn't a stick in her hand. It was a metal fireplace poker.

And everything fell into place. . . . The missing fireplace poker from Billingsly's living room. The crime scene left only as a woman would leave a house, neat and orderly.

Another chopping blow followed the first, this time glancing off the left side of her head. *Run!* her survival instinct screamed. Rachel tried to run, but time seemed to slow and her knees buckled. Blackness swirled, and she fought to remain upright.

The hard object swooped toward her, and she raised a hand to fend it off. Somehow she deflected the blow, but pain exploded in her wrist, and the strength drained out of her arm. The sharp pain, then numbness, radiated from her arm up to her shoulder and neck. Nausea rose in her throat and she gagged.

Naamah charged, dropping the poker and seizing Rachel by the hair and knocking her backward with the sheer force of her weight. Rachel stumbled, falling onto her bottom, landing on something hard and solid in the straw.

"It's all your fault," Naamah said, her voice gradually rising from a rational tone to something far scarier. "I warned you. But you kept nosing around." Still gripping Rachel's hair in a meaty fist, she loomed over her and shook Rachel like a terrier might shake a rat. "First the hat. *Whose hat? Who lost a hat?* You wouldn't let up. Pestering. Pestering. *Who owns a top-hack? Where was it the night the newspaperman died?* Mind your own beeswax!" She yanked Rachel so hard by her hair that Rachel came to her feet to try to escape the pain. Naamah pulled Rachel's hair, forcing Rachel to bend backward.

Rachel's spine struck the lip of the stone trough, and a new agony shot up to her neck. A slideshow of black-and-white snapshots, illuminated by the pulsing throb in her head, flashed behind her eyelids. Naamah's accusing face. A cat running, ears pressed flat against its narrow head, tail stretched full length. A gray cat in the Chupp barnyard. Billingsly's cat. Goat eyes leering through the slats. A black hat in the snow. Billingsly's distorted face trapped in a wall of ice.

"You're no different than she was!" Naamah shook Rachel, making her teeth rattle. "Always pestering him. Tempting him! I know what you wanted. You wanted his baby. Just like that English Jezebel."

"You . . ." Rachel rasped, trying to grasp what was happening. But it couldn't be true. Never in her wildest dreams— "You killed Billingsly? It . . . it was you?"

Naamah paused, panting for breath, breasts heaving. "I had to. He would have told everyone about the boy. Eddie Millman. Printed it in his paper. And they would have laughed. Because I couldn't give Abner a living son. They would have all known it was me who couldn't have a baby. Not Abner. And that woman . . . that *creature* had the nerve to come to Sammy's grave."

Black spots danced in front of Rachel's eyes, but she knew Naamah meant to kill her. She had to keep her talking. Her hands found the top of her head, anything to relieve the pressure Naamah was putting on her scalp. "You went to Billingsly's that night?"

"We took Abner's top-hack," Naamah said, eyes bulging with madness. "We went to his house. He would have written lies about my Abner, told everyone that I wasn't worthy to be a bishop's wife. An Englisher harlot had his baby and I couldn't."

Rachel was trying hard to follow what Naamah was saying. Everyone had always assumed Abner wasn't able to have children because there had been none from his first marriage either. But if he had fathered Eddie . . .

Somehow it was beginning to make sense. "But . . ." Rachel tried to think clearly enough to speak. She must have bitten her tongue because she tasted blood in her mouth. "Sammy was there, wasn't he? In town last Saturday night. He saw what you did."

Naamah's gaze became sly. "How do you know it was me? Maybe Sammy hit him with the poker."

"You tied Billingsly up. You threw water on him," Rachel accused. "You left him to freeze."

"He wouldn't have stopped saying those awful things about Abner. I threw water to wash out his nasty mouth. To shut him up. Water washes away sin. Shuts up a barking dog." She made a sudden movement, spinning Rachel around and shoving her head down.

Rachel saw the water coming toward her. She tried to fight back, but Naamah was too big, too strong. As strong as any man.

Rachel gasped at the shock of the icy water in the stone trough, struggled as Naamah forced her face under and held her there. Rachel clawed at Naamah's coat with her good hand, kicked at her in desperation. Rachel's lungs burned. Water ran into her nose and down her throat. *Dear God, help me,* she cried silently.

Suddenly, she was yanked up out of the water by her hair. She choked and gasped, struggling to clear her lungs and suck in mouthfuls of air. Again, Naamah shook her.

". . . Always losing his hat!" she was saying. "Stupid boy . . . Left it under the bench at church. Left it at the feed mill. Let the wind blow it away at Billingsly's."

"You . . . you committed murder," Rachel whispered hoarsely.

"God killed the Englisher. Not me. God sent the snow. God turned him to ice. For his sins."

"Sammy?" Rachel closed her eyes for a second, afraid she was going to black out. She was dizzy and nauseated. "You pushed Sammy from the loft. So he wouldn't tell."

"*Ne. Mupsich.* Sammy wouldn't climb into the loft. Not even after the cat. I let him take it home that night. In the buggy. To shut him up. He wanted the cat and I let him have it. I spoiled Sammy. But he couldn't hold his tongue. So I hit him in the barnyard, with the shovel, to teach him a lesson. Stupid boy. It wasn't my fault if he had a soft neck." She smiled. "But God took Billingsly and he took Sammy. And now he will take you."

Rachel was shaking all over from cold. And stark fear. "You . . . you can't . . . just . . . drown me and expect no one to find out."

"No?" She shoved Rachel's head under the water again.

Again, Rachel tried to fight, but not as hard as the last time. This time, she couldn't hold her breath as long, and the choking water didn't seem as cold, and the flashes of pictures in her head were fainter.

*I'm going to die here.*

The strange thing was she felt removed from the woman whose head was being held underwater. It no longer seemed so urgent that she care.

And then Naamah jerked her up again and flung her face-down on the floor. Rachel vomited water, curled into a ball, and fought to draw in a breath. "H-how did you get into Billingsly's house?" she asked, panting.

"I knocked. On the back door. He let me in."

The straw on the barn floor scratched Rachel's cheek. One minute Naamah sounded crazy, the next . . . not so crazy. Then crazy again. "But . . . there was no sign you'd been there."

"I cleaned up his mess." Naamah seemed to be babbling now, speaking not so much to Rachel as to herself. "Wiped down the counters. I keep a tidy kitchen. He left the stove on. Just like a man. Nearly burned his steak. Wasting good food like that."

"The robe," Rachel murmured, remembering how out of place it had seemed in the formal living room. Folded neatly, thrown over the back of the chair. Naamah had folded it and left it there; her instincts had been right. And she must have just locked the front door from the inside after she left Billingsly on the porch, and then gone out the back, locking the door from the inside before closing it.

Naamah kicked at Rachel's sprawled body, and Rachel instinctively curled into a tighter ball in the straw, to protect herself.

"Wake up, lazy," Naamah commanded. "You're not dead yet."

Rachel tried to clear her mind, trying to push back the pulsing black spots in her vision. She tried to pray.

"Are you listening? Do you hear me?" Naamah kicked her again. "I brought you the cat. And the poker. The newspaper-man's fire poker. When they find your body, they'll know it was you that killed them both. And maybe you'll even have killed the cat." Naamah laughed. "Wring its neck."

Rachel choked up more water.

Naamah crouched down next to her. "I'll tell you a secret. I'm going to have a baby. Abner's baby. So he doesn't need the harlot." She patted her own stomach. "And he doesn't need Eddie."

Warm blood trickled down Rachel's cheek. She was aware of the cold seeping up out of the stone floor and the weight of her wet parka. She was suddenly weary, so weary. She had to force her eyes open to look up at Naamah. "But . . . the bishop will wonder . . . where you are this morning. Why you aren't in church? He . . . will worry."

"I had a baby, you know, one, two, three, three little baby boys," Naamah went on. "But they all went to heaven. And now I'm having another, a stronger one. One that will grow strong and be smart. Not like Sammy. A boy who listens to his mother." She smiled. "I know it's a boy."

"This won't look like an accident," Rachel croaked. "The police will know. Evan will find you. He'll put you and your baby in jail." She tried to push herself up in the hay, and her hand closed over something hard and cold. *The poker.* She lay down again, wrapping her fingers around the metal.

"I'll drown you and then throw your body in the millrace. It's a good thing the water runs so fast here. It never freezes," Naamah pronounced. "And then everyone in Stone Mill will know. You killed the newspaperman and you killed Sammy and Abner's boy. And you were so ashamed, you couldn't live with yourself."

What Naamah just said took a moment to sink in. Rachel closed her eyes, trying to focus. Her wrist was throbbing with pain. Trying to think. "What did you say about Eddie? You killed him?"

"First you. Then him." She sounded so . . . pleased with herself. "Eddie delivers the paper on Sunday mornings. He'll be here any moment. And I'll be waiting for him. I'll lure him to the barn, tell him you're hurt, and then I'll drown him, too. Water washes away sin. He's a child of sin."

"You can't kill an innocent boy," Rachel argued, trying to push herself up off the floor now, her fingers wrapped tightly around the fire poker in the straw. She couldn't let Naamah hurt someone else. "Not Abner's son."

"Abner won't need him. He'll have our boy. He'll understand. You've talked enough." Naamah reached to grab hold of Rachel's hair again, and Rachel swung the poker with every ounce of her strength.

Rachel slammed the poker into Naamah's knee, and the big woman howled, grabbing her injured leg. "Wicked!" she cried. "Wicked girl!" She limped away and seized a pitchfork from its peg on the wall. "I'll teach you to strike your elders!"

Rachel scrambled to her feet and stood swaying, the poker in her hand. "Naamah, please," she begged. "Think what you're doing."

"I know what I'm doing. I'm running this fork through a snooping busybody, and then I'm throwing your sorry, carrot-haired body in the millpond." She moved forward menacingly, the pitchfork held out. "I never liked you. You always thought you were better than us, with your English ways, Rachel Mast."

Rachel was trapped between the windowless wall of the barn and the goat stall. She knew she couldn't manage to climb over the fence before Naamah ran her through with the deadly prongs of the pitchfork. She had the poker, but a poker against the longer pitchfork wasn't an even match. And Naamah outweighed her by a hundred pounds of sheer muscle and bulk.

"Please, Naamah," Rachel reasoned as she watched Naamah walk slowly toward her, the pitchfork poised. "Think about what you're doing. You don't want to hurt me."

"*Ne,*" she replied. "I want to kill you." The distance between them was narrowing by the second.

"Think of your baby," Rachel heard herself say. She was suddenly feeling so dizzy that she felt like she was going to collapse. Her head lolled, and she felt the strength left in her good arm waning. Her eyes closed against her will. "He'll—"

"Naamah."

A man's voice penetrated Rachael's fog. She blinked, not certain if she'd really heard the voice or if her mind was playing tricks on her.

"Naamah, put that down, wife."

Rachel forced her eyes open.

Abner walked slowly toward them. "The pitchfork is sharp," he said. "You might hurt yourself."

Naamah turned her head to stare at him. "Husband?" Her tone became sweet. "Why aren't you in church?"

"I came for you, Naamah." Abner smiled at his wife, and the scene struck Rachel as being so surreal that she still wasn't absolutely sure that the bishop was there.

"I couldn't give my sermon without you there to hear," he was saying. "You're always there in the front."

"We're having a baby," Naamah told him. "A baby boy. Aren't you happy?"

He held out his hand. "Give me the pitchfork, wife."

"I went to the doctor. Don't you remember? In May our son will be born."

Abner's face creased with sorrow. "There's no baby, wife. I told you that. Again and again. Remember when you went to the hospital? When our last child . . ." He choked up. "You had surgery . . . a hysterectomy. We can't have a baby, Naamah. We had children, but God took them all home. They were born too sick to live in this world."

"Some people should die," Naamah insisted; she was still holding the pitchfork, but she'd lowered it.

Rachel took a step back and leaned on the rail of the goat's stall.

"First Rachel and then Eddie and then the harlot," Naamah

declared. "We can do it together. Help me hold her head underwater and then—"

"*Ne.*" Abner's hands closed over the handle of the pitchfork. "Give it to me, Naamah."

She shook her head stubbornly. She'd lost her black bonnet at some point, but she was still wearing her white prayer cap. "Not until I stick it through her."

"Wife. I am your husband. I am the head of the house. You will do as I say, won't you?" For a moment, the two struggled for possession of the pitchfork, and then Naamah's face crumpled and seemed to collapse like a discarded Halloween mask. She released the handle and began to weep.

Rachel dropped the poker to the straw on the floor. She was shivering violently inside her sodden coat, but she was no longer afraid that she was going to die. And she was suddenly overwhelmed with compassion for Naamah. "She's sick, Abner," she murmured.

Like a puppet with the strings cut, the bishop's wife sank onto the floor. Abner dropped to his knees beside his wife and pulled her into his arms. "She's been sick for a long time, in her mind," he told Rachel. "Since our babies . . ." He trailed off, his voice nearly drowned by Naamah's sobbing. "That's why Sammy came to live with us. Not for Naamah to care for, but so that I didn't have to leave her alone. But I didn't know how sick she was until I realized she'd taken the top-hack to town that night. Taken Sammy with her to Billingsly's house. And then, when I realized she was gone this morning—"

"I had to do it," Naamah wailed. "Don't you see, Abner? It wasn't my fault. Rachel wouldn't leave it alone. God took the newspaperman for his sins. It should have been over. But she kept nosing around. Nosing and . . ."

"Go to the house," Abner said firmly but kindly to Rachel. "Call 9-1-1. Do you think you're strong enough to walk to the house?"

Rachel nodded. She could have walked farther. She could have *run* into the sunlight. She might have died here in the barn, but she'd been spared. So instead of running out of the barn, she paused a moment, bowed her head, and murmured a brief prayer of thanks for her life and a plea for God's mercy for Naamah and Abner and all the heartbreak that would soon come their way.

# Epilogue

Rachel opened her eyes and blinked. It was so bright. Where was she? She smelled roses. She swallowed. Her mouth felt dry . . . her eyes as though they were weighed down with bricks. The ache had returned in her arm, heavy, dull. *Thump. Thump. Thump.* She squinted. Pale green walls and the smell of what? Alcohol? Disinfectant?

A hospital? Was she in a hospital? Impossible. She'd just tried to call Evan on the phone. Why? Why had it been urgent that she talk to him? Why was she in a hospital?

She opened her eyes again and saw roses: bouquets of red roses. And white . . . and yellow. The windowsill, the bedside table, and a rolling stand near the door. There had to be a dozen vases of roses. No wonder the smell was so strong.

"You're awake."

A familiar hand squeezed hers.

"Evan?" she croaked. Her voice cracked and came out as a rasp. "Evan?"

His face blurred and then came into focus. He was leaning over the bed, smiling down at her. "Hey, sleepyhead."

"Where am I?"

"The hospital. State College." He put a finger to his lips. "Don't try to talk. You're going to be fine."

The pounding pain in her arm grew more intense. She tried to turn her head so that she could see it, but she couldn't. Some kind of collar was keeping her head immobile. She touched it with her good hand, noticing an IV line in the arm. "What . . ." she managed.

"The neck brace is just a precaution. Dr. Patel said that should be coming off tonight. But your wrist is broken. It was a bad break; you're scheduled for surgery first thing in the morning."

She closed her eyes and opened them again, trying to follow what Evan had just said. *I'm in State College?* "What time . . . is it?" she whispered. She'd gone out to the barn before eight; the sun had just come up. It was dark outside now. How many hours' time had she lost?

"It's seven fifteen, Sunday evening. You've been sleeping on and off since I got here."

"Naamah?"

"In the hospital as well. She's under observation in the psych ward."

"Here?"

He shook his head. "No, not here." He grimaced. "I'm so sorry. Not much of a detective, am I? She wasn't even a person of interest."

"How's Abner?"

"Taking it hard. He told me what she did. About Billingsly and Sammy. Abner had no idea, not until he figured it out this morning." He shook his head again. "Funny thing is, there was nothing in Billingsly's files about Abner or the Millmans. It's why I was skeptical of your hunch that Bishop Abner, or anyone Amish, had anything to do with Billingsly's murder. There was no need for Mrs. Chupp to have done any of this. Her secret would have stayed safe."

Rachel tried to process what he was saying. "Did she say *why* she thought Billingsly was going to tell Abner's secret or why she thought he knew?"

"I only questioned her briefly, but somehow she got it in her head that Billingsly knew *everyone's* secrets. She thought it was just a matter of time before he told Abner's." He exhaled. "She's mentally ill, Rache. The intake psychiatrist thinks it's all wrapped up in her inability to have children."

"Poor Naamah," Rachel breathed. She squeezed his hand, felt the ring on her finger, and raised her hand to stare at it.

Evan nodded. "I put it back where it belongs."

She smiled, flooded by so many emotions that she couldn't categorize them. "You . . . didn't ask me."

He sat down on the edge of the hospital bed, looking down on her. "I'm asking you now. Will you be my wife? I love you, Rachel Mast. I don't want to be without you." He gathered her hand in his and brought it to his lips. He kissed her knuckles. "Can you forgive me?"

"Nothing to forgive."

"You didn't answer the question," he reminded her. His shirt was rumpled, and a faint haze of beard was beginning to shadow his chin. He looked as though he hadn't slept in days.

"*Ya,* I will."

An expression of relief flooded across his face. "You will? Really? Great." He gave a sigh of what appeared to be relief. "Now I won't have to tell your mother I'd gotten her riled up for nothing. She's downstairs. She and your father. Mary Aaron wanted to be here, but she thought she was needed more at Stone Mill House. She said to tell you that she and Hulda have everything under control. No worries. Your house is well looked after."

She felt dizzy, and she closed her eyes. "Eddie and Sandy?"

"Fine." He leaned down and kissed her forehead. "It's over, Rache. I'll have questions for Bishop Abner, but I doubt that he's involved in any way. The troopers who picked up Mrs. Chupp said that he seemed genuinely stricken, learning what she'd done." His mouth tightened into a thin line. "They said she was pretty much a basket case. Not rational."

"What will happen to her?"

"She'll face murder charges, but she'll be evaluated to see

if she's psychologically able to stand trial. It's out of our hands once an arrest has been made."

All Rachel could think was that Naamah had seemed so normal until she walked into the barn.

"Do you feel strong enough to see your mother and father?" Evan asked.

Rachel's opened her eyes. "They're here?" And then she remembered that he'd just said that. Her thinking wasn't clear.

"They've been here all day. Your mother let me buy her lunch downstairs in the cafeteria. We had quite the conversation. And I think we've worked out a few of our differences."

She looked at him, wanting to ask what he meant, but decided that she didn't have the energy to ask. Each word she uttered seemed an effort, as though she were wading through waist-high snow. "I want . . . to see them."

"I'll get them." He got up, squeezing her hand. "Sit tight. I'll be right back."

*And where would I go?* Above her head, just inside her line of vision, a bag of clear solution dripped and ran down a tube to her arm. A broken wrist? Why were they keeping her in the hospital for a broken wrist? She fixed her gaze on the door.

"Oh, you're awake. Lovely." A pert nurse in violet scrubs came in and approached the bed. "Nice to see you. I'm Arlene. I'll be here until shift change at eleven. Need anything?"

"Water?"

"Certainly." Arlene removed a foam cup from a stack and poured water from a pitcher. Rachel heard the clink of ice. "Just a few sips to begin with." She lifted the cup so that Rachel could drink from the bent straw. The water was cold and tasted wonderful. "Nothing solid to eat tonight. You're scheduled for surgery at nine tomorrow morning." She walked out of Rachel's line of sight. "I'll be back."

More footsteps. Evan's. Her parents entered the hospital

room first. Her mother was pale, and there were lines around her mouth.

"Rachel, daughter," she said in Deitsch.

"*Mam?*" Rachel wondered if she'd drifted off to sleep and was dreaming her parents were here. Her mother talked to her only in her dreams.

"Are you in pain?"

"Not much," Rachel replied, stretching the truth. Her father came to stand on the other side of the bed. He didn't speak; he just smiled down at her, his eyes full of love. "Sorry," Rachel murmured, "to cause . . . such a fuss."

"*Ne.* No fuss." Her mother switched easily to English as Evan brought her a straight-backed chair and she sat on it. "*Goot* doctors, you have. They will put a metal piece in your wrist and make you *goot* as new. They say you will come home tomorrow."

A rush of emotion made it hard for Rachel to say a word. "*Mam.*"

"You should mind your own business. Let the police do their job." Her mother gave a sigh of resolution. "Stubborn you are, and stubborn you will always be, I suppose."

"And from whom does this stubborn nature come?" her father remarked. "The Masts are known for their gentle nature, but the Hostetlers . . ." He chuckled.

"Not now, Samuel," she admonished. "I am talking to our daughter."

"About time, too," he added.

"*Hmmph.*" Her mother sniffed and took Rachel's uninjured hand. "As I was saying, Rachel. You will go your own way in spite of all that I have tried to teach you, but you are a *goot* daughter and we love you." She cut her eyes at Evan. "And I suppose we must learn to love this Englisher son as well."

"He told you?" Rachel managed.

"That you will be married?" her father said. "I knew that for a long time. But we had to hear him say it."

"You'll accept Evan?" Rachel whispered. "Accept us?"

Her mother shrugged. "It is a burden, truly, but one child out of so many . . ." Her eyes sparkled with tenderness. "I suppose I will have to learn to bear it. Of course it would be easier to bear with grandchildren."

Rachel smiled at her as tears clouded her vision. "You'll give us your blessing?"

"I suppose," her mother replied. "For who am I to question God's plan for you?" Her lips curved into a smile. "We could have so easily lost you this morning to Naamah's madness, but the Lord brought you safely through the valley of the shadow. Maybe I have been guilty of having too little faith, both in Him and in you."

"Then it's settled," Evan said, coming to stand at her mother's shoulder. "All we have to do is pick the date for the wedding." And then his eyes narrowed. "I have just one stipulation."

"That is?" Rachel asked.

"That you promise, after we're married, to leave the crime fighting in this family to me."

Rachel managed a weak smile. "I'll try."

Evan gave her his most authoritarian expression. "I'm not convinced."

"Maybe," her father answered, "because she is half Hostetler, and he knows our Rachel all too well." He chuckled at his own joke and Evan joined in.

"I don't see what's so funny," her mother remarked. And then the four of them laughed together, their genuine affection for one another and relief that the nightmare was over echoing out into the corridor and lifting the hearts of everyone who heard.

# GREAT BOOKS, GREAT SAVINGS!

When You Visit Our Website:
## www.kensingtonbooks.com

You Can Save Money Off The Retail Price
Of Any Book You Purchase!

- **All Your Favorite Kensington Authors**
- **New Releases & Timeless Classics**
- **Overnight Shipping Available**
- **eBooks Available For Many Titles**
- **All Major Credit Cards Accepted**

**Visit Us Today To Start Saving!**
## www.kensingtonbooks.com

All Orders Are Subject To Availability.
Shipping and Handling Charges Apply.
Offers and Prices Subject To Change Without Notice.